"An epic
an ode to cultural inheri
and joyously queer romance"
Lauren James, author of *The Loneliest Girl in the Universe*

"A poignant, perfectly formed debut about queer love,
fandom and family"
Lex Croucher, author of *Reputation*

"A lyrical, complex tale of friendship, family, and all the stories we tell
ourselves – true and not – about what it means to love"
Kelly Loy Gilbert, author of *When We Were Infinite*

"Suffused with queer wistfulness and the ache to be known ...
as intimate and revelatory as the first touch of a first crush's hand"
Riley Redgate, author of *Seven Ways We Lie*

"Refreshing, relatable and raw in its honesty, this is the book I wish
I'd had as a queer teen discovering my identity"
Sarah Underwood, author of *Lies We Sing to the Sea*

"Beautifully written with moments of sheer lyricism. A must-read
for humans of all ages and walks of life. I loved it so much!"
Wibke Brueggemann, author of *Love is for Losers*

"So has a uniquely poetic style that sees beauty in the everyday
and makes the familiar feel fresh and new"
Ciara Smyth, author of *Not My Problem*

"A celebration of fannish glee, queer joy and family in all senses
of   s to find
                                                              y"

IF YOU

STILL

RECOGNISE

ME

If You Still Recognise Me contains content that some readers
may find triggering, including references to emotionally
abusive relationships, racism and homophobia.

STRIPES PUBLISHING LIMITED
An imprint of the Little Tiger Group
1 Coda Studios, 189 Munster Road,
London SW6 6AW

Imported into the EEA by Penguin Random House Ireland,
Morrison Chambers, 32 Nassau Street, Dublin D02 YH68

www.littletiger.co.uk

First published in Great Britain by Stripes Publishing Limited in 2022
Text copyright © Cynthia So, 2022
Illustration copyright © Nadia So, 2022

ISBN: 978-1-78895-344-3

A CIP catalogue record for this book is available from the British Library.

Printed and bound in the UK.

The Forest Stewardship Council® (FSC®) is a global, not-for-profit organization
dedicated to the promotion of responsible forest management worldwide. FSC®
defines standards based on agreed principles for responsible forest stewardship that are
supported by environmental, social, and economic stakeholders. To learn more, visit
www.fsc.org

10 9 8 7 6 5 4 3 2 1

CYNTHIA SO

IF YOU

STILL

RECOGNISE

ME

LiTTLE TiGER
LONDON

For my mother, who worries
she didn't do enough to encourage
my creativity as a child – I hope you
can stop worrying now, 媽.

And for Olivia – without writing
this book, I wouldn't have found you.
That alone has made it worth every word.

VOLUME I

CHAPTER ONE

Ritika lets out a whoop when we emerge from the stuffy air of the building where we just had our last exam, and she's not the only one. The school playground fills with cheers, the sounds bursting like fireworks around us. Ritika chats with Mara and Delphine, her friends from orchestra, while I hover by the gates. I gaze up at the school, its cluster of brown buildings smaller today than they've ever seemed before. It wasn't long ago that they loomed.

I think about standing in front of these gates with Joan, under the tree that has always stood watch by the entrance. I was showing her the school I'd be going to for what seemed like the rest of my foreseeable future at that point. The school I'd be going to without her because she was moving to Hong Kong, where both of our families are from. Her dad's job taking her away from me.

"Do you think I'll make another best friend?" I asked her.

"Of course you will. But don't forget me, OK?"

"I won't. You'll still be my best friend even if I make another one. I can have more than one best friend, right?"

"Sure. You can have as many as you want."

I haven't forgotten her. The reverse doesn't hold true, though. I wonder where she is now. Even back then, we were already talking about which university we wanted to go to. She liked the idea of college in the US, the sound of Yale or maybe MIT. "Science sounds cool. I hope I'm good at science when we start secondary school."

I got into Cambridge to study English like I always wanted, and, if I get the results I need, I'll be starting there this October.

Time feels strange and malleable, as though my future – university and life beyond that, *adulthood* – is suddenly so close and blazing in front of me that it has burned a hole right through to my past. As if I could walk through those gates, leaving school forever, and arrive seven years ago, under that tree, where eleven-year-old me is standing with eleven-year-old Joan, and I could pull Joan into the present with me. Drag her by the hand into whatever's coming next.

I step outside the school gates, but I don't go anywhere. I'm still here. Still eighteen. The noon sun warming my skin. And, behind me, my best friend Ritika is still talking to her friends.

Half an hour later, Ritika and I are sitting in an All You Can Eat, eating all that we can.

Spring rolls and prawn toasts soggy with grease, various meats indistinguishable from each other, crunchy stir-fried vegetables doused in a glossy sauce. The food isn't actually that good, but I'm enjoying it, anyway, just being in this dimly lit and mostly empty restaurant with Ritika. An ancient fan slowly spins its arthritic joints, blowing warm air in our faces. Our hands get stickier as we wipe our orange mouths on paper napkins and laugh about nothing, about this giddy feeling that rises in us like bubbles in a champagne glass, this feeling called *end-of-exams*.

But we've promised that we aren't going to talk about them. We're done with those. No use realising now that we've made a mistake on question 3b or whatever. I'm never going to think about maths again.

So we're talking about the summer. The Summer: capital T, capital S. The one big summer of our lives, between school and uni.

"We'd better start booking stuff for our trip soon," Ritika says, spearing a piece of broccoli with her fork. "It's all getting super expensive already."

I groan. I've only *just* finished worrying about exams, and now Ritika is bringing up another thing to stress about. "You know my mum says I have to get a job first before I can think about going on holiday with you."

"Right." Ritika points the broccoli at me. "So get a job."

"Is it really that easy?"

"Elsie. It's not going to get any easier if you keep putting it off."

"You sound like my mum."

We make faces at each other. Ritika eats the broccoli. "Why don't you try that comic shop?"

"Yeah, I've been thinking about it. But I don't know... The guys who work there don't seem that friendly to me? Like, I've never had a bad interaction with them, but I've also never had a *good* one, either. I've seen them chat with other customers but they never talk to me. Which kind of puts me off the idea of working there."

"But you've still been thinking about it."

"Yeah, I guess. I might head over there after this. I've got a copy of my CV with me. It was so hard to write! I didn't really have anything to put on it. Anyway, I'm not a hundred per cent sure I'll actually hand it over."

"You do *love* your comics."

"Only *Eden Recoiling*, really." I can't help but smile because I really, really do love *Eden Recoiling*.

"I haven't read a lot of other things. But I want to use this summer as an opportunity to read more."

Ritika grins. "I bet they have a staff discount."

"Oh! I didn't even think of that."

"How are you smart enough to get into Cambridge, but too stupid to even realise that staff discounts are a thing? It's not fair." Ritika flicks my arm with a finger.

"Ow." I flick her back. "Hey, what's Jake doing this summer? Are you sure you don't want him to come with us on this trip? Doesn't he feel left out?"

"Um," Ritika says. "About that…"

The 'Staff Only' door opens with a distractingly noisy yawn, yielding an old Chinese man with a duster, humming something almost familiar. The woman behind the counter, probably his wife, barely looks up at him, too absorbed in an episode of a K-drama playing on her tablet. I know it's a K-drama because Ritika knows it's a K-drama. She recognised it instantly from the sounds of the actors' voices and the background music. Apparently it's a really tragic romance.

I watch the old man as he walks with shuffling steps, dusting the framed watercolours of lakes and mountains. Vistas of tourist spots in China, I think. Places I've never been.

I find myself staring at this man – his wrinkled forehead, his sagging face, his scrawny arms in that short-sleeved white button-down – and suddenly I'm overwhelmed. Like eating something you don't expect to be so spicy, and it's fine at first, positively bland, but then it sets your mouth on fire, singes your tongue, licks its flame all the way down into your stomach.

My throat hurts.

I feel a gentle touch on my arm. "Hey." Ritika's voice is soft. "You OK?"

I blink and turn back to her, hoping she can't see the wet shine of my eyes. But she's looking at the old man too.

"Yeah. I'm fine."

"Your mum's back today, right?"

"Yeah."

Her gaze shifts back to me, and she squeezes my arm, so I assume she has noticed my tears. "How are you feeling about seeing your grandma again? It's been a while since you saw her, right?"

"Yeah. Eight years. I don't know. I've been too busy with exams to really process any of it… But apparently I'm now crying at the sight of random old Chinese men, so yay?"

I fold my paper napkin this way and that, searching for a relatively grease-free patch to dab at my eyes.

"Here." Ritika pulls out a tissue from a packet in her bag and hands it to me. "It's OK. Better than bottling things up, which – if you want my honest opinion – you have a tendency to do."

"Do I?"

"Yeah, you really do."

I dry my eyes with the tissue. "I have no idea why I'm crying. It's not like I've even seen my grandfather since I was ten. I do remember him, just a little, but it's very foggy. I didn't really feel anything when my mum told me he'd passed away. Which sounds awful. I mean, I was sad for my mum. But other than that…"

"Look, we just finished school *forever*. It's all right to be a bit emotional."

I give her a weak smile. "If you say so. Anyway I think I'll get some ice cream. That'll make everything better."

The freezer in the corner has three big vats of basic flavours – that trio of white, brown and pink that evokes a childlike excitement in me every time – and fruit ice lollies individually wrapped in clear plastic. I bring a scoop of strawberry ice cream back to our table. Ritika frowns at me when she sees it.

"You don't *like* strawberry ice cream."

"I don't? Are you sure?"

I put a generous spoonful of it into my mouth and grimace.

Ritika is right. I hate it. Cheap strawberry ice cream tastes like a child's crayon drawing of a strawberry with no actual fruit involved.

I continue eating it, anyway. It's something to focus on, the task of vanquishing this horrible ice cream.

Ritika rolls her eyes at me and reaches across the table to pat my shoulder. "You can just cry, you know. You don't have to be so weird about it."

"Shh. Let me enjoy my disgusting ice cream in peace."

Ritika chomps on a delightfully noisy prawn cracker

for a while. "Hey, do you ever wonder why your family hasn't been back to Hong Kong in such a long time?"

It is a long time. When my grandfather's illness took a turn for the worse, my mum went over there at last, the first time in eight years, and stayed for the funeral. She's back today, and she's brought my grandmother to stay with us for the summer because she doesn't want her to be alone right now. But I haven't been to Hong Kong since primary school, and all this time I've spent away from it seems more pronounced now.

"It is pretty weird. We used to go every year when I was younger."

"Yeah, you know me and my fam go to India, like, every other year at least."

"I used to ask my mum about it, but she always just gave such non-answers."

After a while, I kind of got used to it. Mum's strained face whenever I asked. Dad's placid smile. *Not this year. Maybe next year.*

Ritika sniffs the air. "Smells like family drama to me."

The old man has moved on to watering the potted plants that line the sill of the front window. He carries on humming. And I think, fuzzily, about how my dead grandfather used to sing to me.

We leave the restaurant, squinting in the fierce light of the afternoon sun. Ritika tells me she's catching a bus home. "Get a job," she says. "Also, movie tomorrow?"

"You don't wanna hang out with your boyfriend?" I tease. "You barely spent any time together while we were revising for exams."

Ritika waves her hand dismissively. "You and I are going to be tragically torn apart in three months. I'll have plenty of time to hang out with Jake."

After her bus arrives, I start walking to the comic shop. As I'm crossing Hythe Bridge back into central Oxford, I pause, looking over the blue railing down into the green stream below.

Crossing the bridge always unearths shards of memory, like an archaeologist digging up bits of pottery, but the memories get a little more washed out every time. Maybe the bits of pottery were vividly painted in the beginning, but now they're faded, smudged, their colours and lines fainter and fainter.

My ex-boyfriend rarely held my hand in public. Sometimes, when we were crossing this bridge, he would reach out, his fingers loosely curled round mine, only for the length of the bridge, and stupidly I held on to every moment of that more fiercely than he ever held on to me. Hard to believe now that something as simple as handholding could've made me so happy.

I still see him everywhere. Every blond-haired white boy is him.

The buzzing of my phone stops me from getting too lost in my thoughts. I assume it's just another message from my mum – I've had a few of those already today. But, when I take out my phone, I see it's not her at all.

For the past few months, there have only been two things making my heart race. The first thing was bad. Every time I opened an exam paper, I'd be terrified that it would turn out to be incomprehensible, filled with questions I was unprepared for: I had missed an entire topic in my revision; I had been taught the wrong syllabus; I had forgotten every single thing I'd ever learned. All frequent occurrences in my exam-season nightmares.

The second thing is happening right now, and it's good. Extremely good.

It's a message from Ada.

> Hey babe, congrats on finishing your last exam! I love you so much and I'm so proud of you. It's nearly 10 a.m. here and I've just woken up after barely any sleep – I stayed up late writing you a fic to mark this momentous occasion! I really hope you like it.

There's a link, followed by a series of orange hearts – Ada's preferred heart emoji colour. Her preferred colour full stop.

I'm desperate to read the fanfic that she's written for me, but not standing in the middle of the street, especially not on this bridge. I want to savour it. Get home, hole up in my room, lie on my bed and linger over every word on my phone. Then I'll read it again on my laptop, where I can easily copy and paste all my favourite parts into a comment and tell Ada in all caps how much I hate her for ruining my life with her brilliant writing when what I really mean is *I love you, I love you, I love you.*

But I think about what else is waiting for me at home.

I know I'll have to see how sad my mum is, and I don't ever want that, but especially not right now. I've just finished my exams, and I want to be *happy.*

I'm definitely going to swing by the comic shop first.

Before I do that, though, I let myself revel in the giddy rush that Ada's message has given me.

> omg i can't believe you wrote me something! thank you, i'm so grateful! i'm just going to buy the may issue of ER and then i'm going to head home and try to read your fic as soon as i can!

> Ahh yay! The June issue of ER is out so soon too! You need to catch up!

> You nervous about seeing your grandma?

> yeah... i just don't remember much about her, so it's weird to think about having her stay with us for months. i don't know what to expect! i feel like it's gonna be so awkward

> Maybe you'll really get along! You never know. Maybe she'll be as cool as my g-ma!

> oh, i hope so. tell your g-ma i said hi! anyway talk later when i'm home! i can't wait to read your fic!

I pocket my phone, and when I start walking again I have to try actively not to skip. Exams are over, the sun is shining, and Ada has written me a fic.

It feels like summer at last.

CHAPTER TWO

The Speech Balloon is only a few minutes away in Gloucester Green, sandwiched between a bubble-tea place and a dusty antiques shop. Inside, I'm greeted by cheerful blue walls and packed white shelves.

There doesn't seem to be anyone here, until a person stands up from behind the till, their back to me. All I see is a blond head of hair.

My heart stops.

I only started coming here after the break-up, looking for something to occupy myself with now that I had all these frightening empty swathes of time. I was armed with a list of recommendations I'd found on Tumblr – comics featuring prominent queer characters of colour. *Eden Recoiling* was one of the first things I picked up, and I got into it so quickly, I barely even remember what else was on that list.

Leo never mentioned he liked comics but maybe he does, and I just don't know about it. I never knew him well enough: he was worse than a stranger to me, someone I thought I knew, but didn't really—

But they turn round, this blond person at the till, and it's not Leo, after all. This person's hair is different, lighter in shade and in volume, a sunlit cloud floating away from their head. They're skinnier too.

They smile at me.

I realise that I'm staring, and I look away without smiling back. I end up feeling horribly rude, and I don't know how to fix that, so I make a beeline for the shelf that I know *Eden Recoiling* is on. The newest issue from May is there. On the cover is Neff, short for Nefarious. Nefarious Warthorn, a male character that everyone in the fandom is obsessed with. He's white, of course, and lean with a cruelly handsome face, and he wears a lot of patterned velvet suits. Nobody can tell whether he's actually evil or not, despite his ridiculous name, and he has a dark and blurry past. Nearly everybody ships him with Hax, the oblivious daydreamer and inventor, a minor character and also a white guy, who perpetually looks like he's just been deposited by a hurricane, with a dazed expression and straggly hair and grease-stained dungarees, one strap unbuckled.

Eden Recoiling is set several decades after an apocalypse, when plagues of locusts destroyed much of the vegetation, and then monsters emerged from underground and killed most of humanity too. The heroes of the comics continue to fend off these monsters, while some of the few plants that remain have gained sentience and mobility.

I roll my eyes at the cover, where Neff is apparently talking to a vine demon. Admittedly, I had a soft spot for him when I first started reading the comics, but then I stumbled into the fandom and realised that he's all everyone wants to talk about, even if there are plenty of characters who deserve just as much attention, if not more.

I take the April issue off the shelf just to look at it because it has Zaria Zero on the cover. I already have a copy of this; it's on my desk at home, and I would just sigh at it whenever revision overwhelmed me. Zaria in an emerald jumpsuit, her beautiful dreadlocks streaked with purple, looking up at a night sky with a pink-hued full moon. I can't help but stroke the cover. Zaria got me through so much. Could I have finished my A levels without her?

I put it back on the shelf eventually and go to pay for the May issue.

"*Eden Recoiling*! Oh my God, I love this series. I don't know anybody who reads it!"

I am not prepared for this interaction. Usually, when I've come here after school, I've been served by an older guy with a scruffy beard, who never really speaks to me.

Occasionally, there was a different guy, beardless but with long dirt-brown hair, also older, also uninterested in conversation with me. The boy in front of me now is probably about my age, and he genuinely seems to want to talk.

"Uh yeah! It's great. I don't know anybody who reads it, either."

Is that true? I don't know anybody *in real life* who reads it, but there's a small fandom online and, of course, Ada.

The boy drums his fingers on Neff's face on the cover. "Ah, Neff. He's fit, isn't he?" He says this not with the detached tone of somebody who's only saying what he supposes *my* opinion would be, like I would expect a straight boy to say, "He's fit" – not that I would ever really expect a straight boy to say that – but with personal conviction in the statement, an audible swoon in his voice.

I blink at him, and he ducks his head, embarrassed, scanning the comic. "Yeah," I say, "but I think Zaria's the hottest."

He smiles at me now, and, unlike when I first entered the shop, I can actually return his smile, even if I'm still nervous.

"Oh yeah," he says. "All the characters in this comic are extremely fit. It's a real problem."

"Yeah, how dare they? Like the world is rebuilding itself after an apocalypse – there's no way they can possibly look that good! It's just so implausible. I can't look half as put-together as them, and the world hasn't even ended in our universe yet."

He laughs. "You're right. Don't they have higher priorities than fashion and personal grooming? Where are all these amazing outfits coming from?"

I set my backpack on the counter, fishing for the right coins from my purse to give to him. As I'm sliding the comic into my backpack, he reaches out to touch the acrylic charms dangling from the zip. They clatter together in his hand. "Wow. Is this Zaria? And Mayumi?"

I nod. I bought them from this fanartist that I really admire. The Neff charm sold out within a few days, but I looked last week and there were still Zaria and Mayumi charms left. Ugh. It upsets me that they don't get nearly as much love as Neff does.

I wish I could draw but I can't. I can't write fanfic, either. I've tried before but I've never managed to finish anything worth posting. The only thing I can do is leave enthusiastic comments on other people's fanworks, and sometimes I make graphics: mood boards, aesthetics and gifs, what people call 'edits' on Tumblr.

As *Eden Recoiling* doesn't have a movie or TV adaptation, I can't make gifs of it exactly, but I take snippets from other things with actors that *could* play characters like Zaria and Mayumi, and overlay them with quotes from the comic and pretty effects. Even if Zaria and Mayumi aren't the most popular characters, I still tend to get over a hundred likes on my posts, which means they must be all right. Ada always gushes about my edits too, so I'm encouraged enough to keep making them.

She has the same Zaria and Mayumi charms. I bought them for her, as a Christmas present.

"I love these – they're so cute! You must really be a huge fan. I'm Felix, by the way."

His expression is just as sunlit as his wispy white-gold hair. I look past him and see the piece of paper stuck to the wall: *Staff Wanted*.

I make up my mind and reach into my bag for my CV. "I'm Elsie," I say.

As I leave the shop, I text Ada again, my stomach bubbling and my hands shaking. I've never given my CV to anyone before *or* met another *ER* fan in real life.

> ahh there was this guy working at the comic shop i'd never seen before and he was really nice and he also loves ER!
> it was so cool!

> That's amazing! So did you hand in your résumé then?

> yeah! you know i was kind of unsure about it at first but this seemed like a sign!

> Aw I really hope you manage to get a job there, that would be incredible!

> Oh and look what I just saw on my dash!

A link appears. I open it up, and it's a Tumblr post by a woman called Sara whose username I instantly recognise. She belongs to the contingent of Neff/Hax shippers; one of her novel-length fanfics is regularly hailed as a classic in the fandom. I've never seen an *Eden Recoiling* fanfic recommendation list that doesn't mention at least one of her works. According to her bio, she's in her late twenties and lives in California.

In this post, she's cosplaying Neff Warthorn in one of his customary velvet suits, hair neatly coiffed, and somebody else is cosplaying Hax, sporting a bedraggled look and sooty dungarees. Against a lush floral backdrop, Neff is down on one knee, proposing to Hax. And what a picture they make – Neff's flawless composure in delicious juxtaposition to Hax's unkempt delight. The caption reads: *I proposed to Macy and she said yes! So of course we celebrated with a Neffax enGAYgement cosplay shoot!*

A ring emoji caps off the post.

Sara and Macy are the dream. Two years ago, when Ada and I just started chatting, Sara was in the middle of writing the fanfic that propelled her to fame. Macy commented on every chapter. She lives in Washington DC but she happened to be visiting California for a work trip, and she posted about it on her Tumblr. Sara, curious about this person whose comments were basically fuelling all her writing at this point, was looking at Macy's Tumblr and spotted that post. They met up in LA and found that they got along better than they could ever have expected.

Two years later, they're still doing the long-distance thing, but Macy is planning to move to LA eventually, and now they're *engaged*.

Sara and Macy have a mini-fandom of their own, and Ada and I, even with our slight grudge against Neffax shippers, still count ourselves as part of it. They're just adorable. They do Neffax cosplay shoots together when they can, and you can see their chemistry in every photo. Fans would often sigh, *I want someone who looks at me the way Sara looks at Macy.*

> THEY'RE. ENGAGED??

> Yeah! Why do they gotta be so cute? And what do I gotta do for this fairytale romance to happen to me?

I could be this for you, I think. *You don't have to do anything except ask me.* Instead I write:

> i'm sure it will happen to you someday, you're a princess <3

> <3 Aw thanks

> Also I love their Neffax cosplays and all, but why does nobody ever cosplay Zaria or Mayumi around here? I mean, we both know why, but still. It's so frustrating!

> > we could

I send it before I can even think about what I'm saying, and, with my heart in my throat, I add:

> > like, imagine if we ever met up and we did a zaria/mayumi cosplay

> Oh wow, that'd be awesome! We would be so perfect I can't believe I never thought of that before

> I guess I never thought about cosplaying since I used to hate getting my photo taken, but I'd totally be down for this now

> You'd be cute af as Mayumi, babe, the fandom won't know what hit them

I hate that I'm standing outside the Speech Balloon because I need to lie down right this second. I already can't believe I even said the thing about us cosplaying Zaria/Mayumi together. But Ada's message has murdered me.

What can I possibly say to that?

Not as cute as you dressed up as Zaria, I'm sure.

We'd steal the spotlight from Saracy.

Do you think we'd have people shipping us?

What would our ship name be? Adelsie?

Which of Mayumi's outfits would you most want to see me in?

I groan. I think about Ada wearing Zaria's emerald jumpsuit. I groan some more.

> you know what? you should just cosplay zaria on your own anyway! i would love to see that

> I don't wanna do it without you! I'll only do it if I can have my Mayumi with me

My heart goes somewhere that isn't this earthly realm.

I can't take it any more. I decide that this is it. This summer – The Summer – is when I'll tell her how I feel about her. I have to. I don't know how – the thought of confessing my feelings, saying, "Hey, Ada, I have a crush on you," out loud over a video call or even typing it in a text feels like it would kill me instantly, turn me into dust on the wind. But there must be a way. There has to be. After this summer, we'll both be at university, and there'll be so much work to do and so many new people. Ada will probably find someone within walking distance to fall in love with, someone who's not an ocean away, and that'll be the end of us. If I don't do it this summer, I never will.

Other people have done it before. Sara and Macy did it. I can do this.

I rub my hands over my face and try to summon enough composure to at least reply.

hopefully one day soon then! <3

CHAPTER THREE

Mum and Po Po are sitting together at the dinner table.

It's startling how much skinnier my mum is after only two months. Two months – that's the longest she's ever been away from me. Seeing her now, it hits me how much I've missed her. Sure, there's been a handful of nights while she's been away in Hong Kong where I've cried myself to sleep, but I told myself that was only because I was stressed about my exams.

Really it was the emptiness of the house, especially when Dad went over to Hong Kong too for a week to attend the funeral and left me all alone. It was me sitting at my desk with my revision notes, and, whenever I pressed pause on my studying playlist and took off my headphones, I could only hear quiet. No TV downstairs, or my parents having a conversation way too loudly with no concept of indoor voices.

It was me waking up on the day of the funeral and thinking about putting on black for something I wasn't going to, and then remembering that it wasn't black but white that was the colour of mourning in Hong Kong. So I wore a white dress to my exam, and then when I got home I found it impossible to concentrate the rest of the day, until I ransacked my room and found, in a crumpled tote bag at the back of my wardrobe, the zippered red coin purse I used on trips to Hong Kong when I was little. It had an Octopus card in it and a handful of coins. Hong Kong dollars. I rolled the pretty, scalloped edge of a two-dollar coin between my fingers.

The final thing in the purse was a key ring, with no keys attached. It was a flat, rectangular piece of white acrylic, in the style of the hand-painted signs that red minibuses in Hong Kong use to show their destination. There were Chinese characters written in red and above them an English translation in blue: *Made in Hong Kong*.

Before he retired, Gung Gung was a minibus driver. He bought the key ring for me, a little piece of his history.

I took it out into the garden and buried it. I felt silly afterwards, kneeling on the grass, still in my white dress, which I'd pulled up over my knees so as not to stain it. It had been so many years since I had seen Gung Gung, and what did I know about him, really? Nothing except the faintest memories. I wasn't sad, not exactly, but I was filled with a kind of longing for all the knowledge that would allow me to be sad. What would life be like for me if, like the key ring, I had been made in Hong Kong? If I had grown up there? If Gung Gung had been a real part of my life, and not just the hazy outline of a man, seen from a distance?

"Yan Yan," my mum says, as I walk into the dining room. It's a nickname for my full name – Yut Yan – that I hardly ever hear. "Where have you been?" All in Cantonese, since Po Po doesn't speak English.

Mum looks like she's holding herself too tightly, back straight and arms rigid. I almost wish I could give her a hug, but people in my family don't really do that. Her taut posture matches her mother's. Sitting across the table from each other, they're nearly mirror images.

"Celebrating the end of A levels," I reply in Cantonese, except the word A levels is in English.

"How was the exam?"

The actual exam seems like something that happened to somebody else a long time ago, or like one of the many dreams I've had about exams. "I think it was OK."

"It's nearly four." Mum actually taps her watch when she says this. "You agreed to be home by two, and you didn't reply to any of my messages. Now greet your grandmother properly."

I nod at my grandmother. "Po Po."

"Yan Yan! So tall now, ah! Taller than your mum, aren't you? And what a lovely dress!"

I can't help but preen a little. I wore one of my favourite dresses today to face my last exam. Not my *favourite* because that's folded up and pushed to the back of one of the drawers under my bed. I haven't put it on since Leo broke up with me because I can still picture the way he looked at me whenever I wore it. The one I'm wearing today I bought earlier this year with my Lunar New Year red envelope money. It's a blue wrap dress with a daisy print.

"Um, thanks! I like your blouse too, Po Po."

"You sound like a white person trying to speak Cantonese, ai yah. And what has your mother been feeding you? Too many potatoes." She shakes her head and then immediately offers me an egg roll from a big square tin made of shiny red metal.

An egg roll. Just one of the many snacks my gung gung used to press into my small hands, insisting that I eat more. I peer down through the golden cylinder and spy the pork floss stuffed in its centre. Pork floss! It's been forever.

I'm still full from lunch, but the egg roll is so tasty, crumbling sweet and buttery in my mouth, with the savoury touch of pork. It's almost enough for me to forget that I apparently sound like a white person trying to speak Cantonese.

"You like it?" Po Po says. "I remember it was your favourite."

"It's delicious. Thanks, Po Po. How are you?"

"The flight was so long," she complains. "My body aches! Even more than usual. This house is very nice, though."

How strange that she's never been here before, to the house where I've lived all my life.

Now that I'm closer, I can see that Mum's mug is actually empty, but she carries on gripping it with both hands. She starts on a long spiel about all the work that's gone into the house over the years, the big bathroom renovated a couple years ago and what she's thinking about doing with the kitchen next year.

Po Po's eyelids are drooping.

"Po Po, why don't you go for a nap?" I suggest. "You must be so tired after the flight."

"Oh, gwaai syun." *Good grandchild.* A verbal pat on the head.

Warmth flushes through me, a sunflower turning towards the sun. I'd forgotten the way those simple words could make me feel. If I'm just a white person speaking Cantonese, how can that phrase make me glow like that?

"We were waiting for you to come home," Mum says a tad sharply. She's always been stricter than my dad, but she seems more intense than usual.

She leads Po Po up to the guest bedroom.

I wash up the mugs they left behind and go upstairs, to the sanctuary of my room.

Being around my mum was like sitting next to someone who's smoking a cigarette. Like I was inhaling all this second-hand smoke, but the smoke was her grief, thick and clouding the air.

It was what I'd anticipated. Why I'd put off coming home for as long as possible. I just didn't want to be in the same room as all that sadness. I wanted to be able to pretend that this was going to be the best summer of my life.

I lie down on my bed and check my phone, clearing away the WhatsApp notifications from my mum asking me why I wasn't home yet.

I sling my arm over my eyes. Po Po is like a stranger to me, but she makes *me* feel like I'm a stranger in this house too, with her comment about my bad Cantonese.

A memory floats up. One summer, when Joan and I were both in Hong Kong at the same time, we went to the Peak. The skyscrapers of Hong Kong glittered below us. "Isn't it weird," she said, "that when we're here everyone looks like us, but I feel even more different than I do when we're in England?"

"It's not weird. I know what you mean."

"We're just like tourists here."

"At least here nobody is yelling *ching chong ling long* at us, though."

"Yeah. There is that."

I roll over on to my stomach, open up Ada's fic on my phone and start to read.

Two hours later, I'm still lying on my bed, phone in hand. I've read the fic three times over, but I haven't managed to leave a comment. I haven't even messaged Ada to say that I've read it.

I just want to roll off the bed and smush my face down into the carpet and become one with it.

For Elsie, the Mayumi to my Zaria. That's the dedication at the beginning.

And the fic is exquisite. Ada's writing always is, but this is special because she wrote it specifically for me. From all the comments I've left on her fics, from all the conversations we've had, she knows exactly what makes my knees weak and my cheeks hot, and she's woven all these perfect details into the story. Mayumi overhearing the cool and serious Zaria talking to a stray fox in a baby voice, cooing at it. Zaria dozing over an open book and drooling, and Mayumi deftly removing it from under Zaria's chin before their research is destroyed by Zaria's drool – but pausing, just for a moment, to watch Zaria's sleep-softened face. Mayumi fastening the clasp of Zaria's bracelet round Zaria's wrist, fingers brushing along skin.

And Zaria and Mayumi's *kiss*. I've read iterations of their first kiss a dozen times – most of them in Ada's previous fics because she's practically the only Zaria/Mayumi writer in the fandom – but, while I lapped it up every time, I've never read one as exhilarating as a real kiss. But this one. Three times I've read it in the past two hours, and each time

I touched my fingers to my lips, felt my breath, quick and shallow in my throat, a pulse of pleasure fluttering through me like the wingbeat of an enormous bird.

Ada wrote this for *me*.

Ada, the Zaria to my Mayumi.

Like everyone else in fandom, Ada and I say *I love you* to each other like it's punctuation. But lately I've been finding it harder to say it to her because I've discovered that I mean it more seriously than I thought. Even just typing those three words requires an effort that feels deeply and nauseatingly physical, like reaching into my own ribcage and turning my lungs inside out.

I still say it to other people in fandom easily. A pretty piece of fanart featuring Mayumi in a tuxedo, an eloquent paragraph or two of analysis about snake symbolism in the comics, and I don't even think for a second before saying *I love you* to the stranger responsible. Meanwhile, my closest friend in fandom has written me this unbelievable piece of art, and I'm just lying here, clutching my phone to my chest, paralysed with feelings that I can't bring myself to articulate.

For dinner, Mum's planned chicken wings marinated in soy sauce, a whole steamed fish, pan-fried tofu stuffed with pork mince, and gai lan with oyster sauce. I make a face when I see the gai lan in the vegetable drawer in the fridge.

Chinese broccoli is too bitter for my taste but, whenever I complain to Mum about that, she just says, "Be thankful I'm not making you eat bitter melon."

I chop garlic while Mum washes the gai lan. Part of me is still living inside that fic Ada wrote for me, the cosy weave of its sentences like a blanket fort, and I nearly slice my own finger open.

Mum doesn't notice. She asks me about the exam again absent-mindedly. Then she asks about Ritika.

"She's all right. We might go and see a movie tomorrow."

Mum looks up, holding a bundle of green under the running tap. "You know you need to stay at home and look after Po Po while your dad and I are at work, right?"

"Po Po is perfectly capable of looking after herself for a few hours."

Mum looks back at the sink and turns off the tap, shaking the leaves energetically. "I brought her here so she wouldn't have to be by herself."

I can't believe this. All my hopes for The Summer feel like they're going down the drain along with the green-tinted water. "She knows how to use a phone. She can call any of us if she needs to. This is the time when I'm meant to be having fun with my friends, Mum, and I can't even go to the cinema?"

"Weekends." Mum sets aside the gai lan in a blue plastic colander. "You can go this Saturday or Sunday. You can do anything you want at the weekend. Believe me, I *want* you to have a good summer with your friends. I didn't want any of this to happen, but it's what's best now."

"Wait, what about my holiday with Ritika? You said I could go to Cornwall with her as long as I get a job first."

"When did I say that?" Mum's brow is creased.

"Um, I don't know. Before exams?" Before everything else happened. Of course.

"You know things have changed since then, Elsie."

"It'll only be for, like, a week!"

"And what about this job?"

"OK, I haven't got a job yet… But I'm sure I can work weekends or something."

"Maybe, if you ask your dad, he can take a week off work to stay home with Po Po when you go to Cornwall. I've used up all my annual leave already. But…" She glances at me. She looks so frail and her small hands, dripping water into the sink, are nearly skeletal. "If you find a weekend job, when will we have time together as a family?"

"Mum, you *just* said I can do anything I want at the weekends. Also, we'll still have every evening together, right?"

Her lips press together in a flat line. "Hmm. Well. You have to find that job first."

"Do you want me to get one or not?"

"I want you to hurry up with chopping that garlic," she says.

43

When Dad comes home, Mum meets him at the door, and I hear them in the hall talking in low voices while I watch the stove. After a while, they come through to the kitchen, and Dad oohs and aahs over the smell of the food.

The house feels better now that he's here. Airier. Dad's always been really good at lifting the mood.

Mum tells me to go and wake Po Po up for dinner. I'm still half in shock and half annoyed by the fact that this summer isn't going to be anything like I dreamed, all because of Po Po being here, so I do this briskly, throwing open the curtains of the guest room and letting the light of the summer evening spill in. Po Po sits up groggily and asks me the time.

"It's seven."

"In Hong Kong?"

"No, it's … two in the morning there, I think? Dinner's almost ready."

"I'm not hungry. I just want to sleep."

"Mum's making soy-sauce chicken wings."

"I know," she says, and I remember that she was with Mum this morning, buying all the groceries. She sighs. "Your mother is trying so hard to make my favourite food for me, and I'm too jet-lagged to even enjoy it."

"Didn't she cook for you while she was in Hong Kong too, the past couple of months?"

"No, of course not. It's my house. *I* make the food."

She relents and comes with me, making her way down the stairs slowly with a hand on the banister.

We have the TV on in the living room, but the volume turned down. As we eat, Po Po keeps asking what's happening on the show, but she does compliment the food too. Mum looks momentarily less ghostlike when Po Po says she likes the chicken wings.

Then two men kiss each other on the TV, and *everyone* at the table turns ghostlike, including me.

I always freeze when there's anything gay on television, as though there's a rainbow searchlight beaming from the screen directly on to my face. I'm used to it being awkward, my parents looking down at their food and saying nothing, and that silence taking on a physical presence, like a clammy fog over our table. But this time, with Po Po here, it's so much worse.

The audible pause in chopstick activity rings in my ears.

This has to be the longest TV kiss I've ever witnessed in my life. It's not even all that passionate – it's a bit unconvincing, to be honest. If anything, the fakeness of it makes it even more excruciating: here I am, having to endure watching this gay kiss with my family, with my grandmother whom I hadn't seen in nearly a decade, and it's not even a *good* kiss.

When it finally ends, Dad offers Po Po another chicken wing.

Mum stands up, her chair scraping against the floor, and walks into the kitchen.

Po Po frowns. She lets Dad drop the chicken wing into her bowl of half-finished rice without protest and eats it with a focused efficiency, discarding the clean bones in the growing pile on the table.

Mum emerges from the kitchen with a glass of water. We all carry on with the rest of our meal.

Probably ten whole minutes later, Po Po says, "It doesn't seem right for a man to be wearing a floral shirt."

The man wearing the floral shirt on TV right now was not involved in the kiss earlier. I'm not sure if he's another gay character, although it seems highly unlikely to me that there would be so many in a single show.

"I love florals. I think they look great on everyone," I say.

Po Po glances at me. "Hmm? Do you know any boys who wear floral shirts?"

I watch as it takes Mum four tries to pick up a piece of tofu with her chopsticks, which is unusual for her. "No, but I wish I did."

God, boys at my school wore the most boring things. I've always thought more boys should dress like Nefarious Warthorn, or, if they can't be as bold in their sartorial choices as Neff, a floral shirt should be the least they could do, once in a while.

Po Po's response to this is to lift a long strip of white flesh from the steamed fish with her chopsticks and put it in my bowl.

CHAPTER FOUR

After dinner, I retreat to my room and message Ada at last.

> your fic is everything, oh my god, thank you. i've read it three times already. i don't know what to say! i'm going to leave a proper comment on it tomorrow but i just wanted to let you know that i love you

It turns out that saying *I love you* to Ada is so much less horrible than watching two men kiss each other on TV while my family sit round me in silence. Baby steps, I guess.

Ada's reply is almost instantaneous.

> Aww, thank you! I love you too! I loved writing it for you, so it means the world to me that you liked it. I'm looking forward to your comment, you always leave the best ones!

How's it going? How's your mom and grandma?

oh my god. we were all having dinner just now and there was a gay kiss on tv and i felt like all of us were going to pass out from holding our breath. it was SO bad. i mean the kiss itself and also how we were all reacting to it. and then there was this other character, unrelated to the gay kiss, who was wearing a floral shirt and my grandma did NOT approve! men? in floral shirts? think of the children!

Oh man, that doesn't sound fun.

i'm going to have to put up with this all summer. i really think i'm going to break before i ever escape to uni. i mean it was just a floral shirt!

Babe, you've got this!

Do you want to do a quick video chat maybe?

I press the video button in the top right corner, and after a couple of seconds Ada's cute shaved head and big tortoiseshell glasses appear. She waves. She's wearing a robin-egg-blue bow tie and a grey shirt with a subtle white floral print. Every time I see any of her outfits, I feel a spike of something in my gut. I'm pretty sure most of it is just the fact that she's so gorgeous, but sometimes

I wonder what it would feel like to dress the way she does. The confidence that would take. I don't think I could do it, and maybe that makes me a little jealous of her. But mostly I'm just in awe of how she looks.

"Speaking of florals," I say, "you look great!"

"Thanks." She smiles. "You do too. So. How was the rest of your day?"

"I bought the May issue of *ER* but I haven't even read it yet because I just couldn't stop rereading your fic."

Ada hides her face behind her hands. "You're too sweet! We should be talking about how awesome you are. You finished your exams, and you applied for your first job ever!"

"I just really hope I get it! But it was so frustrating earlier with my mum. She totally forgot that she said I could go to Cornwall with Ritika as long as I get a job."

"So she's not gonna let you go any more?"

"No, I think I probably still can. I just need to check with my dad, because he'll have to take a week off work to stay home and keep my grandma company. Which is what I'm supposed to be doing the rest of this summer."

"You know my grandma used to live in Cornwall?"

"Oh cool! I don't think you've said."

I know that Ada's grandma, Rebecca – her dad's mum, on the white side of her family – moved to the US from England decades ago, but that's about it. Ada's mum's parents are in Nigeria, and Ada doesn't know them so well.

I've seen Grandma Rebecca a few times before. She lives

with Ada, and she sometimes comes into the room when Ada and I are video-chatting. She always says, "Hello, Elsie!" whenever she sees me on screen. She still has an English accent, mostly.

"Yeah, I told her you were going to Cornwall, and she started reminiscing about it. I gotta say, it kinda feels like she had a crush on another woman back when she was living there."

"What?" That is not what I expected. "You think your grandma is bi?"

"I don't know if she would call herself that. It's not like she explicitly said anything. But she was telling me these stories about her friend Theresa, and she showed me some letters Theresa had written to her. I could *feel* the sapphic vibes. I'd bet my entire bow-tie collection there'd been something going on."

"Wow."

I wonder if Ada would be able to feel the sapphic vibes if she could see the things she and I wrote to each other through the eyes of someone who was an outsider to our friendship. There's a possibility that Ada's just reading too much into things. There's a possibility that *I'm* reading too much into things.

"Yeah, but G-ma lost touch with Theresa soon after she moved here. They only ever exchanged a few letters, and then Theresa stopped replying. That was years and years ago. G-ma got a bit choked up when she told me she didn't know what had happened to Theresa."

"That must suck."

As I say this, it jostles up the memory of Joan again. What it was like to reach out in the dark for a friend and find only a void.

"Man, I'd love to go to Cornwall with you," Ada says. "First of all, hanging out with you IRL would be dope, obviously. Second of all, imagine if I found Theresa!" Her eyes widen, and then she laughs.

I'm thinking about *so many* things at once.

"I wish you could come." I squeeze my pillow, out of frame, so Ada doesn't see. "Do you have the letters?"

"Oh yeah, I took pictures. G-ma said I could. I told her it would be a good idea to make digital copies! Paper's so fragile."

We chat for a bit more, and after we end the call Ada pings over her photos of the letters from Theresa. I zoom in to read them, but it's hard to decipher the messy handwriting. I can tell I'm going to get a headache from this.

I do at least make out Theresa's address, though, written at the top of each letter. I recognise the name of the town – Padstow – from the little bit of trip planning I've done with Ritika. I remember it was recommended on lots of blog posts we found.

We could definitely go there. We haven't firmed anything up yet. I still need to get a job before I can book anything. But, if I do, we could go to Padstow. I look up the address on Google Maps, use Street View to look at the house. White walls and a grey roof. Is Theresa still there?

I run a search on her, but Theresa Bennett is a pretty common name.

I'll send the pictures to the printer in my parents' room tomorrow, when they're at work, so they don't ask me about what I'm doing. Maybe, if I read the letters in full, I'll find more clues.

The only person I've ever written letters to was Joan. When she moved away, she specifically *gave* me a letter-writing set. Pretty sheets of paper with floral borders and bright, colourful envelopes. So I wrote her letters but she never replied.

I sent emails too. Nothing.

So I understand how Ada's grandma must feel, not knowing what happened to her friend.

I want to find Theresa.

I let myself fantasise about it. An old white woman alone in a seaside cottage, watching the boats from her window every day, welcoming me into her home. Boiling water in a kettle on the stove to make me tea.

"Rebecca Hobbs?" she'll ask. "Rebecca still thinks about me?"

And I'll tell Ada about what I did, and she'll fly over with her grandma, and Theresa and Rebecca will have a tearful reunion while Ada and I smile shyly at each other.

It could happen. It really could. It feels like it's *meant* to happen. Ritika and I going to Cornwall, and, that being the birthplace – the beginning – of Rebecca and Theresa's love story, it could be the beginning of mine and Ada's too. It would be the perfect way for me to show Ada how I feel about her. No screen between us. I could say something smooth like, "If this was one of your fanfics, we would be kissing right now," and she'd laugh and take my hand and pull me close—

I throw a pillow over my face and breathe into it. I'm thinking about the scene in Ada's fic where Zaria and Mayumi kiss, and I'm thinking about waves lapping at the shore, and I'm thinking about what it would be like to see Ada in front of me, to hug her, to feel her body so warm against mine, the beat of her heart as wild and thrilled as my own.

I need to think about something else.

I pick up the May issue of *Eden Recoiling*.

I thought *Eden Recoiling* would distract me from thinking about Ada, but it really doesn't because, the moment I finish reading it, all I want to do is talk to her about it.

A vine demon just told Neff about the apple tree. There are no apple trees left in this nearly barren world. But the sentient plants seem to believe in a god they imagine to be in the shape of an apple tree, and there have been hints that one does still exist somewhere in the world. Whisperings about what finding this tree would mean.

And a vine demon just told Neff that he's seen the apple tree.

Turns out that this is what Neff's been looking for all along. He came to Zaria and Mayumi's little town of Muse early on in the story, but never revealed why. When he found nothing, he stayed because he preferred Muse to his own home, which he didn't like to talk about. Neffax shippers have written all sorts of fanfic about how Hax is the reason he's stayed and come up with many different traumatic backstories for Neff.

I go on Tumblr to look at the fan reactions to the issue – I've been on a Tumblr hiatus ever since exams started and avoided spoilers – and eventually I give up trying to restrain myself from messaging Ada.

> hhhh ok SO. the apple tree? do you think neff will go and find it?

Oh you read it! I thiiink Neff will probably try and get someone else to go look for it. You know him, he doesn't like to get his hands dirty.

> right! it's so cool that all those fandom theories were right about neff looking for the apple tree though!

Yeah! What do you think finding the tree will actually do?

idk. i've seen theories about how maybe the apples are poisonous to monsters? maybe people can propagate the apple tree and kill more of them?

Why would the monsters eat the apples though if they're poisonous?

hmm. yeah i have no clue!

the vine demon could be lying too, they're not the most trustworthy

I stay up late exchanging messages with Ada while I make an edit for the fanfic that she wrote me. A fox, a pile of books, a bracelet.

In the end, I go to bed with my mind still completely full of her.

CHAPTER FIVE

In the morning, when I go downstairs, Po Po is in the garden, her back to me. The sight of her pink shawl and her wavy hair, dyed black but with wisps of white showing through, makes me stop still.

It's so strange to see her in our house. I just can't get used to the idea that she's going to spend the entire summer with us. This person that I barely know and hadn't seen in eight years.

She asks me if I can show her round Oxford. I figure it's better than just sitting in the house all day, so we take a bus into the city centre.

I decide to show my grandmother Christ Church first – that's where all the tourists go. But, when we get off the bus, I'm immediately approached by a Chinese tourist who starts asking me a question in Mandarin.

This is a problem because I don't know Mandarin. And neither, it seems, does Po Po. It's not the first time this has happened to me. I always feel self-conscious, shaking my head and telling the person in English that I can't help them, but it also annoys me. It's like a splinter, painful and irritating. Sometimes they even look angry when I reveal my lack of understanding. I don't know why they just assume I can speak Mandarin, and it makes me feel as if there's something wrong with me.

I'm struggling to try to get rid of this person but then someone else brushes in next to me, replying in smooth Mandarin, and the conversation carries on without me.

I study the person who interrupted us – just a glance at first, but then I can't look away. They're about my age, short hair shaved at the back, and they're wearing glasses with a clear frame, a silver stud earring in one ear, and a black bomber jacket and jeans. There's something familiar about them, but I can't figure out why.

When the tourist goes on their way, satisfied, the other person smiles at me. "Elsie Lo?"

It can't be.

She looks so different from when she was younger, but I see it. It must be.

"Joan Tse?"

"Yeah," she says.

"Oh wow. I. Wow."

She laughs.

Oh my God. Joan is alive and she's standing in front of me, *laughing*, and also I really, really think she might be gay. Everything about her appearance screams it.

"Won't you introduce me to your friend?" Po Po nudges me, and only then do I remember she's there.

Joan knows Cantonese too. So I switch to that, except I can't remember what Joan's Chinese name is, or if I ever even knew it. "Joan, this is my po po. Po Po, this is Joan."

"I'm Tsz Yu," says Joan. "My family name is Tse. Nice to meet you, Auntie."

"'Auntie'!" Po Po exclaims. "I'm not so young."

"I haven't seen Joan in years, Po Po." It still feels more natural for me to call Joan by her English name. "Since I was eleven."

"Oh, so about as long since you came to visit me in Hong Kong," Po Po mutters.

Yeah, the last time I went was the year before Joan moved over there. Nonsensically, though, it feels like it's been far longer since I last saw Joan.

"Joan lives in Hong Kong too. What are you doing in Oxford, Joan?"

"I'm starting uni here in September to study physics," she says. "I'm moving in a couple of months early."

"You got into Oxford?" Po Po asks, eyes immediately bright. "You must be very clever! Our Lo Yut Yan here is going to Cambridge. I don't know why she didn't also choose Oxford when she already lives here. Why do

58

children these days always have to move far away from their family?"

I rub the back of my neck, embarrassed. "Joan, do you want to sit down somewhere and catch up?"

"Yeah, of course," she says, "Elsie."

We end up in a café across the street. I can't stop looking at Joan, privately noting all the ways she's changed.

Joan and I speak in Cantonese so Po Po won't feel excluded, but Po Po doesn't really join in the conversation. I want to speak in English, not just because it's more comfortable on my tongue, but because I don't want Po Po to be able to listen to us. I want it to just be me and Joan because there are things I'm desperate to say that I can't with my grandmother sitting right beside me.

Joan takes a sip of her coffee. "So how come you haven't been to Hong Kong in so long?"

I look at Po Po, who's staring through the café window at a woman with a pram outside, the baby waving its tiny hands, making noises we can't hear through the glass. "I don't know. We just haven't. Mum went just recently for my gung gung's funeral, and Po Po came back here with her. Po Po's staying with us this summer."

"Ah, I'm sorry to hear that." She touches Po Po's hand and offers her condolences, although Po Po is barely listening.

"But you didn't go to the funeral?" she asks me.

"No, I had exams."

"So we really haven't been in the same country at all since we were eleven," Joan murmurs, her eyes meeting mine, and the softness of her voice shocks me, strikes something in me that rings like a church bell.

I slurp too much smoothie through the straw and cough. "So *why* are you here? I know you said you're moving in early, but why?"

"Things at home were getting a bit much," she says. "I just wanted to be on my own for a while. I only arrived a few days ago."

On her own. What does that mean? Does she mean that she doesn't want to see me, either? She's the one who didn't keep in touch with me, after all. Maybe she would rather never see me again. Maybe I'm an intruder upon her solitude.

"But it's really good to see you again," she adds.

Perhaps she can see how unsure of myself I look. I avoid her gaze and stare at her hands. How easily she patted my po po's hand just now. I feel like, if she touched my hand like that too, I might be less doubtful of her sincerity. But she doesn't, and there have been so many years of silence between us, too many to overcome with a few minutes' shallow dialogue.

Still, I want to believe her.

The woman with the pram outside the café finally moves

on, and Po Po, bereft of this distraction, starts to quiz Joan on where she went to school in Hong Kong, which part of Hong Kong she lives in, what her parents do.

Joan seems to hold up well under this interrogation. The Joan I remember was … shy. The sort of girl who hid behind other people – hid behind *me*, more accurately. She never said a word in class. She also used to have pigtails. This Joan has a low, warm voice. Though it isn't loud, she speaks with the surety of the sun. She moves differently too, again like the sun, with its broad sweep of light over the land. I can't begin to imagine this Joan having pigtails.

My phone buzzes with a call from a number I don't recognise. I normally wouldn't pick up, but I'm thankful that it's giving me something to focus on that isn't Joan's hands.

I walk outside and answer. "Hello?"

"Hi, is this Elsie Lo?"

"Yeah."

"Hi, Elsie. I'm Nathan Cutler, owner of the Speech Balloon?"

Oh my God. "Oh! Yes! Hi, Mr Cutler."

"Felix passed your CV on to me. Do you think you could pop into the shop today for a quick chat?"

"Um? Yes? I could probably come by in about fifteen minutes? Is that OK?"

"Sounds great! I'll see you soon."

I stare at my phone and blink. Did I just get a job interview? What does a quick chat *mean*? I go back inside the café but I don't sit down. "Joan, could I ask you to do something for me?" I ask in English.

"Yeah?"

"Do you mind if I leave you with my grandmother here for a bit? I told my parents that I would look after her all day, but I've just been asked to go in for, like, a job interview, I guess? Right now. I promise I won't take long. I know it's a huge ask, but—"

"No problem," she says quickly, with none of the reluctance I was expecting. If our roles were reversed, I would have ummed and ahhed for a minute and replied in a flat monotone to express just how put-upon I felt.

I switch to Cantonese. "Po Po, you and Joan are getting along so well, I'm so happy. I just have to leave you for a little bit because I applied for a job at a shop yesterday, and the owner wants to see me. I'll be as quick as I can. You and Joan keep on chatting, and when I come back maybe we can order some food?"

Po Po doesn't look too displeased. She seems to have warmed to Joan.

"When you get back, Po Po will have told me all your secrets, and we'll be conspiring against you," Joan says, perfectly charming.

She knows none of my secrets, I think, but I smile at them both as I leave.

"So what do you think of my shop?" Mr Cutler asks. He's been telling me to call him Nathan but, having only just left school, I'm not sure I'm ready to call grown-ups by their first names yet.

"Um."

This quick chat really is very informal. We're just walking round the shop and talking, and I've been babbling about *Eden Recoiling* for at least ten minutes.

"I love it here! I think it's amazing that we have an independent comic shop, and I've always tried to support this place as much as possible and buy from here instead of getting digital copies online."

I hesitate a little, wondering if I should say anything more. But there's something about Mr Cutler that makes me feel like he would listen. His face is attentive, interested.

So I venture: "But I also know that comic shops aren't always the most welcoming to people who aren't men, and, while I wouldn't say that I've personally found this to be a massive problem at the Speech Balloon, I do think that making this place as inclusive as possible should be a priority, and I'd like to help with that."

This is terrifying. I tack on, "Plus, I'd love to work weekends."

"Weekends, huh? We could definitely do with more

help then. And, honestly, Felix has been saying the same thing, about making this place more inclusive."

"Oh really?"

We've come back round to the checkout counter and Felix, who is manning the till, pipes up. "Yeah, there's still some of Pride Month left to go – I've been thinking we should do a display of LGBTQ comics and LGBTQ creators."

"That would be so cool!" I say.

"You should definitely hire Elsie," Felix says to Mr Cutler. "Then we can make the display together."

"All right, Elsie, you're hired. Can you start this weekend?"

I blink. I have a job! "You mean tomorrow?"

"Yep."

"I can do that, absolutely, yeah! Thank you!"

Mr Cutler goes through everything I need to know about starting, and then he retreats to the staffroom and leaves me with Felix.

"That was easier than I expected," I say. "He's so nice!"

"Yeah," Felix says, looking down at his shoes. "He is. Also, I should probably tell you now before I leave it for too long and it gets weird. He's actually my dad."

"Mr Cutler is your *dad*?" Although now that he says it, the resemblance is pretty clear. They both have the same fluffy blond hair, the same gentle face. "Is that why I got the job?"

"It's certainly why *I* got the job," Felix says.

I shake my head and tut. "Nepotism is real."

Felix laughs. "I'm looking forward to working with you."

"Same," I say, and I realise that besides the staff discount – which Mr Cutler just confirmed, a whole twenty per cent off! – the thing I'm most excited about is the fact that I'll get to hang out with Felix. I don't have a lot of friends, and I don't *want* a lot of friends, but sometimes I wish I didn't find socialising so difficult. With Felix it's easy.

There's nothing like meeting someone and feeling comfortable with them instantly. That to me is the closest thing we have to magic in the world. The inexplicable connection that we just feel, right away, to some people, when with the vast sea of humans we have to work hard to get anywhere at all.

Or maybe that's just me.

I text Ritika as I leave the shop.

> i have a job! i'm going to sell COMICS! i'm also probably going to be BUYING a ton of comics! but i will be sure to save some money for our trip. speaking of, trip planning session this weekend after i finish WORK?

> YESSSSS thank god congrats girl. CORNWALL HERE WE COME!

CHAPTER SIX

"So, this Joan," Po Po says on the bus home, "she's very well-mannered. But such a naam zai tau!"

Boyish-looking. The word tugs at something inside me – my sense of who I am, neatly ordered, seems to come toppling down, falling apart into a jumbled mess of memories and feelings. I remember hearing that word the last time I was in Hong Kong. My relatives whispering it to my parents about me.

When I was little, I was the boyish one with short hair, who refused to wear skirts and dresses outside school. I wonder where that girl is now. Did Joan and I swap identities somehow? Did our souls fly across the sky in the smoky trail of airplanes, finding each other's bodies with more success than my letters ever found her?

Po Po said naam zai tau the way I've noticed she says almost everything, with mild and airy criticism. Men wearing floral clothing. The greasy fish and chips she was subjected to at lunch after asking me to order something for her that's good in England. Me choosing to do English at uni instead of something that would set me up for a more lucrative career. She treats all of these things with the same slight disapproval.

"I was a naam zai tau as a kid too, right?" I ask.

Po Po looks at me. "Yes," she says. "Running around like a boy in big trousers. But you've turned out well. You wear such pretty dresses now."

I look down at my sundress. Florals again, ha.

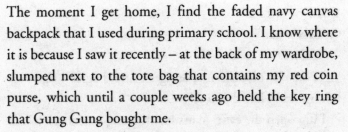

The moment I get home, I find the faded navy canvas backpack that I used during primary school. I know where it is because I saw it recently – at the back of my wardrobe, slumped next to the tote bag that contains my red coin purse, which until a couple weeks ago held the key ring that Gung Gung bought me.

I unzip the backpack and shake it upside down. A chunky grey pencil case falls out with a thud, followed by a clear blue plastic folder. Inside the folder are the remnants of a letter-writing set: several sheets of paper, still pristine and unused, and unlabelled envelopes in various colours. There's also a bigger square envelope addressed to me, ripped open, a greetings card tucked within.

I slide the card out. It's got an illustration of a sleeping tiger on it. One of the first conversations Joan and I ever had was just me asking her about all her favourite things and telling her mine. "What's your favourite colour?" She said apple green. I said blue. Every single shade of blue.

Favourite book? Movie? Season? I don't remember the answers to any of those other questions now. I just remember we had different answers to them all, until I asked about her favourite animal, and she said tiger, and I pounced on her and said, "Oh my God, me too!"

She liked tigers because they seemed strong, but quieter and less annoying than lions.

I liked tigers because of the stripes.

"Just because of the stripes? What about other animals that have stripes?"

"Like what?"

"Zebras?"

"They don't look as nice as tigers. Also, I agree – tigers are strong, and I like that too."

I flip open the card. Joan's handwriting covers every inch of the inside, narrow and neat.

Dear Elsie,
I'm sorry that I'm leaving. I can't imagine what it's going to be like when we can't hang out every day any more. I feel like I miss you already. Is that silly to say? I want to cross that out.

But I'll leave it because it's true.

Anyway, I'm giving you a letter-writing set so you have to write to me. I hope it helps to make sure you don't forget me.

Also, writing things down means you can say things that you wouldn't otherwise. At least for me. I know I don't say a lot. Teachers are always telling me I should speak up more in class. I like that you give me the space to just be quiet if I want, and that's the kind of space that makes me want to speak. And you always listen to me. I'm nervous a lot of the time that I don't have anything important to say. But writing a letter is like... It's like giving myself that space. When I opened this blank card and I started writing, I had to believe that what I'm saying is important enough to write down and give to you.

And I'm running out of space now. I'm sure we'll see each other when you next go to Hong Kong, but, until then, please remember to write! I want to know about everything.

Your best friend,

Joan

I close the card and insert it back in its envelope. Back into the folder. I can't think when I last looked at it, but there was a time when it stood on my desk, until I gave up on the notion of ever hearing from Joan again.

But she's back. She's really back. I have her number, and I can contact her whenever I like. She gave it to me without any prompting. So that has to mean she actually wants to talk to me. That, despite the years she let sink into a canyon of silence between us, we might be able to become friends again.

But can I just wave away those years? I wish I had a record of the letters I sent to her. All the things I tried to tell her that she showed not a scrap of interest in.

And then it occurs to me: I do have a record. Not of the letters but the emails I wrote when the letters got no response. They should still be in my sent folder.

But, as soon as I recall this, I also realise I probably don't really want to reread them. They would just be embarrassing reminders of my life at eleven.

Maybe another time. Not right now.

Right now, I have somebody else's letters to read.

Becca,

I reread your favourite book the other day. I treasure the copy you gave me, and I still enjoy the story very much, although this time round I can't help but think that the romance is a little too easy. I find that love in real life isn't easy at all. But, that complaint aside, it's a pleasure to revisit a book that I know you adore. It's a little like spending time with you. Just a little. But not quite enough.

The stray cat that used to come by often hasn't made an appearance in a long time. I think maybe it liked you more than me, and it doesn't care to see me without you. Whenever I saw you play with the cat, I liked to imagine having one of my own, but now I've realised that I just liked watching how happy the cat made you. I don't dislike cats, but I don't think I'll get one as a pet, after all. No matter how much I long for companionship, I think a cat would be a poor substitute for the person I truly want with me.

Yours,
Tessa

I'm sitting on the floor by my parents' printer, holding the letter. I think about how many books in my room are there because of Leo. I've been meaning to take most of them to a charity shop, but I just haven't got round to it.

Our romance started with a book that he claimed was his favourite.

In the beginning, I saw him all the time in the library and didn't know his name. In the shafts of light falling through the big windows in the library, his hair was champagne-gold. I would grab a seat where I could sneak furtive glances at him as I read or did my homework. One time, he whispered a *hello* to me when he came in later than me, brushing past my seat. Another time, he slid a book across the table to me, and I opened it up and it had a note inside saying, *I think you'll like this one.*

I stayed up all night reading it.

I returned the book to him and told him that I loved it. We had a chat outside the library, about books, about school, about teachers and friends and family. The shock of him having noticed me in the first place was one thing. The shock of feeling so understood by the book he recommended to me, when we had never talked before that, was something else: heady and beguiling.

He asked for my number. I gave it, starving to be fed more of this feeling of being understood, as though it was a syrupy pudding, golden and rich and dense.

And he did feed it to me, by the spoonful, as we started to text each other every night, forming our own private little book club. Within days, I felt like he knew me better than anybody else in my life. We hung out more and more often, perusing second-hand books in the quiet corners of bookshops, pointing out the strangest titles to each other and laughing, then shushing ourselves as if we were still in the library. We went to museums with rooms to get lost in, and he would make up his own stories about the exhibits, fascinating and odd tales that felt like he was creating a new world for me, for us.

We kissed for the first time in one of these museums, me rapt in one of his stories and him stroking my cheek with his thumb, leaning down to close the gap between us. No one around us to tell us off when he pressed me up against a glass display case with precious things inside.

Afterwards, he winked at me and said, "I'd prefer it if

you didn't tell anyone about us, OK? Isn't it cool that we just get to have our own secret world?"

"Yeah," I said, breathless.

And it was good. It really was at first.

I blink away tears.

I just want that again. I want to feel like I'm in the middle of a love so big it becomes its own world.

And I really think that there's something here, in Theresa's looping handwriting that took some effort to read. Something that resonates with what aches at the centre of me. It would be incredible if I could find a way to reunite her and Rebecca after all these years. It would be proof, wouldn't it, that love can last? And, if there can be a happy ending for two people who haven't seen other in years, there can be a happy ending for me and Ada.

I'm going to find Theresa somehow, and Ada will see that and understand that I did it because I love her, because I want with her what I'm going to make possible for Rebecca and Theresa.

At dinner, I tell my parents about Joan and the Speech Balloon.

Mum actually looks slightly dismayed that I managed to get a job. "So you'll really be busy every weekend?"

"Yes. But I'll still be around when I'm not working, which

is, like, *most* of the time. I do want to go to Cornwall with Ritika, though." I smile at Dad. "Dad, do you think you can take a week off work next month?"

Dad glances at Mum. "I'll check with my manager, but it should be OK. Anyway that's very exciting! Your first job!" He puts a mountain of braised pork into my bowl of rice, which I take as a reward.

"Thanks, Dad."

"How's Joan?" Mum asks. "You two were really close. She used to come over all the time, didn't she? What was her favourite food … stir-fried egg with shrimp? Why did you lose touch again?"

"She moved to Hong Kong…" I trail off, thinking again about how Joan was the one who cut contact. A giant's shadow, lumbering, passes over my heart. Mum still remembers Joan's favourite food, and Joan couldn't even be bothered to write me an email.

But I notice the same shadow passing over Mum's face, and I realise that she's probably thinking that the reason I lost touch with Joan is because we stopped visiting Hong Kong.

"Joan's well," I say. "She really seemed to get along with you, Po Po. Isn't that right?"

Po Po makes a vague noise, picking up a piece of tofu with her chopsticks. Tonight's tofu dish is steamed, with shrimp. I'm too afraid to even attempt to go near that dish with my chopsticks. The tofu will surely crumble if

I try, and then Po Po's bound to have some words for me regarding my ineptitude with chopsticks.

"Why don't you invite her over for dinner?" Mum says. "I'd like to see her again. Do you remember her, Oscar?"

Dad nods. "She played lots of instruments, didn't she?"

Dad loves music, and he and Mum both tried to get me to take one up as a child, but they've never been too pushy, and I got away with remaining completely unmusical. Being such close friends with Joan as a child, I saw how her time was constantly eaten up by piano practice and violin practice and bassoon practice, and, while I liked going along and listening to her play, I didn't have any interest in doing so myself. Ritika's often busy with orchestra commitments too, which means we can't always hang out. I'm glad I have more room to breathe in my life.

"Yes, you should tell her to come," Dad continues with enthusiasm. "We'd love to have her over."

I see in my mind's eye how different Joan is now. How she might walk through the front door of our house and cause my parents to freeze, bewildered by this stranger, supposing at first sight that Joan is a boy. The idea of them seeing this new version of her kicks up a scattering of fear in my chest, like dirt from the hooves of a galloping horse.

"Maybe," I say.

CHAPTER SEVEN

I wake up early and wade through all the dresses and skirts in my wardrobe, trying to pick out what to wear for my first day at my first job.

It comes to me again, the phrase naam zai tau. I think about Ada and her bow ties. I think about Joan and her … everything.

After changing several times, I end up wearing a mustard-yellow top with a forest-green suede skirt. I throw on some simple make-up and head downstairs to find that my mum has made breakfast. Po Po is sitting at the table, halfway through her bowl of macaroni soup. It's a traditional Hong Kong-style breakfast. I haven't had it in a long time.

I hurry through my bowl, having spent too much time deciding on an outfit, but the macaroni is like a warm memory of childhood, a taste that undoes the knot of nerves in my stomach. Dad comes in from pruning shrubs in the garden, and, while he and Mum are talking about where to go today, whether to show Po Po Blenheim Palace or take her shopping in Bicester Village, I leave for work.

I've walked from home into the town centre a million times before, but today the walk feels different, longer somehow. The nerves come back, gathering in a flock.

But, the moment I walk into the Speech Balloon and see Felix grinning at me, the flock scatters.

"Morning, *co-worker*," he says.

"Morning to you too, co-worker."

Mr Cutler – Nathan – waves. He's standing by the counter, eating a bagel. "Hey! Good morning, Elsie! Glad to see you haven't changed your mind about wanting to work for us!"

"No, not at all! I'm really excited to start."

"Excellent. Let me show you everything you need to know. I'll also be finishing this bagel as we go. I hope you don't mind."

"No, sure. Please do."

The rest of the morning flies by as he teaches me how to shelve comics, do inventory, operate the till and other bits and pieces while constantly offering me biscuits. After a late lunch of sandwiches from a nearby café, I work with Felix to put together the Pride display.

I have several recommendation lists that I've saved on my phone written by people whose opinions I trust. Felix and I agree on twenty titles, a few of which I've read – the rest I immediately ring up at the till for myself.

We arrange the books on a small table and print out rainbow flags to make bunting. Customers come in while we're still working on the display, and one girl with blue hair lights up at the sight of it and starts chatting to us about a title featuring a trans girl main character that I haven't read, but Felix has. She buys a whole load of the other titles, including *Eden Recoiling* – probably because I gush about it for ten minutes – which sends me reeling with so much excitement that I have to sit down on the floor next to the display for a second.

"Cute," Felix says, standing back to admire our work when we've put the finishing touches on the glittery Happy Pride sign.

Nathan comes over and gives Felix a side hug, clapping a hand on his son's back. "This looks great. Well done, both of you! Let me take a photo, for our social media."

There's glitter in Felix's hair. And in mine too. We pull goofy faces with our arms round each other's shoulders, and I forward the picture on to Ada, who immediately responds with a string of exclamation marks and rainbow emojis.

Before the shop closes for the evening, I make another sign that says COME IN FOR OUR PRIDE DISPLAY! to go by the front door, ready for the next day.

I can't remember the last time I was this tired, my feet sore and my legs aching from standing all day, but I don't mind it one bit.

My parents ask me about work at dinner, after I get shown the pictures of Blenheim Palace that Po Po took on her phone. I don't know how to tell them about the Pride display, but I do tell them that I had a great day and a busy one. Mum piles more spare ribs into my bowl of rice in response. "You have to eat more – you must be so hungry."

When I've consumed as many spare ribs as I can, I go upstairs to my bedroom and sprawl out on my bed in relief.

I take out my printed copies of the letters from Theresa, rereading some of them as I massage my feet. The bad handwriting still gives me a headache, but, since I've already done the work of deciphering them, they don't require as much effort to read now, and I can just soak in the longing that I feel expressed in the words.

Becca,
Remember when I took you to the rock pool and we had such a beautiful summer afternoon, with only the gulls squawking overhead and those adorable little crabs to keep us company? I think of that day often. Does Howard make you feel like that

day did? Nothing makes me feel like that, Becca. Nothing.

When we were younger, you talked of opening an ice-cream shop. Sometimes I dream of opening one now, then maybe that might entice you back here to see it, even stay and run it with me. Fanciful, I know. Mostly I just dream of leaving Cornwall, though. There's little for me here now that you're gone.

Although I did chase down a thief the other day who tried to snatch some poor woman's purse! A thief! Here in our little town. You wouldn't think it. But I tackled the villain and returned the woman's purse to her, and the police came and questioned us all, and the scoundrel was arrested. So there was that bit of excitement at least. I'm the hero of the moment. Laurels have been bestowed upon me.

I do always wish you were here. That would be sweeter to me than any glory.

Yours,
Tessa

I close my eyes, thinking about that rock pool. Thinking about Ada, and a beach at sunset, and ice cream. Ice cream… I'm almost asleep when I think of it.

What if Theresa *did* open an ice-cream shop?

I pull up Google Maps on my phone and search for all the ice-cream shops in Padstow. There are several but none of them are called Theresa's or Tessa's Ice Cream, which would have been a helpful clue. Not all of them have any contact info, either. I check the ones that do have websites – well, Facebook pages – and I can't find any mention of Theresa Bennett, only close-up pictures of ice cream that make me hungry again.

After some more scrolling, I find that the two highest-rated shops have been profiled on a local news website, but they're both owned by people who aren't called Theresa, although one of them *is* run by a woman who must be close to Theresa's age called Lily Newham. In the photo in the article, she's wearing the quirkiest, most extremely orange outfit I've ever seen, in front of her equally orange shop.

I stare at the picture for a while, so tired that I'm nearly about to break into hysterics over this woman's ludicrous ensemble – an orange party hat? An orange bobbly knitted vest? – and then I put my phone down.

OK. That didn't work.

But maybe Theresa owns one of the other shops that I can't find any extra information about.

I *know* I'll find her. I can feel it.

CHAPTER EIGHT

On Sunday night, I go to see a movie with Ritika.
The cool dark of the cinema is a blissful relief from the
heat outside, and, as the interminable ads play out on
the massive screen, I say, "So, I want to look for somebody
while we're in Cornwall."

"Who?" Ritika says, through a mouthful of popcorn.

"You know Ada?"

"Uh, that girl from Tumblr that you totally have a
crush on? Yeah, you talk about her *all the time*. Doesn't
she live in New York?"

I cram popcorn into my mouth and don't say anything
for a moment.

It always disarms me how easy it is with Ritika.
I wasn't draping rainbow flags round myself at school,
but I wasn't completely closeted, either. I told a few

people, who were all straight as far as I know. There were a few out queer kids at my school; they were all white, and they hung out with each other a lot, but I didn't feel like I could be a part of their group. I admired how much they felt able to be themselves, and I was jealous of the friendship they'd found with each other. But it didn't seem like it was for me for whatever reason. And the people I was friends with – the people I told – they were all accepting. None of them reacted negatively.

But I just didn't feel like I could talk about it openly with them. Except for beautiful Ritika Ghosh, who could just casually go, "Your crush on Miss Weston is so obvious. Jesus, you need to stop looking so lovestruck in class or I'm going to have to slap you," and make me laugh and feel giddy with joy that this was OK. I was OK. We were OK.

Which is why she's probably the only person from school I'm going to stay friends with.

"She has a grandma called Rebecca," I say, "who used to live in England. And apparently was really close to another woman, Theresa Bennett. I mean *really* close. Then Rebecca moved to the US, and they kind of lost touch. I want to see if I can find Theresa."

"How many years has it been since Rebecca moved?"

"Um, forty or so."

"There's no way you're going to find this woman. Why do you want to do it, anyway? Has Rebecca asked you to? Because that would be really weird."

"No, she hasn't."

"Has *Ada* asked you to?"

"No."

"Then why? You just want to impress her or something?"

I grab more popcorn and let my silence speak for itself.

"Ugh, this is the worst plan I've ever heard. You aren't going to find Theresa, and, even if you did, Ada won't hook up with you just because you found her grandma's long-lost friend. She lives in New York! What do you think she's going to do – move here for you out of gratitude?"

"I know it sounds ridiculous. But we were planning to go to Cornwall, anyway, and then Ada told me about all of this! Don't you think it feels kind of like... I don't know, like fate?"

Ritika raises an eyebrow. "You know what? OK. OK. I'm into it! I'm into your grand love story!"

I choke on a kernel. Ritika thumps my back, and I shove her away. "Seriously?"

"Yeah, I want to see what happens. You always hear these stories about people who fall in love despite never having met in real life. If you become one of those, I do *not* want to be someone who stood in the way of true love! I'm rooting for you."

I have no idea how to react to this. "Thanks?"

"You're welcome. So we're planning the trip after this?"

"Yeah. Let's do that."

84

"Is that what love is supposed to feel like, do you think?"
Ritika asks.

We're in her bedroom, as cosy and familiar to me as my
own. I love its deep purple walls, the succulents lining the
windowsill. There's an odd one out, a clay model of a Venus
flytrap with googly eyes that Ritika made when she was ten,
which manages to be menacing and cute at the same time.
I call it something different every time – today I've named it
Billy. Above Ritika's bed is a wall of her favourite romance-
novel covers, featuring many a hunky and bare-chested man.
We spent a free period at school last year printing those out
in the computer room and giggling.

The film was good, a fun comedy, the sort of movie that
feels like summer distilled, the bright energy of it rolling
down from the screen like the greenest slope of grass.
I laughed a lot and heard Ritika laughing beside me.
It featured a queer romance too, which was the main reason
why I had to see it with Ritika – it's not something I'd ever
watch with my parents.

When the two women on screen kissed each other,
I thought breathlessly of Ada. I wanted to remember what it
was like to kiss someone like that. The way Ada wrote about
kissing. *Like a summer storm, like thunder breaking through
the sky after the long, unbearable heat.*

Next to me, Ritika was rattling what was left of the popcorn, annoying me as much as a 5 a.m. alarm wrenching me from a good dream. But later, as the credits rolled, she said, "That was brilliant. I was in hysterics! And that kissing scene – that was hot, right? You thought it was hot?"

I bit my lip and said, "Yeah, it was."

And now we're in Ritika's room – she's sitting cross-legged on her desk chair, and I'm curled up in a corner on her plush grey ottoman, knees tucked under my chin – and we're still talking about the movie. Or, I guess, about love.

"I think so," I say nervously. "I mean, I've only really experienced it once, and … maybe hindsight colours my memory of it, but it was intense. This is going to sound stupid but … it really felt like the beginning and end of everything."

"Really? That's what it was like with Leo?"

"Yeah."

"Huh." She squints. "And that's… You were happy together? Sorry, I know he broke up with you, and that really hurt, and you don't like talking about it, but… Well. This is the most you've ever told me about it, so I'm just curious. The way you describe it, I can't tell if the intensity was good or bad."

"It was both, I guess? When we were happy, it was the happiest I'd ever been. I didn't even know such a feeling was possible. But … I think I was also really sad a lot of the time. But I thought it was worth it? Like, when you love someone, you try your best to stay strong and weather all the bad things and stick with them no matter what. That's what love is."

"Is it?" Ritika says.

I rub my cheek against my knee, feeling self-conscious. "I don't know. Like I said, that's just my one experience of it."

"But why were you sad?"

I clench my jaw. I hate talking about it. But I think it's more that I'm not sure how. It's like being told to clean up a really, really messy room. You just don't know where to start. Instead, you stand there, surrounded by all that dust and dirt and disarray, and just keep staring at it in blank despair.

Why *was* I sad when I was with Leo?

He got really angry with me once because I said I had too much homework and couldn't hang out. We were walking through a park, and he literally took off his shoe and threw it at a tree, past my head.

It seemed so absurd that I didn't realise I was shaking until he put his arms round me and said, "Did you think I was going to throw it at you? No! Hey, baby, I'm never going to hurt you. You know that, right? I couldn't ever bear to hurt you."

He then hobbled over to pick up his shoe, and we laughed about how silly he looked with only one shoe on, and I spent the rest of the day with him, after all, even though it meant I had to stay up late to finish working on my history presentation.

Sometimes he would want to kiss and fool around, and I wouldn't be in the mood, but he'd say, "I've been feeling so depressed. This will make me feel so much better." Or, "I hate myself so much right now, and this is the only thing that helps, you know that." Or, "This is making me feel like you're not really attracted to me."

And so I would make out with him, and he would touch me and pull on my hair too hard, but he would call me beautiful, and look at me like I was his *lifeline*, the only thing keeping him afloat, and it made saying no to him harder each time.

When I got all A*s in my GCSE mocks, he yelled at me. And then half an hour later he called to apologise for all the terrible things he'd said. He was just so stressed about A levels and university applications. He was afraid of failure and worried that he wasn't clever enough, and he didn't want to think about how I would probably have an effortless time with A levels and uni applications when it was my turn, because I seemed to swan through everything academically speaking. He explained all this, and then he bought me dinner and told me I was the most important person in the world to him. He made me promise I'd never leave him because he didn't know what he'd do without me.

I shake my head. My eyes are watering. Why, even after

two years, does he still make me feel this way?

"I really don't like talking about it. But I will say… At the time, it almost seemed like it was proof that it was real, and that I loved him, because it wasn't all sunshine and rainbows, but we were still committed to each other. But I guess love doesn't have to be that way, does it? You and Jake have been together for over a year now, and he doesn't make you miserable, right?"

"…Right. He's the nicest boyfriend you could hope for."

Jake made Ritika a chocolate cheesecake for her birthday last year; I had a slice and it was *divine*. When I picture Jake Milner, I see him in an apron, arms dusted in flour, butter smeared on the tip of his nose. Everything about him seems sweet. It wasn't just for her birthday – he bakes little treats for Ritika all the time. Brownies and cupcakes and cookies, no special occasion necessary.

"Exactly. Your relationship seems perfect, and I'm just so happy for you."

Ritika flips open her laptop lid. "We should probably actually book our trip to Cornwall now."

"Oh yeah, sure."

I remember something I haven't asked Ritika. I've been thinking about Joan, even though I still haven't messaged her since we saw each other. I'm waiting for her to message me first, which she hasn't done. But I've been imagining her coming with us to Cornwall.

"Actually, there's this girl I used to be best friends with

when I was little. I might have mentioned her to you before – Joan Tse?"

Ritika blinks, twirling a strand of her hair. "Oh. Yeah, I remember. You said she moved back to Hong Kong?"

"Yeah! So, basically, I bumped into her a couple of days ago. She's starting uni here this year, and she moved in early. I think I'd really like it if she could come with us. I haven't asked her yet, but would that be OK with you?"

Ritika narrows her eyes. "You guys haven't seen each other in years, and you immediately want to go on holiday with her? Didn't you say she never got in touch with you after she moved? She didn't even bother to, like, send you an email or anything to let you know she was still alive!"

"Yeah, I know." I let my fingers slide over the spines of the books on the shelf next to me. "I'm gonna see, if we hang out together for a bit first, what it's like. And, if it looks as if we're going to be close again, then I really want to spend more time with her and reconnect. Also, you're both into music, and I think the two of you would get along."

Ritika sighs. "I have to be honest, I don't love this. I don't want to stop you from inviting her, but I'm not friends with her. I liked the idea of just the two of us going on holiday, you know?"

"And I'm so excited to be going on holiday with you! But Joan coming along will be fun, trust me. Look, how about we hang out together first, all three of us? And then, after that, you can decide whether you're cool with her coming or not."

"Fine." Ritika taps her foot against the side of her desk. "But we really have to sort this trip out soon, OK?"

"Yeah, we will," I reassure her.

Once I get home and answer my parents' questions about work and about the movie, not acknowledging the fact that it was about a gay relationship, I head to my room and sit staring at my phone for a while, as if I can will a message from Joan into existence just by glaring at the blank WhatsApp chat between her and me. I know I could text her myself, but I want some proof that she really cares, after ignoring me for so long.

I end up messaging Ada instead, telling her about the movie.

Oooh I need to see that!

you do! also i've already looked up the movie on ao3 and there's no fic for it yet): it would be so cool if you wrote some!

Oh, you know me! I can only have one hyperfixation at a time! I can't write fic for anything else other than ER

well, i'm so glad you're writing for ER <3

> i got another person to buy a copy of ER today!!

Yay! Work is going well then?

> yeah, i'm enjoying it! my co-worker felix is super nice, so that's really great!

You know, you two kinda look cute together in that pic you sent me yesterday...

> nooooo! ada! i like him but i'm not into him like that!

Aw, and here I was thinking maybe that could be the start of a great summer romance for you...

> stop writing fanfic about me and felix in your head already!

I'm sorry, but that selfie you sent me today? I can't believe people aren't falling over themselves for a chance to kiss your gorgeous face. You can't blame me for wanting to write fanfic to fix that!

I clobber myself with a pillow repeatedly. I don't want *anybody else* to kiss me, only her. I want her to be my great summer romance; my great romance, full stop. My "grand love story", as Ritika called it. I want her to be the person I'm still in love with when I'm eighty.

I haven't told her anything about my plans for when I'm in Cornwall. I want it to be a surprise if I do find Theresa. And I haven't said anything about Joan yet, either. Joan's presence in my life just seems so uncertain still. Telling Ritika about it made me feel as shy as a girl on a first date.

My phone buzzes again. But it's not Ada.

It's Joan.

Hey, it was so nice to see you the other day. We should make a time to hang out again.

I reread the message over and over, trying to find a way to make it sound less detached than it looks on the screen. Have I waited two days for this?

Then I realise that it says *typing...* underneath her name. She's still writing.

I wait for the message to appear. When it finally does, I wonder why just three simple words took her so long.

I missed you.

CHAPTER NINE

On Wednesday, the June issue of *Eden Recoiling* comes out, and after breakfast I quickly pop out of the house to buy it.

It's not Felix at the till of the Speech Balloon, but the older guy with the beard who I've seen lots of times before and never really spoken to. He usually works there on Wednesdays – comic release days.

I tell him that I work here at weekends now and ask him if I can use my staff discount. He lets me, and I look around me and marvel again at the fact that I work here. The glittery Pride display in the centre of the shop still makes me grin.

I run home once I have the issue, and I go outside to sit in the garden with Po Po and start reading it immediately. When I'm done, I message Ada.

> **HELLOOOO WE NEED TO TALK WHEN YOU'VE READ THE NEW ISSUE**

I start idly searching for photos on my phone that I can use to make an edit, and I look at what people are saying on Twitter and Tumblr.

After lunch, I go out for a walk with Po Po, and we have a look at the outside of Oxford Castle, which Po Po doesn't really care for.

In the evening before dinner, I finally get a text from Ada.

> **OOOF. Just read it!**

> **ughhh MAYUMI**

> **MY BABY. I can't believe she's going off on her own...**

As Ada predicted, Neff absolutely doesn't want to do the dirty work, and he's told Zaria and Mayumi about the tree. But Zaria thinks it's too dangerous since there's been a surge in monsters lately, and more plants also seem to be gaining sentience for reasons they can't figure out yet. They don't even know what the apple tree will actually do, or if it's real, or anything.

Then Mayumi *flashes back* to conversations she's had with Zaria in the past, where Zaria talks about what life will be like one day if they can figure out a way to get rid of the monsters completely, and they can just rest. They've spent so long fighting them and holding their fragile little town together, but Zaria talks about wanting to *live*. To have the space to simply be. And maybe then there will be time to think about more than survival. To think about what they actually want to do for the rest of their lives. And Zaria looks at Mayumi *meaningfully* when she says that. Apparently, Mayumi also feels the same because, after this flashback, she heads off on her own to find the tree. Every time I think about it, I want to scream. There just seems to be this ... undertone.

IS IT ME OR WAS THAT REALLY GAY THOUGH?

It's not just you!

GOD DO YOU THINK MAYBE THEY REALLY ARE MUTUALLY PINING

I really hope so!

WHAT IF MAYUMI GETS INJURED WHILE SHE'S OUT THERE ALONE AND ZARIA COMES AND SAVES HER...

Ahhhh STOP! That's too much. I don't have time to write this fic right now!

> nooooo you have to write it i'm gonna die

> OK! Fine! I'm gonna try my best to get it done before camp... I only have a week!

Ada is working at a summer camp for middle-school kids this year. It's a camp she went to herself when she was younger, and she still has a couple of friends from it. They're all going back this year as counsellors.

> you can do it!! i'll cheerlead you as always!

> Thanks! Btw I loved the edit you made for that fic I wrote you! Just thinking about it now makes me want to start writing

> yessss that was my goal

She tells me she's firing up a Word document, and I tell her how I can't wait, and the next two days pass quickly as she sends me snippets of what she's writing, and I reply with fire emojis in reaction to them.

I decide to invite Joan over for dinner the following Friday. It's Thursday evening, and my mum has just got home from work. I heard the front door open and movement downstairs. As I leave my room, snatches of her conversation with Po Po drift up to me. They both sound so tired. I think they try harder to sound cheerful when Dad and I are around.

I tell Mum that Joan is coming over tomorrow night and that I'm going out for a walk. "I'll be back before dinner."

Twenty minutes later, I end up at the bubble-tea shop next to the Speech Balloon. I get my favourite – rose milk tea with tapioca pearls, half ice, half sugar – and I sit down and watch people walk past the glass front of the shop. I came here on my own a lot after the break-up. What I like about bubble tea is the texture of the pearls, the time it takes to chew each one, like mulling over a thought.

When Joan and I first met, there were no bubble-tea shops in Oxford as far as I can remember. By the time she left, there were plenty. One of the last things we did together before she moved was have bubble tea.

I pull up my email on my phone and open the sent folder, sorting by oldest to newest.

I roll a pearl on my tongue and bite into it.

Hey Joan!
Thought I'd send you an email. I've written you a few letters, but haven't got anything back. I hope everything's OK! How is Hong Kong? And school?

School here is pretty weird without you. It's nearly Christmas and I still haven't got used to not seeing you around yet. Mum's been badgering me again about how I should learn to play an instrument like you. Ugh! I just don't want to. I miss hearing you play, though. Especially the bassoon.

Hi!

Did you have a good Christmas? I had a good Christmas. Auntie Susan and Uncle Jeremy came over from Australia because they wanted to have a wintry Christmas for once. Uncle Kevin came down from Manchester too, so that was nice.

Then we went to see my ye ye and ma ma in London for New Year. I wore a dress. It's just something I'm trying out. I guess it feels like what I should do to ... grow up? I don't know, but it made my grandparents really happy.

Remember when I told you about how my po po bought me a dress as a present and she asked me to try it on and I refused and threw a big tantrum and everything? It feels a bit silly now. I gave the dress to you when I came back to England, and you looked really pretty in it. I think I just never wanted to look pretty before, but now I kind of do? Everybody else does, you know?

It sucks that the holidays are over and I have to go back to school. But anyway Happy New Year.

Joaaaan,
Literally, where are you? Hello??? Did you give me the wrong
email address?

You're probably not actually reading this, but whatever.
I miss you. I've been finding it a bit hard to make friends.
It wasn't hard with you. I feel like I never used to worry
about everything so much, but now it's all I know how to
do. Everything was easy and then BOOM. Everything is so
overwhelming all the time now. And you left before that
happened so maybe you don't even know me any more?
OK, none of this makes sense but you're not going to read
it anyway.

Have you ever liked a boy? We never really talked about
them. Girls at school go on about it a lot. Is this new or did I
just kind of miss it before? I think there are cute boys in my
class but – I'm not sure if any of them would like me back.
You said you were going to an all-girls' school, right? Is it
difficult to meet boys there?

I'll stop bothering you. I just hope you're OK.

Part of me has wanted to be angry at Joan for the radio silence, but I'm no good at holding grudges. All eleven-year-old me wanted was to hear from her again. Eleven-year-old me would have been overjoyed.

I just hope she has a good reason for falling out of touch. And I hope she means to stay in my life this time.

I swallow the last tapioca pearl whole and head home.

On my way back, I find myself in the street that Joan used to live on, a mere five-minute walk away from mine. It looks much the same. Her old house seems like it's had a fresh coat of paint, but otherwise I don't think it's changed much. I wasn't here that often, though. Joan preferred to hang out at mine. Her mum wasn't the best cook and, if left to his own devices, her dad would probably just make instant noodles for every meal, so Joan had dinner at my house a lot. Plus, her parents' favourite hobby was arguing.

"Your parents actually like each other," she once said to me.

I hold my arms round myself for a moment, standing in front of a house that Joan no longer lives in, feeling the heat rising like a ghost from the sun-warmed pavement.

CHAPTER TEN

I answer the door on Friday night to see Joan in a light blue linen shirt and navy chinos that come down just past her knees. Her hair is gelled back, neat and a little shiny. She doesn't have her earring in, and I have a strange urge to look closely for the hole in her ear, but I step back quickly.

And walk into my mum.

"Joan!" Mum squeaks, sounding a little shocked. "Look how you've grown! It's wonderful to see you again. Do you want a drink? Coffee, tea?"

"Hi, Auntie, it's so good to see you too," Joan says. "Water is fine."

I watched her go through at least three coffees in that café the other day. My mum doesn't let *me* drink coffee – not that I want to since I've had it outside the confines of home, and I'm not a fan. Still, I would appreciate being treated like an adult, same as Joan.

But Joan does look more like an adult than me, somehow, even though we're the same age. It's not that she's taller – she's actually shorter than me – but maybe it's her presence, something about the way she carries herself.

Mum goes back into the living room, and I linger in the hallway with Joan. "Hi," I say belatedly.

"Hi," she says. She looks at the photos on the walls. "These are new."

"Oh, there's lots of new stuff in the house. Wait till you see the bathroom."

"It still feels like coming home," she says, as she kneels down to unlace her brown Timberland boots.

I look at the shaved hair at the back of her head. By the time she straightens, I've turned away.

At dinner, Joan tells my dad that the only instrument she still plays is the bassoon. She dropped everything else when the pressure of secondary school got too much. I'm happy that she kept up with the bassoon; I always thought it suited her the most. She asks my dad whether he's still going to classical-music concerts and compliments my mum's cooking several times. My mum smiles and keeps piling more and more stir-fried egg with shrimp into Joan's bowl of rice, and Joan eats all of it.

Joan even asks my po po how her friends are. She asks after them *individually*, by name. Even my mum's mouth hangs open. I don't think she can name that many of her mother's acquaintances. Po Po spends every morning chatting with those people on the phone, before they go to bed on the other side of the world. They all have WhatsApp, or WeChat, and send each other pictures and stickers and voice messages. I took Po Po to the Botanic Garden yesterday, and she spent an hour taking photos of flowers and sharing them with her friends on social media.

After dinner, my parents and Po Po and Joan play mah-jong. I listen to them, the clattering sounds occasionally drowning out the TV when they're shuffling the tiles. My parents rarely break out the game. You need four people. I tried to learn when I was younger, but we don't play enough for me to remember how. Whenever we do, which is only when Uncle Kevin or Auntie Susan comes to visit, I always have to stumble awkwardly through it all over again, and it's no fun when you feel like you're just slowing everyone else down. And also losing. Badly.

Joan and my family only play a few rounds together. Po Po wins but Joan seems to hold up pretty well against everyone else.

"Let's see this bathroom then," Joan says to me in English, after she's finished helping my parents pack up the mah-jong set and stow away the foldable mah-jong table with its bright green surface.

I lead her to the bathroom and switch on the lights. The ventilator fan starts up its whirring. Joan makes a show of appreciating the new fixtures, the tasteful shade of grey paint on the walls.

I make a face. "You're such a suck-up." I cross my arms and lean against the doorjamb. "My parents are going to disown me any minute and adopt you instead."

Joan rubs the back of her neck and laughs a little stiffly. "I'm sorry. Living in Hong Kong has really hammered that whole filial piety and respect-your-elders thing into my head."

"You were always like this. My parents love you. They literally would not stop bothering me about inviting you to dinner."

"They love me, do they?" she says, smiling.

Inanely, I want to repeat, *They love you.* Instead I say nothing. I just look at her hand, pressed flat on the bathroom wall.

"I actually do need to pee," she says.

A few minutes later, she finds me in my bedroom and does a double take at all the posters and artwork I have up on one wall. "Wow, Elsie. This is amazing."

That wall is pretty much just a massive Zaria/Mayumi mood board, though much less obviously gay than the stuff I make for Tumblr and for Ada, so it won't arouse my parents' suspicions.

It's still hard for me to believe that Joan is really here, after all these years. Here in my bedroom, I especially feel that I can't look at her directly, or she'll vanish.

But, when I glance at her out of the corner of my eye, I see how solid she is. So much more solid than pigtails-and-ribbons Joan, so much more solid than *me*. I don't need to worry about her vanishing; I need to worry about *myself* vanishing. The sight of her in this house, in this room – Joan, naam zai tau, short hair and linen shirt and chinos – reduces me to feeling like a hollow projection of myself, as though she could reach out and put her arm straight through me.

"Yeah, um. I'm really into this comic. It's called *Eden Recoiling*. Have you heard of it?"

Joan shakes her head. "No. I don't really know a lot about English comics. Obviously, there's DC and Marvel, but beyond that… I read a lot of manga, though."

"Cool. I'd love to read more manga. You know I work at that comic shop now, so I'd be really happy to have some recommendations."

"I can give you some."

I think of the letters and emails I sent. How much time I spent wondering if maybe Joan didn't care about me.

How that turned into me wondering if maybe nobody wanted to be friends with me at all. After Joan, I didn't really have any good friends for a while. Not at school, anyway. I discovered fanfiction and had friends on Tumblr. At school, I felt like a ghost.

I want to be friends with Joan again, but I still don't know why we ever stopped.

"Joan," I say haltingly, "I … I need to know why you dropped off the face of the earth. It really, really sucked. I felt like our friendship didn't matter to you, but now… You're back, and I'm not sure how to feel about it any more."

Joan's shoulders sag. She gestures to the bed, to the space next to me. "Can I sit down?"

I want to say no. No, she can't sit down on my bed where I lay awake thinking of her when I was eleven, twelve; just last week. She should sit on the chair at my desk. But then she'd be facing me, looking at me. If she sits next to me, wouldn't that be easier?

So I nod and feel the mattress shift under me as she adds her weight to it.

"I'm a lesbian," she says.

Even though I'm done with exams, I'm still having dreams where I'm told that I have an extra exam left to take, on a subject I didn't even do. I wake up with anxiety like a tightly crumpled wad of paper in my chest, thinking, *Oh God, it's morning. I have to go to school and take this exam that I'm not prepared for*, and then the golden daylight would reach through my window with gentle fingers, smoothing out that piece of paper in my chest, carefully ironing out every wrinkle.

This is just like that. Like waking up to peace.

Hearing Joan say that she's gay puts me at ease. It's something I kind of already knew – I was ninety per cent sure from the moment I laid eyes on her with this new haircut and fashion sense. The confirmation isn't a surprise, but it is a relief. I didn't have to do anything for Joan to give this to me, this admission, of her own accord.

"I'm bi," I say.

"Oh." *She* is surprised. "Oh my God, Elsie. Really?" She starts to laugh. "When did you— When did you know?"

"When I was fourteen or so? There was this actress on TV... Anyway, what does this have to do with anything? I mean, I'm glad you told me, but…"

She kicks her feet; she's wearing one of those pairs of paper-thin slippers that my parents have taken from hotels and keep for visitors. "I … I knew about myself when I was younger than that. At that age, I was convinced I couldn't tell anyone, but it was all I could think about. I didn't know how to tell you. Especially since we couldn't talk in person. And my dad… He's very homophobic. He said that gay people were a bad influence on others, and they shouldn't show that stuff in the media and all that crap. It wasn't even like they ever had gay characters on TV in Hong Kong, apart from as a joke sometimes. Anyway, I didn't want to be a bad influence on you, so I just couldn't keep in touch. I wanted to, Elsie. Really. But there was all this other stuff going on in my head. Not to mention my parents divorced, and my dad remarried, and it was messy. I felt like, if I was going to talk to you, everything I wanted to say would be so negative. I'd just be complaining about my life, and I didn't want to be like that."

It stuns me, this picture of Joan's life that was so different to what I'd envisioned, which was that she was simply having too much fun to remember me. I wish, so badly, that I could have been there for her. I hate that she was as alone as I was.

"I would've listened. You could've told me anything."

"You say that now, but I don't know. It would've been a lot for you as an eleven-year-old."

"*You* were eleven too! And you had to deal with it all on your own."

I realise that I'm turning now to look at her, anyway, even though we're sitting side by side. I want to see her. I want her to see me.

But she doesn't look at me. She stares straight ahead. "It's all in the past now. I really do want to be friends again."

I don't doubt her sincerity, after the information she's just entrusted to me. The precious gift of her vulnerability in this moment is something I can almost hold in my hands.

"Your dad… He's still homophobic?"

"Yeah, that hasn't changed."

Joan's rolled up her sleeves, maybe while she was in the bathroom, and the dark hairs on her arm are now on display. Another new thing about her. They look soft.

"Have you told him that you're gay?" I ask.

"I don't think I need to tell him. I've made it pretty obvious with the way I look. You knew it."

"Yeah."

"That's why I was trying to wait for you to message me first. I mean, I was scared maybe you might've seen how different I looked and not wanted to hang out with me again, in which case I wouldn't have wanted to be friends with you, anyway. But that would've *hurt*, Elsie. And I couldn't… In the end, I couldn't wait."

You missed me, I think with a pure, sweet shock, like a slurp of freezing-cold milkshake hitting the roof of my mouth. "And I wanted you to message me first because I thought maybe *you* didn't want to talk to me. Considering that, from my perspective, it felt like you abandoned me, you can't blame me."

"No, I can't. But you can't blame me, either, for being worried that you might be homophobic."

"No, I know how that feels."

She takes a deep breath. "Right." She laughs again shakily. "You're bi. Elsie, wow."

Now that it seems we've got all the difficult emotional stuff out of the way, I can finally revel in the wonder of coming out to someone who's just come out to me, and not just anyone but Joan Tse, my best friend, whom I believed for years I would never see again. I feel like diving into a technicolour ball pit and screaming my head off.

"How did you realise that you were gay?" I ask.

"Oh, just this girl at school."

"Have you ever gone out with a girl?"

"Yeah. One but we broke up. You?"

"No. I… I had a boyfriend for a bit. There's this girl I know from Tumblr, though, and we talk all the time, and I kind of have a crush on her. So I hatched this plan…" I tell Joan about Ada's grandma and Theresa and Cornwall.

"You want to go there?" she says.

"Ritika and I were planning to go, anyway! And then Ada tells me all this. Don't you think that's like … fate? I feel as if I'm meant to find Theresa."

Joan makes a vague noise that sounds neither like approval nor disapproval. "Well. Good luck?"

"Do you wanna come with me?"

"You want me to?"

The hope in Joan's voice sounds like the hope in mine. I've been afraid of getting her back briefly only for her to remind me that I don't mean anything to her. But … I believe her. I believe that she missed me.

"Yeah."

Joan smiles at me but then she shakes her head. "I have to say, Elsie, I don't know about this plan.

It's been decades since these two women were last in contact. Theresa stopped writing. If there was anything between them in the first place, Theresa's probably moved on."

"*You* regret not keeping in touch."

Joan rubs a hand over her face.

"Even if she's moved on or whatever, it'll be nice for Ada's grandma just to know what happened to Theresa. To get closure."

"Closure," Joan echoes.

"Yeah. Just look at these letters!" I rifle in my bag for them and hand one to Joan.

After a few minutes, she puts the sheet of paper down.

"Well?" I ask her.

She pinches the bridge of her nose. "I wish everyone was taught calligraphy," she says, and I burst out laughing.

CHAPTER ELEVEN

After Joan leaves, I immediately feel bad about asking her to come to Cornwall without Ritika's OK first. I really didn't plan to do that, but it was just … Joan's face. The unrestrained delight on it when I told her I was bi. The way her eyes crinkled.

Having confirmation that Joan is gay, like I thought she might be, and knowing that she must have been as lonely as me when she first moved to Hong Kong, when she was figuring out her sexuality and couldn't confide in me, I immediately wanted to reach out with everything I had.

But I did tell Ritika I would wait till she'd met Joan first, and I failed to stick to that, which is terrible of me. I pick up my phone and fire off a text to Ritika.

> hey, i hung out with joan just now.

i'm sooo sorry but i already asked her if she would wanna come with us to cornwall! i'm sorry! i was telling her about ada and i got too excited about it and had to invite her!

elsie! you said you would wait!):

i know i'm sorry!): why don't i ask joan to hang out with us tomorrow night? we can go get dinner?

ok but if she and i don't get along then it is on YOU to uninvite her from our trip!!

it's not going to be that drastic. she's nice!

and what about the fact that she stopped talking to you?

she explained why, and i can understand it, so we're not going to hold that against her any more. i really am sorry though!

hmm. ok! fine, let's get dinner and i will make up my own mind about her

I switch to my chat with Joan.

hey, it was really great to hang out tonight!

Same! Thanks so much for inviting me. Talking to you made me really happy. Also...

Your mum is an incredible cook!

aw, i'll tell her

it made me really happy too :)

you free tomorrow night to have dinner with me and my friend ritika? she wants to meet you! and she'll be coming to cornwall too.

Yeah, I'm free tomorrow! Just let me know when + where

In the morning, Mum has this new sharp energy to her, like she might give me an electric shock if I stand too near. She hasn't been her normal self ever since she got the news that Gung Gung was ill, but this is different. She's humming as she darts round the kitchen, accidentally dropping cutlery on the floor several times and making a discordant melody out of clanging pots and pans.

"It was nice to have Joan for dinner last night," she says with an almost frightening level of enthusiasm. Po Po, I can see, is outside in the garden, sipping tea.

"Yeah, she had a good time. She told me to thank you for her."

"I forgot to ask her about her family." Mum puts a bowl of congee in front of me. "How are they? I remember her mother, lovely woman…"

"Her parents are divorced now." I blow on a spoonful of congee to cool it. "Her dad remarried. But other than that I don't know much."

"Remarried?" Mum says with cartoonish surprise, as though she's never heard of such a thing. "Oh. Well. Does Joan live with her mum?"

"Her dad, actually. But she's here on her own now."

"On her own! She must be very lonely… You should invite her over more often. We have so much food in the house, we need more people to eat it." She stares at her own half-eaten bowl of congee and stirs it. "You'll be going off to uni soon too on your own. Time goes by so quickly. I wouldn't have recognised Joan. She's all grown up."

Dad leans across me to retrieve the table salt. "I was glad to hear that she's still playing the bassoon." He sprinkles salt into his congee. At least *he* seems normal.

"Yeah, same. I really want to hear her play again. Mum, I'll definitely invite her over more."

"Why don't we all go to a concert?" Dad says.

"Will Po Po be into that?"

Mum scrunches up her nose. "I don't think so.

She'll probably fall asleep and start snoring, which would be quite embarrassing. Maybe just the two of you can go with Joan while I stay with Po Po."

Dad's mouth twists. "It would be nice if you could come! But I'll have a look at what's on." He appears to make a note on his phone. "Are you off to work today, Elsie?"

"Yeah."

"We must come and see this comic-book shop some time, maybe buy something. Your mum used to read a lot of manga as a kid. It'll be a trip down memory lane for her. You do sell manga, right?"

"Yeah, of course, but – what? I didn't know you like manga, Mum. Joan reads a lot of it too."

Mum shifts in her seat. "I'm sure she won't be familiar with any of the things I used to read – that was so long ago. But yes, maybe we'll come to the shop! I'd like to see you at work."

The idea of my parents coming to see me is almost as embarrassing as Po Po snoring loudly at a classical-music concert, but I suppress my wince and keep eating.

After I wolf down my congee, I try to escape as quickly as I can, but Mum corners me in the hallway as I'm slipping on my shoes. She presses an apple and a cereal bar into my hands to take to work and says, "I know I might have been a bit taken back last night when I first saw Joan – she used to be such a pretty child! – but it really was nice to have her to dinner. You two used to be inseparable."

117

Is Mum acting so weird because of the way Joan looks now? Does she realise that Joan is gay? I can't figure out whether all of this means she knows, and she's OK with it, or she's not OK with it, but is trying to hide it or just hoping she's wrong, *or* she has no idea, but is put off by the way Joan looks, anyway.

I wish I could ask her outright.

As I walk down the street, I think about Mum's lament that Joan used to be pretty, and it hurts. A bee-sting hurt.

And inseparable! God. Leo and I seemed inseparable to me once. And now I've spent the past two years trying to figure out what it means to be without him. Some days it feels like something I'll never understand, like quantum physics.

I want to fight the idea of me and Joan becoming inseparable again. To think of yourself as inseparable from someone is nothing other than an invitation for the world to pull you apart.

At the end of the day, Felix walks with me to Westgate because he's meeting friends there too. I'm in a terrible mood because a customer got upset with me for not having a book in the shop that he'd ordered on the phone yesterday, but Felix tells me funny stories about the last woman his dad dated, and, by the time I see Ritika and Joan outside the restaurant where

I agreed to meet them, I'm feeling much better.

They're hovering on opposite sides of the restaurant door. "Ritika! Joan!" I call to them. They look up at me and then at one another.

"Hi," Ritika says, leaping towards me and eyeing Felix. "Have we got another unannounced guest?"

"This is Felix," I say. "But he's not joining us for dinner. He's got his own friends."

"Aw, I would love to have dinner with all of you some time, if you'll have me."

Joan's presence gently makes itself known at my elbow. "Hi, everyone, I'm Joan."

Ritika waves. "Hi, I'm Ritika. Felix, you should definitely come hang out with us at some point."

"Sure," Felix says. The genuine warmth in his eyes is so charming. "All right, nice to meet you both. I'll leave you to it!"

He glides away.

Which leaves Ritika and Joan shuffling their feet.

"*Food*," Ritika says, and grabs my arm and drags me into the restaurant.

"So how did you two meet?"

We're digging into all the food that's just arrived. Joan's never had Lebanese food before, and I had to remedy that immediately. I'm still getting used to it, the idea that I can enjoy new experiences with Joan now, that she doesn't live in the ever-receding landscape of the past, but she can be here with me, sharing mezze, the three of us pulling apart a large, steaming-hot flatbread and dipping it into the houmous and baba ganoush.

"We went to the same primary school, and we lived really close to each other," Joan says. "We got the same bus to school and back."

The memory bubbles up inside me. "Yeah." I lick the smoky, garlicky taste of baba ganoush from my lips. "Joan's parents used to buy her these paper cartons of Vitasoy from the Chinese supermarket, so she'd have one to drink every day after school. I remember being really jealous, so I asked her if I could have a sip. Then I begged my parents to buy me some, and we had Vitasoy-drinking competitions on the bus home to see who could finish it the fastest."

I can feel it as I talk, the sensation of pushing the sharp end of the straw out of its flimsy plastic wrapper and poking it through the tiny foil circle at the top of the paper carton. My muscles tensing as I poise my mouth above the straw, readying myself to drink with all my might. Every time I finished first, I'd punch a hand in the air, whooping out loud. Every time Joan finished first, she just lowered the carton with a quiet, triumphant smile. And then, after the huge, breathless gulps of sweetened soymilk, we would sit there next to each other, giggling, clutching the caved-in cartons until we got off at our stop, the plastic straws chewed to a disgusting state.

Ritika prods my cheek. "Aw, that's so cute."

I roll my eyes and bump my shoulder fondly against hers.

"How did you two meet?" Joan asks.

"I joined Elsie's school in the sixth form, and one day she showed up in the music rooms, wanting to listen to somebody practise an instrument. I was like, *What the hell?* But I let her listen to me practise, anyway."

I nibble on the edge of a sambousek, careful not to burn my tongue on the melted cheese encased inside the pastry. Joan is asking Ritika what she plays, leaning forward with interest. I think about how I had instinctively sought out that music to comfort me.

When I was little, I would listen to Joan practise her many instruments after school. Sitting cross-legged at Joan's feet while she played, closing my eyes and travelling to the fantastical places that the music took me. When she played music – especially the bassoon – I thought I could hear her true voice. She was timid the rest of the time, but never when she played.

When I started sixth form, I was lost, more alone than ever. A summer of discovering *Eden Recoiling* and crying over Ada's fanfics hadn't been enough to heal me from the break-up with Leo, and being back at school, walking daily through corridors where he had shot me glances filled with secret meaning, brought it all back, vinegar-sharp. Sixth form was a lot more stressful than I'd anticipated too, the leap in difficulty from GCSE to A level unexpectedly giant. I stared at the yawning chasm that I was apparently going to have to jump across, and I didn't know how to handle it.

One day, I ended up in the music rooms after school. I looked through the glass panes in the doors. Behind the first couple of doors were people I already knew and was intimidated by, but behind the third door Ritika was playing the violin. I didn't recognise her. So I knocked.

Ritika didn't ask me too many questions. She let me sit cross-legged on the floor with my eyes closed while she carried on playing. She let me do this again, and again, and we started going for burgers afterwards, and suddenly it was the Christmas holidays, and Ritika and I were messaging each other inane things, cat gifs and terrible takes on Twitter and updates about our families, and I realised that, not only were we friends, we were *good* friends. And, between our hang-out sessions and my video calls with Ada, I'd made it through the autumn term.

Now, sitting with Joan and Ritika as they trade stories about orchestra, I remember all of this. Have I thought about this before? How, if it wasn't for Joan's music saturating my happiest childhood memories, I wouldn't have gone to the music rooms that day and asked Ritika if she would mind an audience? Joan is the reason I have the joy of Ritika in my life. The thought is like a towel fresh out of the dryer, warm and clean and soft in my hands. If it's not new, it *feels* new.

When Joan gets up to go to the bathroom, Ritika whips round to me. "OK, you did not mention that she's *hot*!"

"What?" I drop the falafel I was about to eat back on to my plate, and it rolls around a little.

"Joan. You didn't tell me that she's hot! Is *that* why you're so desperate for her to come on this trip with us, huh?"

"Ritika, I do not know what you're talking about." I nudge the falafel back and forth with a fork. "I've never thought of Joan like that. I'm not saying she *isn't* hot but – I'm still having trouble getting used to the fact that she exists like this now. She's not the eleven-year-old Joan that I remember any more. Also, I'm trying to win Ada over, remember?"

"Oh right. So you definitely don't have any –" she waggles her eyebrows – "*intentions* towards Joan?"

"Oh my God. No! Shut up. Please just eat." I stuff the falafel into her mouth instead, and, while she gobbles it down, I ask, "So what do you think, anyway? Are you happy for her to come on our trip?"

"Lucky for you, yes," Ritika says. "I like her. She seems nice. We should really start booking everything. After this?"

"Yeah, after this."

Joan comes back to the table, and we scoff down more flatbread, and lamb kibbeh, and spicy potatoes, and Joan and Ritika carry on talking animatedly – well, Ritika is animated, and Joan radiates interest in her own calm way. They're getting along, and the food is good, and I wrap myself in the cosy towel of this moment and don't ever want to let go.

CHAPTER TWELVE

There's just over a week left till the trip. I'm counting down the days.

"Hey, do you want to grab dinner after this?" Felix asks as I'm arranging some comic books on the shelves nearest the till.

"Sure," I say without thinking, slotting a slim volume back into place. Then I swivel round to look at him. We haven't really spent time together outside the shop yet, apart from last Saturday when we walked to Westgate together. "Hang on. Dinner dinner or dinner ... date?"

He cracks up. I love his laugh. It's a full belly laugh, noisy and infectious, and he laughs so easily, at things that are only a little bit funny, or for no apparent reason at all. I've often heard him cackling to himself inexplicably when there are no customers around, and it makes me have to bite my own laughter back.

"Dinner dinner! I'm not asking you out on a date. I hope you aren't offended. I'm not interested in dating girls right now, anyway."

"I'm not offended. I'm not interested in dating guys right now, either."

"Oh?" He sits up straight and beams. "See, *this* is why I want to get to know you better!"

A customer comes in, and we resume our work, but when the shop closes fifteen minutes later I throw out several suggestions of places to eat as Felix locks up.

"I don't really mind," he says. "I'm not, like, super into food or anything. As long as it's edible, I'm good."

I put the back of my hand on my forehead and close my eyes. "Did you really just say 'As long as it's edible, I'm good'? I feel physically hurt by that statement."

Felix laughs. It really is such a wonderful laugh, the sweet crunch of it like toffee apple. "Good thing this isn't a date then, right?"

"Yeah, thank God. Let's just stick to pizza."

It's a busy Saturday night in the pizza place. I get one laden with tuna and olives, and Felix orders a simple margherita.

"So," he says. "You said you're going on holiday soon with your friends that I met last week?"

I rip out a slice of pizza with my hands, relishing the

golden strings of mozzarella stretching until they break. "Yeah. We're going to Cornwall. And it's only for five days, during the week, so don't worry. I won't be abandoning you for our weekend shift."

"Sweet! What are you going to do there?"

"Chill on the beach? Also, I'm on this ... mission to win over the girl that I have a crush on."

"Oooh." He puts down the pizza slicer and rubs his hands together. "Who do you have a crush on? Is it Joan?"

"What? No!" I can see why Felix might have got confused, since Joan is one of the people I'm going on holiday with. "It's not... It's not her or Ritika. You don't know this person."

"OK. Who is it? Don't make me sing that song from *Grease*."

"What?"

"*Tell me more, tell me more,*" he sings.

"Ah." I smile and try to take a bite of my pizza, but it's too hot. "Well, it's this girl called Ada that I met online. She writes *Eden Recoiling* fanfic. I started chatting to her about two years ago, and we both love the same characters—"

"Zaria and Mayumi?"

"Yeah. She writes about them. We got to talking about how rare it is to see representations of ourselves in media, you know, since we're both queer and not white. She lives in New York, but we still talk pretty much every day."

Felix makes a sympathetic noise. "Long distance is tough."

"I haven't told her that I have a crush on her." I pick up the pizza slice to try again. "Have you done long distance then?"

"You still haven't told me what your grand plan is."

He hasn't answered my question but I'm sure I'll get to the bottom of it eventually. "Right. Ada's grandma used to live in England when she was young, and she had a close friend here. They lost touch when she moved to the US. I'm trying to find her."

"Ada's grandma's friend?"

"Yeah. Apparently, Ada's grandma still thinks about her all the time. Her last-known address is in Cornwall."

"Wow, that would be pretty cool if you found her! But I don't see why that will help you win Ada over. If she has romantic feelings for you, she has romantic feelings for you. If she doesn't, she doesn't. She's not going to fall for you just because you've found her grandma's friend. Why don't you just tell Ada that you have a crush on her?"

"And what makes *you* such an expert in romantic feelings, Felix?"

I don't know why but I feel completely comfortable talking to him about this. There are people I've known for *years* at school that I can't talk to with anything approaching this degree of ease.

"I'm no expert." He rolls up a pizza slice from the pointy end to the crust and attempts to cram the entire thing into his mouth like some kind of pizza cigar.

I gape at him while he chews. It takes some time. "What do you mean?"

He wipes his mouth on a napkin. "I've never done long distance. I've never been in any kind of relationship."

"Oh. But... You... Really?"

"Don't look so shocked." He flips his hair back. "I know I'm very handsome. I'd be such a catch, right? Alas." He starts to roll up another slice.

"Have you kissed anyone?" I ask. Maybe he means that he's made out with people, or even had sex with them, but he's just not been involved with anyone in a more lasting way.

He shakes his head. "It's truly tragic. I'm a fabulous kisser, and there's no one to appreciate it."

"How do you know you're fabulous at it if you've never done it?"

"Oh, I just *know*." Grinning, he holds my gaze for a second, and then he shrugs and sighs. "It doesn't really bother me as much as I'm probably making it sound. You know how sometimes other people expect you to be a certain way, so that even if you're not really like that you end up kind of acting like it?"

What a question. Isn't that just what it's like to move through the world? I often catch myself pretending to be something I'm not, and it's not a deliberate disguise. It's just habit. Or like a face mask, something you put on but then you absorb its essence into your skin, so that even if you peel off the mask it's already in your blood, a deeply ingrained part of you.

"Yeah," I say gently.

"I... There's this guy." Felix doesn't inhale the whole rolled-up pizza slice this time, but takes a small, thoughtful bite of it. "I met him in Spain while I was travelling. We had a bit of a spark. But ... I tried to imagine myself kissing him or sleeping with him. And I couldn't. I realised that I've never really imagined myself kissing anyone or having sex with somebody that I know. Famous actors? Sure. Characters from a comic book? Yep. But nobody I've ever had a crush on." He pauses. "Does that make sense?"

I nod. "So you think you might be ... ace? Like asexual?"

"I thought maybe that was it. My sister told me she has a friend who is ace, so. But I've been talking to this guy for a few months, and ... I don't know. I've started considering it more. I still can't imagine it, but ... he's all I can think about. But should I ask him to come to England to see me even if I might not want to do anything?"

"It doesn't have to be about sex. The two of you can figure it out together. You should just tell him what you've told me and, if he still wants to see you, he wants to see you."

It's so easy to give other people advice that I find impossible to take myself. I'd much rather the opposite, but unfortunately that doesn't seem to be how life works.

"You're right." Felix takes a swig of his beer, and I sip

my Coke. I don't drink alcohol. "Anyway, when I say I'm not interested in dating girls right now, what I mean is I'm not interested in dating anyone who isn't him."

"And Nefarious Warthorn, *whew* – am I right?"

Felix chokes on the third pizza slice that he's tackling. After he finishes spluttering, he says, "Yes, when I said characters from a comic book, I should have just said Neff Warthorn."

We spend the next five minutes counting all the ways Neff is the dreamiest man ever. Then Felix asks, "So, what about you? Is it just that you want to date this Ada girl, or why don't you want to date guys?"

"Well, I *do* want to date Ada," I say. "But also things were … not the greatest with my ex-boyfriend." I think about Leo's arms wrapped round me. I used to think I couldn't possibly belong anywhere other than in his arms. "He's the only person I've ever dated. I really want to know what it's like to date a girl, and Ada is… She's wonderful. If I'm going to start dating again, I want it to be her."

"Well, I hope it all works out for you! I'm sorry to hear that about your ex."

I remember how, when I first saw Felix in the shop, I thought for a split second that he was Leo. I look at him now, and I can't believe I ever made that mistake. They're nothing alike. There's something so clear and unguarded about Felix's face, a light in it that's summery and bright, that makes you want to unlatch every window and throw them all wide open, to air out a space in your heart that was previously closed off and cramped and dark.

But, then again, I felt that way about Leo in the beginning. I thought: *Here is a face that makes me feel safe. Here is a face I can tell all my secrets to. Here is a face that understands me.*

I shake off the memory. "I hope it works out for you too. What's his name?"

"Daniel."

The way he says the name, I feel the nervous dream of it, of tending a patch of soil where you want love to grow, and I recognise it so well.

I get home and find my parents sitting on the sofa, watching what looks like a true-crime documentary. Mum's leaning against Dad, and he's massaging her shoulder as they watch. She looks relaxed for once, eyes half closed.

"Where's Po Po?" I ask.

"Went to bed early," Dad says. He pats my mum's head. "Your mum could probably do with having an early night too."

"It's tiring having to spend so much time with my mother," Mum mumbles into Dad's shoulder, and then her eyes open fully and dart to me. "You didn't hear me say that." She yawns and stretches and leaves the room.

"I guess it must be a lot for Mum," I say, as her footsteps fade up the stairs. "Having to take care of Po Po all by herself. Like why has it all fallen on her and not Auntie Susan or Uncle Kevin?"

"Well," Dad says, "Auntie Susan will be moving back to Hong Kong after this summer to live with your po po, and – anyway, it's just complicated."

"Why?"

"I don't think I'm the best person to answer that question."

"Hmm." I take the space that my mum vacated, the leather still warm.

"You hate true crime," Dad says. "Should we switch to something else?"

"Leave it on if you want."

Dad puts on something else, anyway, a food show, but I tune it out as I think about what Felix said. About how he doesn't understand why finding Theresa will help me win Ada over.

I guess it doesn't make sense to other people. But I just think that, if I can find Theresa, it will be the universe's way of telling me that Ada and I belong together, and I believe that Ada will understand that, even if no one else does. I hope – I really hope – she already does have romantic feelings for me, but this will just be the thing that clinches it. That tells her I'm worth the ocean between us.

And the more my friends think that finding Theresa is impossible, the more I want to do it. I've been dreaming about telling Ada that I have a crush on her for months, and it just seems impossible. But the idea of finding Theresa isn't nearly as daunting, and, if I can track her down, what does that mean for other impossible things? Besides, maybe I won't even have to tell her. Maybe Ada will get it – the momentous way I feel about her – without me having to say anything when she sees what I've done for her. And that'll be proof that she feels the same way about me.

I just don't want to have to say it out loud. To say that you love someone, and to be met with indifference, with cold silence, even with scorn... I remember Leo leaving me in that school corridor after his last exam. I'll always remember it. I begged him to change his mind because I loved him, and he told me he'd never loved me.

If I find Theresa, Ada will understand how I feel, and everything will fall into place.

I don't care if it doesn't make sense to other people. It makes sense to me.

CHAPTER THIRTEEN

I dream about Leo. He says, "I'm sorry. Can we try again?"

I nod and I hold him. He kisses me, and it feels like a star burning against my lips.

When I wake up, I'm so angry.

It's been months since my last dream about him. I was having so many dreams about exams instead, which was just a different kind of stress. But I thought maybe I was free of it all now. Why am I so weak in my dreams?

I pick up my phone, and I go to my chat with Leo.

The last time he messaged me was almost exactly a year ago.

hey, i'm back in oxford. might be nice to hang out?
kinda miss you

what happened to that girl you had a crush on?

we went out for a while but it's over. i can't stop thinking about you

sometimes i don't know if i'll ever find anyone like you again

i just feel so bleh all the time and you were the only thing that's ever made me feel ok

I press my hand against my eyes.

I check his Instagram. I'm awake earlier than usual, and I have half an hour before I need to change for work. He doesn't post that much. There are sporadic selfies, pictures of pints at the pub. I scroll carefully to make sure I don't accidentally like anything. Every time his face appears, there's one particular person who pops up in the comments.

nice jacket, they commented on one post where Leo's wearing a navy jacket that seems new and crisp and makes his eyes look bluer. They follow up with the addition: *also your face is pretty nice too.*

Leo's replied: *thanks. your face is OK too i guess ;)*

An actual winky face.

I open up the person's profile. Emily. No surname. She's East Asian – some of her captions are written in Korean. She's pretty. Long hair blowing in the wind in one of her photos. She's wearing a beautiful silky white blouse and a checked miniskirt. The wind in the photo feels like it's whistling right through me.

Leo's liked all of her photos but he doesn't comment on them, not like she comments on his.

The last girl he was with was Asian too. And then, before that, there was me.

I put my phone down. I get up and try to find something to wear.

The dresses in my wardrobe all stare back at me.

Mum isn't downstairs in the living room. "Where's Mum?" I ask.

"Sleeping in," Dad says. "But I made waffles! You look nice."

Mum rarely sleeps in, but she did make that comment last night about being tired.

"Oh. Thanks."

I picked a simple blue cotton dress, and then I stared at myself in the mirror for ages, but couldn't figure out what I was looking for. I tied my hair up into a ponytail and then let it loose again. It didn't make much of a difference. Something was still off.

Dad's waffles are good. Po Po seemed to have barely touched hers, though; she's already outside in the garden, engrossed in her phone.

I point to the plate she left behind, with the remains of a waffle still on it, drooping sadly with syrup.

Dad shrugs. "Po Po doesn't have much of a sweet tooth, I suppose. I offered to make her some vermicelli noodles instead, but she said she wasn't hungry."

I try to focus on my waffle, drizzled with chocolate sauce, and forget about Leo. But it's not working.

I text Ritika.

> hey, how was your day yesterday?

oh it was great! it was delphine's birthday and there was a barbecue at her house. like half the people from orchestra were there. we had sooo much food

delphine's flying to paris today so i'm hanging out with mara. think she wants to do some shopping for her holiday in portugal next month

> how's jake? was he at the barbecue too?

no he didn't come

are you guys OK? is something up? you haven't really talked about him in a while

yeah idk. it's whatever

???

shhh don't worry about it, it's not a big deal. how's everything with you?

are you sure?

yes i'm sure, how are YOU

i'm ok. day's off to a bit of a bad start but i've got a call with ada tonight which always cheers me up. we haven't been able to chat in ages

and i'm sure work'll be fun too. i really like working at the speech balloon with felix. idk i guess until this summer i had never really had queer friends irl and i didn't realise it just makes such a huge difference!!

not that i don't love you i totally do, you're the best <3

There's nothing for a few minutes. I finish my waffle, and then I get a sparkly heart emoji from Ritika.

love you toooo, sorry your day's off to a bad start): what happened?

it's stupid really. just a bad dream

When I check Tumblr on my lunch break, I see somebody lamenting the lack of Zaria/Mayumi fan content in the *Eden Recoiling* tag. They're clearly a newcomer to the fandom. I check their profile: *Gracie. Black nonbinary lesbian. 19. They/them.*

I send Gracie some messages, pointing them in the direction of Ada's fics, and include a link to a couple of other blogs.

I write:

> it's so good to see another person who ships them!
> we should chat

And I make sure to follow their blog.

"What are you grinning at?" Felix asks, bumping his shoulder against mine.

"Oh, I found somebody else who ships Zaria/Mayumi, and I've just told them all about how incredible Ada's writing is."

"Aww, you're so *smitten*," Felix drawls, smushing his cheeks with his hands.

I laugh.

But, as soon as there's nothing else to distract me again, I go back to thinking about Leo, the memories of him like an abyss I could vanish into entirely.

The way he would smile at me sometimes, eyes half shut, haloed in an aura of cat-in-sunlight peace, and I would feel like the only person in the world who had ever seen that expression on his face. I'd feel lucky, and it would be like a fist clenched round my heart.

I try not to revisit these memories if I can help it. But most days I still think of him, anyway, in fleeting moments, just feeling the ache of his absence from my life.

Maybe it's the distance, the two years I've gained between now and then, but today I wonder if maybe his presence in my life hadn't ached in just the same way.

Hadn't loving him, even back then, felt exactly the same as missing him now?

I pull out one of the letters from Theresa.

When you were here, the ocean used to look full and glittering and playful, and I loved it for its endlessness, how it went on forever. Now it looks empty and too deep. The horizon too far in the untouchable distance.

Too deep, like it could drown you.

Maybe loving someone shouldn't feel like missing them. Like you're constantly reaching for something that isn't close enough. That isn't there at all.

Seeing Ada laugh on my laptop screen, I feel my heart loosen a little. I've been filling her in on what's been happening over the past couple of weeks, how I've been reconnecting with my best friend from primary school.

"Joan's been around a few more times now, though, and my parents love her, but my mum is still being weird sometimes, and I'm just like... Does my mum *know* that Joan's gay? Does my mum even know that lesbians exist?"

"She must know," Ada says. "Right?"

"I don't know! My mum has literally never acknowledged the existence of gay people."

"I tried to ask my dad if he knew anything about G-ma's old gal pal back in England, and it was the first time he'd even heard the name Theresa, so it's like why does Grandma feel as if she can tell me about her, but not Dad? Is it because she's getting the queer vibes from me?"

I look at Ada's face, her shaved head, her yellow bow tie and lavender shirt. "I mean, you are positively *radiating* queer vibes."

"Yeah, well, it doesn't seem like anyone else in my family has caught on yet –" Ada is only out to her brother and not anyone else in her family – "so maybe you're right, and your mom has no idea about Joan."

"Maybe. But then I have no idea why she's being so weird."

"It's just a difficult time for her right now, isn't it? Her dad passed away recently, and now her mom, who she hasn't seen in eight years, is living with her."

"When you put it like that… She did say it was tiring being around Po Po again." I tap a pen against the edge of my desk. "You know, I was talking to my dad about it, and I found out that Uncle Kevin didn't go to the funeral. Which is weird. And, like, come to think of it, Uncle Kevin never really talks about going back to Hong Kong, either. So I asked Dad if Uncle Kevin's been back there in the past few years, and Dad just kind of brushed it off. He says he doesn't talk to Uncle Kevin enough to know."

"That's your mum's older brother, right?"

"Yeah. I know Auntie Susan, who lives in Australia, was at the funeral. She went to see my grandfather just before he died. Like my mum did."

"Do you think something happened with Kevin and your grandparents? Did they fall out?"

"I can't think of any other reason."

"It must be a pretty big deal if Kevin wouldn't go to his dad's funeral."

I pop a chocolate button in my mouth to sweeten the discomfort of this train of thought. "I guess. What was your grandpa like, if you don't mind me asking?"

Ada's grandpa passed away a few years ago, before I knew her.

"You know, he was a pretty cool dude. Some of my

143

friends who are also mixed race don't get on well with their white grandparents, but I lucked out with mine! He really liked going to see plays. I saw a *lot* of plays with him. They usually went over my head, especially when I was younger. But yeah, he was nice. Not very chatty, but he was like … a quiet thinker. He really liked reading non-fiction books about world history and travel. And nature."

"Did he and your grandma seem like they were really in love?" I want to complete Rebecca's story, beyond what I've gleaned from Theresa's letters. I want to know if she found happiness again, or whether nothing was ever the same for her after Theresa.

"Oh yeah, I think so. Grandma was, like, huge on PDAs. She was always kissing his cheek and holding his hand. He liked to put on this really serious, philosophical front but around Grandma he was always so silly and cracking the stupidest jokes to make her laugh."

"That's so cute," I say.

"Yeah. I miss him a lot."

She sighs and tears open a packet of Doritos. I munch on another chocolate button. I like it when we're both snacking on a call with each other. I've never had a meal with Ada, but this is as close as we can get.

"I'm sorry. I would've liked to have known him too."

"Yeah. Anyway. It's so good to catch up with you. I've been super busy."

"How's it going with setting up stuff at the camp?"

"It's going great. The campers will be here real soon! You know that fic I was working on? I was hoping I'd have posted it by now, but I think I can still get it finished before the kids arrive. Oh! By the way, I just got an incredibly long comment on one of my fics. An entire essay! This person said you recced my fics to them?"

"Yes! That must be Gracie. I think they're new to the fandom, and I saw they were looking for Zaria/Mayumi stuff on Tumblr."

"Oh cool. I was just opening up their Tumblr before you called me. This is so wild. I've never received such detailed comments before. Aside from your comments obviously. I feel like my ego is blowing *up*."

"You deserve all the long comments! You're such an amazing writer."

Ada does a mock bow. "You're too kind. Yo, it looks like Gracie is an artist! They have a whole sideblog for their art."

I pull up Gracie's Tumblr as well and find the link. Even knowing nothing about the fandoms they'd created fanart for, I'm stunned by their art. Their use of colour is just so striking. It's hard to look away.

"Wow."

"Man, I hope they draw *Eden Recoiling* fanart. Their stuff is amazing."

"Yeah."

I scroll through Gracie's Tumblr. There are lots of reblogs

of gifsets from sci-fi TV shows and superhero movies, but after a while a selfie post crops up. They have long, waist-length box braids, and they're wearing silver lipstick. I click on their selfie tag. There are more bold lipstick colours, bright against their dark skin: turquoise, lilac, orange.

Ada would like that orange lipstick.

"Ooh, they're cute too," Ada says. She's clearly discovered Gracie's selfies as well.

"Yeah."

"Anyway, I should probably go keep working on this fic. Don't wanna keep my adoring fans waiting, since I apparently have more than one now."

I laugh. I feel better again. There's just something about Ada. She makes the world a little lighter. "Yeah, you should write. When do your campers get there?"

"T-minus two days. I'm excited! I hope they like me." She grins.

"They'll love you," I say, and I reach out to stoke the curve of her cheek where it dimples.

CHAPTER FOURTEEN

It's warm the day we set off for Cornwall, even at nine in the morning. The train is packed and horrible inside, though it looks like people have opened all the windows they could.

Even so, the heat can't dampen the excitement I feel. I keep fiddling with the pendant of my necklace. I can't help but think about Mayumi setting off to find the apple tree on her own. Hopefully, I won't get into the trouble that she does in the fic that Ada posted from camp, though, where Zaria cradles a bleeding Mayumi in her arms, having come to Mayumi's rescue just in the nick of time and slain the offending monster. She snaps at Mayumi for going off on her own, but, even while she's outwardly snarling, she's tenderly checking Mayumi's wounds and cleaning them.

And then they kiss.

I swoon again just thinking about it.

By some minor miracle, my friends and I manage to get seats together. Joan doesn't seem too bothered by the heat. I suppose she's used to it, living in Hong Kong, but Ritika fans herself with a newspaper somebody left behind on her seat, and I hold my water bottle desperately against my neck, even though it's long since imparted all the coolness it can to me.

I'm sitting next to Ritika, so I do catch a bit of the breeze from her makeshift fan, but it's just stale air, as warm as anywhere else. Joan has the seat opposite me, and she's wearing a white tank top with a black-and-white photo printed on it of a pixie-haired woman in profile, and baggy quarter-length jeans in black denim. I gaze across at Joan's bare shoulders and think about asking her who the woman is, but the heat feels too heavy on my tongue.

"Tell us something else about Ada," Ritika says. "I need to know more about your future girlfriend."

"Well, she's our age, she's going to Columbia in the 'fall', as they say, and she has no idea what she's going to major in yet. Which is wonderful for her but it really annoys me that over here we have to choose what we'll be studying at uni so early. Anyway, her dad is from upstate New York and he's white, and her mum is Black, from Nigeria. She's working as a camp counsellor at a summer camp she used to go to in middle school, and she says it's going pretty well, but a kid called Joshua has now become her mortal enemy. She writes amazing fanfiction, but I think you're sick of me gushing about that." I grin at Ritika.

Joan lights up. "She writes fanfiction?"

"Yeah."

"I write fanfic too," Joan says. "But in Chinese."

"Oh cool! What for?"

"It's all anime and manga fandoms."

"Now I *really* need to get into the manga you like so that I can check out your fanfic! Although I'm terrible at reading Chinese."

"I can … attempt to translate some of my shorter stories?" Joan offers. "If you're really interested in them?"

"Oh, that would be so cool. I don't want you to do it just for me, though. Maybe you could put up your English translations for other people to read too?"

"That's a good idea. Ritika, do you read fanfiction?"

"Not really."

"I saw you on AO3 once on your phone!" I yell.

"That was a one-off!" Ritika yells back. "I was just checking something out! It doesn't mean I read fanfic all the time!"

Joan smiles. "I find fanfic so freeing. I was writing about girls kissing girls before I had the chance to kiss a girl, and it connected me to other people who embraced that part of me."

"Yeah! I mean, I don't write it, but that's how I feel about reading it too. I still haven't kissed a girl, but I get to live vicariously through my favourite fictional characters."

"Oh hey," Ritika says, elbowing me, "have you shown Joan a picture of Ada yet? She's *so* cute."

I scroll through the photos on my phone. I have a bunch of Ada's selfies saved, and I show Joan and Ritika one of my favourites, a recent one from the New York Pride march two weeks ago. Ada is with her brother, one arm round his shoulder, and she's wearing a rainbow bow tie. Her face glows in the sun, and the photo feels like the warmest thing in the world.

"Oh, Elsie," Ritika says. "I really hope this works out for you."

"Yeah," I say.

My eyes land on the most recent thing I saved in my photo roll, which isn't a selfie of Ada. It's a piece of fanart that Gracie drew a few days ago that looks so close to the actual style of the comics that it's like Zaria/Mayumi becoming canon before my eyes. Underneath it, Gracie had put a quote from Ada's fanfic. *Like a summer storm, like thunder breaking through the sky after the long, unbearable heat.*

The tags had said:

#stayed up late reading this author's fics #woke up thinking about this author's fics #could not get this image out of my head until i drew it #please all of you have to read eden recoiling and then also all of ada's fics immediately

Ada was having lunch at camp when she saw it, and she said she had to walk out, go to the bathroom, which was in a shed, check no one else was there and then scream out loud.

I mean, I understand. Or I don't really. I'm not a writer, so I'll never know what it's like to have my words brought to life like that. I worry, a little, that I can't compete with Gracie. All I have are my edits, collages of things other people have created.

But it's OK. I clutch Theresa's letters in my bag. They're only printed copies, not the real thing, but I've handled them so much in the past few weeks that the pages have become dog-eared.

I'll find Theresa. I'll tell Ada. It'll work out.

As we step off the second train we've been on that day, Ritika groans and stretches. "Thank God we're here. I did not realise how long this would take."

"We still have to catch a bus," I say.

Ritika throws her hands up. "You're joking! We've been travelling for *hours*."

"You were *there* when we planned this all out!" I say.

Ritika crosses her arms. "I am not a detail-oriented person."

We find the bus stop. There's a shelter but it seems to be cooking a pocket of steaming-hot air under its roof. We end up perching lightly, rather than sitting, on the bench, leaving as much space as we can between us, and we nibble half-heartedly at the sandwiches we packed that morning.

"I can't believe we have to do this all over again at the end of the week," Ritika whines.

Dazed by the heat, I imagine myself as a wax sculpture melting away into a misshapen lump. I don't want to move to take my phone from my bag. I'm half worried that I'll find a useless, gloopy hunk of metal.

"Are you regretting coming along?" I murmur to Joan, while Ritika mutters to herself about global warming.

I can feel Joan turn to look at me, even though I'm staring at my sandals. "No," she says. "I'm enjoying this."

"Uh. What?"

She laughs. "I don't mean the heat. Or the waiting. But I don't mind it, either, the waiting. I'm patient. I can wait a long time. But this is fun. It's an adventure. With you."

It's my heart that's the useless, gloopy hunk, which is the only explanation I can think of for what comes out of my mouth next. "If I hadn't run into you that day by chance, would you have come to find me?"

"Why do you think I moved in so early?"

"I specifically asked you that. You said you wanted time on your own."

"Time away from my family."

I glance at her. Turning my head requires physical effort. Her forehead shines with sweat. Her upper lip too. I probably look even more of a mess than she does; I can feel the hair plastered to the side of my face. My eyes flicker to her bare upper arm. If it wasn't so hot, I would lean against her, put my head on her shoulder. It's something Ritika does to me all the time. It would be easy if I didn't feel as if my skin would burn and crisp up like crackling if I came into contact with anyone else's body heat.

"You definitely said time on your own."

"Maybe I did, but I know what I meant."

By accident, I meet her gaze, and out of that useless, gloopy hunk of muscle and blood in my chest a skittish beat makes itself known. It's still a functional heart, after all, fragile and pumping. For a moment, I realise it wouldn't be easy to touch Joan at all, but only for a moment before that thought slips away from me in the heat, like a drop of sweat.

On the train, we'd occupied ourselves with the pack of cards that Joan brought with her, but here on the bus it's more difficult to play. I sit with Ritika, who opens up one of her trashy romances. She buys them from second-hand bookshops, actual paperbacks with white creases on the spine and raunchy covers and pages falling out, and she reads them everywhere, even in front of her family, who don't seem to care. Her mum finds the wall of risqué romance-novel covers in Ritika's room hilarious.

If I try to imagine reading anything like what she's holding in front of *my* family, I have to bury my face in my hands. My parents would probably try very hard to pretend they didn't notice and avoiding mentioning it, but Po Po would *definitely* comment, in that scandalised tone of hers.

Admittedly, I do read fanfiction on my phone in public sometimes, but I angle it away from other people whenever anything remotely sexy is happening.

I can't read on a moving vehicle, though; it makes me dizzy. I put on a podcast about comics, but several times I feel a phone buzz, and it isn't mine, so it must be Ritika's.

I hit pause on the podcast. "Who are you ignoring?" I ask her.

She keeps her eyes on the page. "Jake."

"Why?"

"Does there need to be a reason?"

"What's going on with you and him?"

"I don't want to talk about it."

I think about how, when I was with Leo, I believed fervently that he was everything I wanted, even when he wasn't treating me well. Nobody had known about our relationship at the time, of course, but, if anybody had, would they have had any sense that it wasn't the perfect thing that I convinced myself it was?

"Wait. He hasn't done something ... horrible, has he?"

"No! Oh my God, no."

"Are you sure? It's ... not always easy to process if bad stuff is happening."

Ritika blinks. She lays her book down in her lap. "I am one hundred per cent certain that he's not been horrible. That is not what's happening here."

"OK."

She turns to me. "Is that what it was like with Leo?"

My eyes flick towards the seat in front of me, where Joan is sitting. I wonder if she's listening to our conversation. "Yeah. I guess so. I … I feel like I'm still processing it all, two years later."

Ritika's shoulder nudges against mine, a vague sense of comfort. "If you do want to talk about it, I'm here, you know."

I almost want to. But it doesn't feel like the right time. We're on a bus, and Joan might be hearing this, and I don't want to dredge it all up again. I want to be over it. But I know I'm not. I'm still working through it, and I'm not ready to voice any of it out loud yet.

I press my hand against the phone in my pocket and will Ada to message me, to provide some kind of distraction from this conversation.

My phone buzzes at that exact moment, and when I pull it out it really is Ada.

I swear she knows, somehow, when I'm thinking of her. More often than not, she manages to message me at the exact moment that I need her to. It's one of the many reasons why I believe the universe wants us to be together.

It's a selfie of her with trees in the background, a leafy-green setting flooded with morning light, and she looks sleepy in an adorable way, eyes half shut. It's strange seeing her in a camp T-shirt instead of her usual dapper outfits, but she looks good no matter what. The caption reads: *Awake too early after our campfire! Craving more s'mores. Would happily eat some for breakfast.*

"Hey, look, Ada sent me another selfie." I tilt my phone at Ritika.

She glances at it obligingly. "Oh cute! I've never had a s'more."

"Me neither." I wrap my hand round Ritika's wrist and squeeze briefly. "I'm here too, if you want to talk about whatever's going on with Jake."

Ritika nods. "Yeah. OK."

CHAPTER FIFTEEN

"Where first?" Ritika asks when the bus drops us off in Padstow. "We go to the address you've got for Theresa?"

It's strange. Now that we've actually arrived, I want to put off what I came here for. "Maybe we can get some ice cream first?" I suggest.

I'm nervous. That's what it is, I think. Theresa is here, or she isn't. I don't want to find out if it's the latter.

Ritika says, "Oh, come on, don't chicken out now. Let's go and find this address first and *then* ice cream."

"Fine," I grumble, but I'm thankful to Ritika for giving me this motivational push. I pull up the address on Google Maps and start following the directions.

We walk up into the residential part of town, turning this way and that. The houses glare in the sun. As Joan and Ritika are discussing whether or not mint-chocolate ice cream is a disgrace – I'm on the side of mint chocolate, for the record, and so is Joan – I come to a halt. "This is it."

We've already staked out this place virtually on Google Street View – I've done it *multiple* times – but there's nothing particularly memorable about it. The house is painted white, like many other houses on this street, the door a muted rainy-day grey.

Ritika and Joan both stand there, looking at me.

Ritika folds her arms. "It was *your* idea. I'm not knocking on some stranger's door."

"Yeah, I'm afraid you have to do this on your own," Joan says.

I pout at them but I approach the house. If I was nervous before... Sweat trickles down my neck like melted ice cream down the side of a cone. The thought of that – the ice cream that awaits me at the end of this, whatever the outcome – is the only thing that pushes me forward.

I ring the bell. Above me, a seagull calls out as if in harmony. I look up at it. It's settled on the roof next door, surveying its realm.

Eventually a man answers. White, balding, in his fifties. Glasses with a silver frame. He squints at me. "Yes? I didn't order any takeaway."

This throws me before I realise what conclusion he's jumped to. I'm not even *holding* anything that can be mistaken for a takeaway delivery. I have my phone in my hand and my backpack slung over one shoulder, and that's it.

"I'm not here to deliver a takeaway. I'm looking for somebody called Theresa Bennett. She lived in this house a long time ago."

"Don't know her," the man says, and my heart plummets. "It's just me and my wife here now. We moved in twenty years ago? I don't recall the name of the family who lived here before us. Sorry I can't help you. Have a good day."

He shuts the door.

I turn back to Joan and Ritika. "Well, that was successful," I say mildly.

"Aw." Ritika pats my back. "I'm sorry. That sucks. I know I told you you wouldn't find anything, but honestly I really wanted to be wrong."

"It's OK," I say, putting on a smile that doesn't seem to sit right. "Ice-cream time now."

Joan's hand hovers in the air near my shoulder, but doesn't land anywhere. I feel its warmth, anyway. "Are you sure you're OK? You really wanted to find her."

"Yeah, I really just want to find some ice cream right now."

Joan cocks her head sceptically, but she goes along with it.

The harbour front swarms with sunburnt people and shrieking children. There's so much red, raw skin on display, but I can almost forgive all of it for the sight of the boats bobbing on the water. It fills me with a sense of peace.

There are a number of ice-cream shops to choose from, as I remember from looking them up before, but I pick the one with the longest queue, and we join it. I'm pretty sure I recognise the attention-grabbing orange shopfront, which reminds me of Ada and draws me to it even more. I think it was one of the ones with lots of good reviews, and a long queue is always a good sign that there's something worth waiting for.

"You said you're patient," I say, grinning at Joan, who smiles back.

"I'm not," Ritika grumbles.

The queue starts outside the shop, though thankfully an awning – bright orange like the rest of the shop – provides some shade. I take a snap of the awning against the clear blue sky above to send to Ada later because I know she'll think it's pretty. I notice then that there's a rainbow-flag sticker on the shop window, which makes me smile.

"So how are you feeling about not being able to find Theresa?" Ritika asks.

"I'm fine."

"It's pretty anticlimactic, isn't it?"

"I guess it hasn't really sunk in that I've failed. Like a part of me still feels as if I'm going to find her."

"How?"

"I don't know. It's just a feeling."

Truth be told, I was crestfallen when it wasn't Theresa who answered the door. But it's hard to feel really, truly bad when I'm standing in front of such a picturesque sight, the water glittering blue before me.

We all take pictures of the harbour while we wait.

When we reach the front of the queue and enter the shop, I see that the people serving ice cream behind the counter are all young and white, except one – white, but not young at all. She has to be over sixty at least. Staring at her, I remember why I recognise this shop: she's wearing the exact same outfit I saw on the internet, only it looks even more bizarre and magnificent in person. An orange party hat with a large misshapen splat of white cloth atop her grey hair, presumably representing an upturned ice-cream cone, and a white apron over an orange bobbly knitted vest over a white short-sleeved blouse, and a pleated orange skirt to boot.

"Hello, my dears," she says. "What would you like?"

"Um," I say, stupefied by the sight of her in person. The outfit is real! It's not just a weird dream I had!

"I'll have the honey and ginger," Ritika says.

"I'll have whatever you recommend," Joan says.

"Chocolate orange is our signature flavour."

Of course. That explains all the orange.

"Great," Joan says. "I'll have that."

"Oh," I say, attempting to recover from my speechlessness. "I'll, um, I'll have the sea salt."

"Excellent choices!" the woman – I'm trying to remember her name from the article – declares.

Ritika mutters to me, "Didn't you say Theresa Bennett wanted to open an ice-cream shop?"

"What's that?" the woman asks, tilting her head.

I figure I might as well try. "We're looking for someone called Theresa Bennett," I say. "Do you know her?"

The woman shakes her head, and I think she's going to tell me that she can't help me, but then she sighs. "I thought that's what I heard."

"What?"

She smiles enigmatically. "How about I get you your ice cream first, and then I'll meet you outside?"

Ritika gasps and grips my arm so tight that I feel like it's going to break. I pay for my ice cream and try to stay calm.

Outside the shop, I exchange glances with Ritika and Joan, as excited as little kids over ice cream.

The woman comes out after us, in her full orange glory, having taken off her apron. She introduces herself to us as Lily Newham – that's what it was! – and we tell her our names. "Right then, let's find somewhere to sit and talk, shall we?" She marches over to a bench that is promptly vacated once its occupants notice her hovering.

"Do sit!" she says.

There's only really room for two more on the bench. Ritika, ever quick to react, sits down on Lily's right. I'm about to gesture to Joan to take the remaining space, but she pulls her bomber jacket from her backpack and spreads it out on the ground and makes that her seat instead.

I plop myself down to Lily's left. I've been so caught up in the suspense that I still haven't started on my ice cream yet, but Ritika's already halfway through her scoop. I notice the liquid ice cream already coating one of my fingertips. Licking up the rivulet, I taste, finally, the ice cream I've been dreaming of. Milky and smooth with a bright tang of salt, like a note plucked from an instrument.

Joan's eyes flicker up at me as she takes a soft bite of her own ice cream, and I feel the slow, cold glide of the ice cream down my throat.

"So, why are you all looking for Theresa?"

"She was friends with my friend's grandma," I say. "Rebecca Hobbs – well, Rebecca Lathey, before she was married."

"Rebecca!" Lily says. "I remember Rebecca. We were never really friends, but I got the impression that she and Theresa had been close. Didn't she move abroad?"

"Yes, to the US. She still talks about Theresa sometimes. I wanted to see if I could put them back in touch."

"Oh, Theresa left. Moved away not long after. Not so far as the US, though. She said she was only going to go for a short while, to stay with a friend in Plymouth. But she never came back."

"Do you know anything more about where exactly she went? Or about her friend?"

"I think her name was … hmm … Catherine? Yes, Catherine Overfield."

I jot this down on my phone.

"I did look Theresa up in the phone book once, years ago. I wanted her to come and see the shop. She always talked about how it would be nice to open an ice-cream shop. I thought maybe she'd hear about how successful my little business was doing and come and have a look for herself. We've been featured in the news, you know, and we're rated highly on travel websites. My niece does all the online marketing for me, so I have her to thank for that."

"Theresa's missing out," Ritika says, dusting the crumbs of the devoured cone from her hands. "Your ice cream is *amazing*."

"It is," Joan agrees. "I'd come here all the time if I lived nearby."

"Same," I chime in. "I'm sorry she hasn't come to see it. It's a wonderful shop."

"Thank you, my dears, you're all terribly sweet. I think it's a wonderful shop too. I actually met my wife through it!"

Joan is the first to recover from her surprise. "Oh, that's lovely! How long have you and your wife been together?"

"Going on twenty years. She's a writer. Came here to stay for a week at a little bed and breakfast just up the road to finish her novel – stopped by for an ice cream every day – and she's practically never left!"

"That is *so* cute," Ritika gushes, while I continue to sit there in stunned silence.

I know I came here to try to find an old woman who is

164

– I hope – gay. But I've never actually met a queer person outside my own age group, and to see a woman my po po's age who is gay and married to another woman – it affects me in a way I can't put into words, can't begin to understand what to do with. It expands inside me like a balloon being inflated, filling up my ribcage, a feeling too big to contain. I think it could float up into the sky and take me with it.

Lily has a picture of her and her wife Eva as her phone lock screen. She shows it to us, and Joan shifts closer to see the photos, her shoulder a hair's breadth from my knee. They're in a garden or a park somewhere – flowers abound in the background. Lily has her arm round Eva. The balloon pushes and pushes against the confines of my chest, gentle but insistent. I find my voice somehow.

"That's beautiful."

CHAPTER SIXTEEN

The Airbnb room is overly warm and sparsely furnished, and the beds are shabby, but it's just about an acceptable level of clean. It was the best option we were able to find at short notice during peak season.

After speaking to Lily, we sat in a café, and I looked up Catherine Overfield online, where I found a Facebook page for a catering company in Plymouth that hadn't been updated in several years, which listed Catherine Overfield as one of their friendly team members. I called the company, and they said Catherine didn't work there any more, but refused to give me any more information, which was fair enough, since I was just a random caller.

After more googling over a bottle of icy lemonade, I turned up a deli called Fields of Food in Truro, owned by a mother-daughter duo. Catherine and Meredith

Overfield. I gave the number a ring and got someone who was neither Meredith nor Catherine. They didn't sound like they could be much older than me. "You're looking for Catherine? She's not here right now. But I work here. Did you want to order something?"

"No, I … I know a friend of hers, I'm trying to find out where she is…"

It was too difficult to explain over the phone, and I've always found phone calls mildly terrifying, so I wasn't surprised when the person hung up on me.

I consoled myself with free fudge samples from the shop next door, and we wandered round the town some more, although Ritika's phone kept buzzing, and she kept ignoring it, which was concerning. I bought a postcard, though I'm not sure whether I'll keep it to adorn my bedroom wall at home or send it to Ada eventually.

Sitting on the bed I claimed in our Airbnb room, the one closest to the door, I run the tip of my thumb over one blunted corner of the postcard. I think about what Ada's face will look like when I tell her that I've found Theresa. I know I haven't yet, but… The glow of Ada's face is real in my mind, like the sun-glossed sea on the postcard.

"So what are you going to do?" Ritika asks.

She's standing by the open window, poking her head out as the sky beyond her darkens by degrees. Joan's gone for a shower, and neither Ritika nor I move to switch on the lights. I like how it feels as the light fades from the room and everything leaches of colour, transforms into shadows.

"About what?"

"About Theresa."

"I'm going to go to Truro, see if I can explain myself properly in person and try to find out if Catherine knows anything about where Theresa is. Truro isn't far from here. We can go one day this week." I've already noted down details of how to get there.

"Well, good luck with that. I'm not going to come with you. I hope that's OK."

I blink at Ritika, the dark curly waves of her hair tumbling down her back. She doesn't sound angry, just tired. "Is something wrong?"

"It seems like a waste of money, that's all. And time. All this travel is really expensive and exhausting. It's a lot of effort to go to for nothing."

I think about the day I've had. It doesn't feel like nothing to me. I haven't found Theresa, sure, but I've found *something*. An orange ice-cream shop by the sea and a woman with a peculiar hat.

"I understand," I say, even though I don't.

"You're still going to go, though, without me?"

"Yeah. I think so. It shouldn't take more than a day."

"This was meant to be *our* holiday, you know."

"What do you mean?"

Ritika whirls round. In the dim room, framed against

168

the thinning light from the window, it's hard to make out her expression. "It was meant to be our holiday. I came up with the idea of coming here, before you decided to take over the whole thing with your little project, and now you're just going to leave me here for a day by myself?"

"Joan will—"

"Joan's obviously going to go with you," Ritika snaps. "She's *your* friend."

"I haven't asked her yet. She might not—"

"Seems to me like she'll go with you anywhere."

"What?"

"She said as much today, didn't she?"

"Did she?"

Ritika snorts. "Look, I didn't mind that you decided to bring her along on *our* holiday. But this is annoying! It's annoying, and I'm annoyed."

"I thought you liked Joan. You're getting along! You spent, like, an hour today talking about your favourite K-pop group!"

They were singing and dancing on the pier. I never thought I would see Joan *dance*, movements as fluid as the water lapping against the boats in the harbour. I must have watched Ritika do that particular dance several times before, but suddenly the choreography looked sharp and dazzling, something newly in focus. Like putting on a new pair of glasses and marvelling at the precision with which the world presents itself to you afresh, the vivid details previously inaccessible to you. Ritika and Joan laughed afterwards and collapsed together on the pier, sweat-soaked.

"Yeah, I like Joan. She's cool. But I also can't forget the fact that she didn't speak to you for *years*, and then she just swans back into your life and you're instantly best friends with her again. Have you ever thought maybe you forgive people too easily?"

My face does something then, I'm sure. Something pinched and dismayed. Ritika has struck a nerve she doesn't know about. How sometimes I thought that, if my heart wasn't so pliable, things with Leo might have gone differently. If I wasn't so ready to forgive him, despite the way he mistreated me, he wouldn't have hurt me as much. I know that's not true, but it doesn't stop me from thinking like that.

The bathroom door opens, and Joan steps into the room.

"What are you two doing sitting in the dark?"

She flips the switch, and the bare light bulb dangling from the ceiling casts its white glare over us. Under the light, Joan's hair shines wet. The hem of her grey shorts peek out from underneath the massive navy tee that she's wearing.

"My turn," Ritika announces, grabbing her toiletry bag and heading for the shower.

Joan sits down on the bed opposite mine and scrubs her hair with a towel, mussing it more and more. "Is everything OK?" she asks, as I watch her.

"She's annoyed at me."

"You two were fine before I went in the shower. What happened?"

"Well, I said I would maybe take a day this week to go to Truro and see if I can keep following Theresa's trail, but Ritika doesn't want to come. She feels like I'm abandoning her."

"Maybe we should go another time."

"It's just so much easier to get there from here. We have time this week. I have to do it now or I don't know when I'll have the opportunity again."

Joan drapes her towel round her neck and tames her hair with her hand. "OK. It's your decision. Do you want me to come with you?"

"Only if you want to."

"I want to."

It's so simple. And it feels so good to hear, like *I want to* means the same thing as *I care about you*. But is it really that simple to negate all the years I spent wondering if I'm not worth caring about? *Maybe you forgive people too easily.* I know Joan had her reasons for not getting in touch, but are they enough? I'm terrified of my own weakness. Seven lost years sit like a stone between us.

"Joan."

"Hmm?"

"You said earlier… If we hadn't bumped into each other that day, you would have still got in touch with me, right? To tell me you were back in Oxford?"

"Yeah, of course."

Of course. As if it doesn't need stating, even though hearing it stated barely reassures me. "But, really, when were you going to do that?"

"I'd only been in town for a few days. I was still settling in, getting used to talking in English all the time again. And I was dealing with some things in my head. About my family. Not that I'm finished dealing with those things now…"

"What things? Can you tell me?"

Joan considers this. "Now I know why you and Ritika were sitting in the dark," she says wryly. "It's easier to talk about things like that."

"I can switch off the light again if you want," I offer.

"No, it's fine." Joan sits up straight, as if the better posture lends her emotional strength. "I was in Scotland with my dad and my stepmum on a pre-uni holiday. We were in Edinburgh and it happened to be Pride… My dad was not happy about it. I decided I'd had enough, and I realised that I could actually leave. I didn't have to put up with him any more. I talked to my stepmum first, and she said she would support me no matter what. She earns a lot more money than my dad. Overseas tuition fees are extortionate, so I had to have her on my side or I wouldn't be able to afford to go to uni here. But she promised she'd still pay for that and for my living expenses. So I found a sublet in Oxford, and I booked my train ticket, and I left."

"God. I'm so sorry. But I'm glad your stepmum is supportive, at least?"

"Yeah, well, I've always had a better relationship with my stepmum than my dad. Her best friend is gay too. But before I left … I had an argument with her. I said I couldn't understand how she could stay with my dad if she actually cares about me and her best friend. How can you love someone who's homophobic if you also love people who aren't straight?"

I hmm in agreement.

"She said I just didn't understand. Relationships are complicated."

"Have you spoken to her since?"

"Yeah. We still chat on WhatsApp. She tried to talk to my dad about it, but he got angry about how she let me leave, and he flew back to Hong Kong. She's just been travelling round Scotland on her own. She's in the Isle of Skye now. She sends me really beautiful photos… I feel bad. Like it's my fault if they separate or divorce. Even though my relationship with my dad has never been that positive. But she seems so sad, and I hate seeing her hurting like this."

Joan looks down at her hands, rubbing circles in the fleshiest part of her palm. "I know I'm lucky to have her on my side. I'm lucky I don't have to worry about money. But I'm just so confused about what the right thing to do is here."

Hearing the distress in Joan's voice makes my heart roll

down into my stomach like a bruised apple. I get up from my bed and go to sit on hers.

"It's not up to you. It's not your fault. Your dad is homophobic, and you did your best to get away from that kind of toxic environment. Now it's just up to your stepmum to decide what she wants to do."

"I guess you're right. But I still feel like I've done something wrong."

"You haven't. I'm sorry that you're going through this, but you've done nothing wrong."

Her mouth twists. "Sorry. It's a lot... I didn't realise how much I needed to talk to someone about it till now."

"I'm glad you feel like you can talk to me." I lean my shoulder against hers ever so slightly, and she leans back, just perceptibly.

We sit quietly, saying nothing in a warm silence, until Ritika comes back into the room, and we spring apart a little awkwardly. The air acquires a strange frost again, winter in the middle of summer.

I think about telling Ritika about Leo, but I can't. This day is already overwhelming enough, and it still doesn't feel like the right time. All I know – and I know this fiercely – is that I'm right to forgive Joan, no matter what Ritika says.

CHAPTER SEVENTEEN

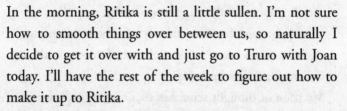

In the morning, Ritika is still a little sullen. I'm not sure how to smooth things over between us, so naturally I decide to get it over with and just go to Truro with Joan today. I'll have the rest of the week to figure out how to make it up to Ritika.

"What'll you do?" I ask her. She's come with us to the bus stop, at least.

"I don't know," she says, kicking a pebble at her sandalled feet, coral-painted toes peeking out from beneath the hem of her canary-yellow maxidress. "Might go and find a beach to sit on like a loner."

"Ritika, come on." I kick another pebble towards her. "We'll be as quick as we can. We'll be back way before dinner. Maybe tonight we can watch that K-drama that you've been telling me I should watch for weeks now?"

"Oh, which one?" Joan asks.

Ritika says the name of the show, and Joan grins and says she watched it last year. Ritika says it only landed on Netflix recently. They start talking about it, and I put my hands over my ears to avoid spoilers because I'm actually serious about wanting to watch the show.

I see Ritika crack a smile and shake her head at me, and she takes both of my wrists and pulls my hands away. "No spoilers," she says solemnly. "We'll watch it tonight. I'll make you stay up until we at least finish episode five. The ending to that will blow your mind."

"OK. Are you really going to just sit on a beach?"

"Yeah, maybe. I did bring several books."

"I told you Jake could've come on this holiday with us."

"Oh, for God's sake," Ritika sighs. She looks up at the sky, cloudier today. "We broke up."

My train of thought screeches to a cartoonish halt in my head. "What? When? What? Are you OK?"

"Yeah, I'm fine. I broke up with him a few weeks ago. I just didn't know how to tell you."

"A few weeks ago?"

"Yeah. After we finished exams."

I can't help it. It's like I've been dragged back in time to the end of Leo's last A-level exam, the school corridor outside the exam room where he'd left me crying and alone, feeling the walls closing in on me like I was stuck in a trap-ridden tomb in some stupid adventure movie. The same constricting sensation wraps its fist round me now. "Wait. Just to clarify. You dumped him."

"Yes, I did. Anyway." She stares into the distance. "I think that's your bus. I'll go. See you later." She runs away, sandals pattering down the pavement.

"Er," Joan says, as I stand there, watching Ritika disappear down the street, comet-like in her billowing maxidress. "Are we getting on this bus or do you want to go after her?"

"Let's get on the bus."

If it wasn't for Joan steering me into a seat, I would feel completely unmoored from the present. I vaguely register her hand on my elbow.

"Are you OK?" she asks. "You seem more upset than Ritika that she broke up with her boyfriend."

"I feel so bad that I had no idea. Like the fact that I'm her best friend, and she couldn't even tell me… And because the moment she told me about it all I could think about was how my own ex-boyfriend dumped me. Ugh." I put my head down in my lap.

"Well. I think tonight you two need to have a good long talk about it. That should probably take priority over the K-drama."

"Yeah."

The bus rumbles around me. I think about the last snow day we had this year before exam worry really set in, Jake and Ritika and I building a snowman together. Ritika shoving a snowball down the back of Jake's coat and him screaming, the two of them laughing as they wrestled each other into the snow and kissed, a pile of woolly hats and scarves, while I exchanged a long-suffering look with the snowman and his stone eyes.

"They seemed happy," I say. "She's never said a single negative thing about Jake to me. I don't understand why they would break up. And why she didn't want to tell me. She's been weird about it for a few weeks. Why did she feel like she had to hide what was going on? I'm just worried about her... What if Jake was secretly awful, like my ex?"

"Look, talk to her tonight and clear things up."

"Yeah." I pick at a peeling bit of the seat next to my thigh. "Yeah."

I take out my phone and text Ritika.

Hey, whatever's going on, i just want to be here for you, ok?

There's no reply.

"Your ex was awful?" Joan asks after a while.

"Mm-hmm. But... It was complicated. I don't really like to talk about it."

"I ... I'm sorry I wasn't there," Joan says in a voice that feels like sunlight on my cheek. "Those years after I moved to Hong Kong. I wish I'd kept in touch."

"I mean, life wasn't all bad." I lift my head up. "I did find it hard to make friends after you left, though. It all feels like kind of a blur now. I mostly just read a lot of depressing books I was probably too young for. We had this book club at school, and I hung out with some of the girls from that. They were nice but, I don't know, I just didn't fit in, really. We read this really good novel, and I was convinced the two main characters should've been gay, but no one agreed with me, so I went looking for reviews of it online to see if *anyone* understood. The chemistry! The yearning! And that's how I found fanfiction, which helped a lot. I read fewer depressing books and a lot more slow-burn, novel-length fanfics that end happily after all the angst. They were a much better escape, I think."

"Yeah." Joan's eyes crinkle with amused understanding. "The novel-length fanfics featured heavily in my life too after I moved back to Hong Kong. There were a few girls in my class who really liked this anime series, and I always heard them talking about it, so I ended up watching it, and I told them, and they said, 'But have you read all the fanfiction yet? That's the whole point of watching the series! For the fanfic! It's better than the show!' And they were right."

"Yeah. Sometimes the fanfic really is better. Also, it made realising I was bi and accepting myself so much easier. It's just … really wonderful to have this space where being queer feels like the norm, and queer characters get to have different love stories and find themselves and each other and be happy in a million different ways, over and over again. You know?"

"Yeah, I know."

Joan and I look at each other. In my mind, I'm flicking

through the endings of all my favourite fics, the tentative touches and first kisses. The euphoria when my two favourite characters finally get together after everything the author has put them through, and I'm in bed in the dark at 3 a.m., laying down my phone and exhaling what feels like a whole world's worth of air from my lungs. I remember so many different endings, so many different ways I've experienced the same joy.

I wonder how Joan's favourite fics end.

After a bus and a train, Truro is a cheering sight, hanging baskets of flowers a sweet peppering of colour against the white and grey buildings throughout the city centre, the cathedral's three spires peering over them all. We pass several art galleries before we find the deli, its window stamped with the words FIELDS OF FOOD in a gold retro font, a curtain of linked sausages serving as the backdrop. When we walk in, we're greeted by several members of staff, none of whom look like Catherine or Meredith in the photo on the website. It's not quite noon, so the lunch rush hasn't begun yet, but there are a few customers enjoying cups of tea, chatting.

"OK. Here goes nothing," I say under my breath. Joan gives me a reassuring smile.

I bite my lip and go up to the counter to speak to a tall person with chestnut-brown hair in a bun, a simple gold necklace with a pendant that's shaped like a holey wedge of cheese catching the light. "Um. Hi. I would like…" I glance at the selection of savoury food on display, golden quiches and colourful salads and a panoply of sandwiches. "Uh, a sausage roll, please. Also, I was wondering, is there any way I can speak to Catherine?"

"Catherine? She's not here at the moment. I can definitely get you that sausage roll, though. You want it to go or for here?"

"I'll eat it here, thanks."

A sausage roll is placed on a cute yellow ceramic plate for me. "What do you need to speak to Catherine for?"

"It's … personal. I think she might know somebody that I'm looking for."

"Hmm. Could you elaborate?" The tone is friendly, more encouraging than whoever I spoke to on the phone.

I wonder how much detail to go into and begin a halting explanation. "Um. I'm just helping my friend's grandma. She used to know this woman called Theresa Bennett who I think Catherine knows as well. My friend's grandma wants to know where Theresa ended up, so I've been helping her look."

"Right… That's not like any request I've ever had to deal with before. Well, Catherine is away on holiday at the moment, I'm afraid. Every year she and Meredith go to this place in the middle of nowhere with no reception for three weeks, so there's no way to contact her."

"Oh. All right."

"Is there anything else I can get you?"

The world shrinks and shivers around me as I panic, thinking that as soon as this conversation ends I won't have anything left but this *sausage roll*, and no other clues as to how to locate Theresa.

"I might get the ham-and-brie sandwich," Joan muses, briefly touching the chilled glass behind which all the food sits. Her fingers leave behind gentle impressions on the glass. I watch them fade, and in that span of seconds I manage to have a productive thought.

"Actually, I'll have a lemonade as well. And some carrot cake. Also, is it possible to leave a message for Catherine?"

"Oh yeah! Of course. It'll be a while before she gets back, but I can pass it on for you. I'll just write it down on my phone and set a reminder for myself."

I dictate a message and give my phone number, and ask for her name – Isabel – and then I pay for all my food. Joan gets her ham-and-brie sandwich and a coffee, and we sit down and eat our early lunch. I simultaneously regret not getting something more interesting than a simple sausage roll and marvel that it's so tasty. Joan lets me have a bite of her sandwich. It's good.

"So, it looks like we'll have to wait," Joan says.

"Yeah."

"Are you OK?"

"I guess." Now that I don't have the next step of my

search for Theresa to worry about, I'm thinking about Ritika again. "Hey, you said you had a girlfriend, right?"

Joan blinks. "Yes, I did."

"Did you break up with her or was it the other way round?"

"Are you asking me about this because of what happened with Ritika?"

I nod.

"OK. Well, I broke up with her."

I hate that this annoys me, but it does. None of my friends know what it's like to be dumped. To have the person you love stand in front of you and tell you that they just don't want you any more. "Why?" It comes out almost petulant.

"It wasn't a serious thing. We had fun but I realised that I didn't really want to be with *her* specifically. I just wanted to be with a girl, and she was the first girl who ever wanted me. She felt the same way too – I was just the first to put an end to it."

That's a bit more reassuring to hear. "So she wasn't upset?"

"No, she was fine. We stayed friends. She's with somebody else now. We weren't even together for long, just a few months."

"So have you been keeping in touch with her even here?"

"Yeah. I have a group chat on WhatsApp with my friends. It's been strange because they're mostly using it to plan things I can't go to, all these dinners and movies, but I do pipe up occasionally. Most of them are queer.

They're very important to me. I don't know how I would have got through the past few years without them, so I don't want to lose them. I'd love for you to meet them."

"I guess, now that my mum's been to Hong Kong for the first time in eight years, maybe the mysterious ban's been lifted, and I can go there too at some point soon."

"I mean, after uni, when you get a full-time job and you're making enough money to afford it, you can go to Hong Kong whenever you want, even if your parents insist on the mysterious ban."

I stare at her. This hasn't really occurred to me. The tension of the past few minutes dissipates immediately as I laugh. Of course. It's still far off, the end of uni, but it's not unimaginable. I'm having a taste of freedom already, going on my first holiday without my parents. Of course I can go to Hong Kong on my own one day, no matter what my mum and dad think. But it still feels like it would be so wrong, even though I have no idea why we stopped going to Hong Kong for eight years.

"What's so funny?" Joan asks.

"Nothing," I say. "I just got hit by this realisation that I'll actually be independent someday. Anyway, I'm so jealous that you have loads of queer friends."

"You have me," Joan says, stirring her coffee. "And Ada—"

"I love her but she doesn't live here."

"Neither do my friends."

"Yeah, but you *did* share the same physical space with them for a long time."

"True. But you also have Felix."

"I didn't have you or Felix until less than a month ago!"

"You can't have been the only queer person at your school."

"I wasn't. I just wasn't friends with the others. I told you, I find it really difficult to make friends. Ritika is kind of like the only person from school I would really consider a friend now. I've never felt fully myself with anyone apart from her."

And she doesn't even feel as if she can tell me that she broke up with her boyfriend. Are we really fully ourselves with each other?

I let this thought sink in, like the sugar dissolving in Joan's coffee.

"Hey." Joan nudges me by pushing her empty plate against my hand. "You'll talk to her later, OK? You'll be all right." As though she can read my mind.

"Yeah. Thanks."

I dig into my carrot cake. It's perfect, not too sweet, moist and nutty with tangy cream-cheese icing, and I close my eyes and lose myself in the dreamy taste of it for a moment.

Joan clears her throat. "What is up with this mysterious ban, anyway? Do you have any idea what's behind it?"

"I don't know. Uncle Kevin is the only one who didn't go to the funeral, though, and you'd think he'd come down to see us now Po Po's here, but he hasn't visited yet, and I haven't heard anyone even suggest it."

"That's kind of strange."

"Yeah, right? I don't feel like I'm going to get anything out of my parents after all these years, so I think maybe I'll try talking to Uncle Kevin about it. I've been meaning to message him to tell him I've got a job at the Speech Balloon, anyway. He loves comics."

"Your Auntie Susan lives in Australia, right? Do you know if she's been back to Hong Kong at all in the past eight years, other than for the funeral?"

"I don't know. We don't really talk about it. I barely see Auntie Susan that much as it is. I think I've seen her maybe three times in the past eight years? I know she and her husband are planning to move back to Hong Kong soon, though, to live with Po Po when she returns there after the summer."

"Hmm. As terrible as this is going to sound, it's kind of a relief to think about other people's family drama rather than my own."

I shake my head at Joan and push my carrot cake towards her. She carves out a spoonful and a trickle of delight runs through me at the blissful expression she makes when she eats it. I offer her more.

"It's funny," she says. "I got carrot cake in this café in Edinburgh when I was with my stepmum, and she found the concept of putting carrots in a dessert so strange."

"Did she like it?"

"I think she prefers chocolate cake."

"Oooh, have you had carrot halwa before? I had it when Ritika's parents invited me over for Diwali last year, and it was so nice."

"No, what's that?"

I look up a recipe with pictures online and show Joan. I think about Ritika's house last November, lit with candles and crowded with family, a dozen conversations happening at once under the same roof. The happy noise of it, a hubbub of warmth and light against the creeping, silent dark of winter.

Even on her own, Ritika is all that noise and all that light for me. I hope she can find something similar in me too.

CHAPTER EIGHTEEN

On the train back, Ada messages me about the turbulent romance between two of the other camp counsellors.

I swear they've like already broken up and got back together twice in the short time that we've been here. And now they're sneaking off into the woods to make out. You want to place bets on how long it will be till Kayla comes and cries on my shoulder again?

oh no! i hope for your sake that they stay together at least till the end of the camp this time

I signed up to look after kids, not people my own age!

lol i'm so sorry

um, speaking of relationship troubles, apparently ritika's broken up with her boyfriend and this happened weeks ago and she didn't even tell me

What??

yeah. i'm just really confused. Why wouldn't she tell me about it? i feel like such a bad friend

): Oh babe. I'm sure there's a good reason. Sometimes some things are just really hard to talk about! Like you and Leo. I think you said you never really talked to anybody else about that

yeah. i mean ritika knows that i went out with a guy called leo who dumped me and that it was, how shall we say it, a majorly devastating event in my life

but nothing much beyond that

but like that break-up happened before ritika and i were friends. this is something she's going through currently

I think that whatever happened with you and Leo is something you're still going through currently too, you know.

...):

i hate that but i guess you're right

hugs

what fun camp activities are happening today?

I've got to supervise a play rehearsal in a minute.
They're putting on Macbeth

oh! cheerful!

The kids voted for it

I told Gracie about it and they said they directed a student
performance of Macbeth and it was a disaster

They think it's because the lead actor kept slipping up and
saying Macbeth in the theater

But my little thespians seem to be taking the curse very
seriously and they are only referring to it as the Scottish play

haha that's cute

gracie's really into the theatre then?

Oh yeah they're a huge theater person. Did I tell you that I found out that they live in New York?

omg really?

Yeah! They go to NYU. They've just finished their freshman year.

oh wow!

Yeah, I was so happy when I found out we live in the same city! I think we'll get to hang out after I come back from camp!

that sounds great!!

Yeah!

OK I have to go. I'll talk to you later! <3

I put my phone down. My heart's throwing a tantrum. It's not *fair* that I've been friends with Ada for two years, and we haven't been able to meet each other in real life, but Gracie and Ada can think about meeting up casually just like that, when they've known each other for barely a week.

It's *not fair*.

Joan says, "Was that Ada?"

I nod.

"How's she doing?"

I tell myself I'm being childish. Am I going to be jealous of the entire population of New York City? Ada and I will always have our own lives.

"She's busy at camp. And dealing with other people's relationship drama. But I think she's having a good time. I keep wanting to tell her about how I'm looking for Theresa, but I can't, so that's weird."

"You could just tell her."

"No way! It's going to be so much cooler if I find Theresa and suddenly give Ada the news out of nowhere."

Joan shakes her head at me. "I don't understand it, but it's up to you." She turns to look out of the window, but then she looks back and says, "So you really think there's a possibility that Ada likes you back, right?"

"Oh." I rub my knee nervously with one hand. "Um. I don't really know? It's so hard to tell. But maybe? I hope so? Ugh, I don't know."

"OK," Joan says. "And you think that, if she really does like you back, you'd be happy to do the long-distance thing?"

I shrug. "I just know that I really like her. I guess if she does like me back then we'll try our best, won't we? Lots of people manage long distance just fine."

"Hmm. Yeah, I guess you're right."

"It does scare me, though," I say quietly. "The idea of being in a relationship again. Long distance or not."

"Because of your ex?" Joan asks, just as quiet.

It's been a *day*. Maybe I'm finally ready to talk about Leo with someone, and I feel safe here with Joan. "Yeah. I still think about him a lot. It's taken me a while to admit that he wasn't good to me. I really loved him. But I don't know if he ever really loved me."

"What makes you say that?"

"He said he did but he didn't care about my feelings nearly as much as he cared about his own. I think he was just using me to feel better about himself. And when he broke up with me he told me he never actually loved me. Also…" I think of Emily's Instagram. The Korean girl that Leo might be having a thing with. "Have you ever heard of something called 'yellow fever'?"

Joan raises an eyebrow. "The illness?"

"No, something else. It's a term that Ada mentioned to me a few months ago. Her best friend Bella Chung found out that the white guy she was dating had slept with a string of exclusively Asian girls before her. He had a fetish for Asian women – yellow fever."

"Oh." Joan nods. "Yeah. I've seen people like that in Hong Kong. I didn't realise there was a name for it in English."

"I've noticed stuff at school before too – mostly just guys making disgusting comments, though it didn't happen to me personally. But it seems like it's more talked about in the US. I looked up the term after Ada brought it up, and it was all articles about Asian Americans."

"You think that your ex had yellow fever?"

"Maybe? It wasn't … obvious. He wasn't ever like, 'Asian women are so hot.' But it looks like, since we broke up, the other girls he's been dating are Asian too. And it makes me rethink some of the things he said to me when we were together."

He was always talking about how cool it was that my family was from Hong Kong. I told him that I was born here and didn't really know much about it, that I went there as a child, but I haven't been back in years, and he was so disappointed. It was his dream to travel in Asia, and he wished he had the money to do a gap year there. But he didn't, so it was his goal to get a job teaching English there after uni.

On the surface, there was nothing wrong with any of that. But then I would tell him that I was insecure about my appearance, and he would say, "You are so much more beautiful than every single white girl I know." And he'd tell me that he liked how shy I was, and he would comment on me being delicate and small, and how precious that was to him. At the time, I needed those compliments. Now, though, the memories leave a bad taste.

"That's horrible." Joan's shoulder presses into mine, a firm and comforting weight.

"It doesn't actually make a difference, right? He was already shitty. It's just another thing to add to the list."

"It does make a difference," Joan says. "I understand why that would hurt even more. You deserve someone who really sees you."

I blink. It's been messing me up ever since I started reading about it. The idea that men who have yellow fever only see Asian women as submissive and obedient playthings that they can dump all their problems on and then discard. The idea that Leo saw *me* as that. On top of all the other things that he's done to me, this is a unique and different pain. That he never even saw me at all.

But I didn't truly believe it back then. That I deserved to be seen.

I do now, though. I do. And being seen requires being open about myself.

Joan looks at me, soft, patient.

I want to be seen.

When our bus gets back into Padstow, I text Ritika. She still hasn't replied to any of the various other texts I've sent her today.

hey, we're back. where are you?

you can't avoid me forever, we're on holiday together

who's bottling things up now?

meet me at the harbour

I tell Joan about Ritika's text and she says, "I'll head back to the Airbnb. Leave you two to talk."

When I get to the harbour, Ritika is sitting on a bench. It's easy to spot her sunny yellow dress, even though her face is obscured – she's bought a straw hat with a wide brim and a red ribbon from somewhere. It looks really good on her.

I sit down next to her.

"I like your hat."

"Thanks."

"What did you do today?"

"Walked to a beach. Came back and saw some baby lobsters. There's like a lobster hatchery here. It's pretty cool. You?"

I update her on what happened in Truro, and then we fall into silence.

Ritika is usually so chatty that she tends to be the first to break any silences between us. But she's not speaking now. When it gets too unbearable, I venture, "Ritika … I don't know what I said or did to make you feel like you couldn't talk to me about what was going on with J—"

"I'm the horrible person," Ritika interrupts, a blank stare on her face.

"What?"

"I'm the horrible person," Ritika repeats. "You were worried that Jake was actually horrible, and you didn't know about it. Well, it's me."

"What do you mean?"

196

"I didn't love him," Ritika says. "I kept thinking I would fall in love eventually but, after we'd been going out for, like, half a year, he told me that he loved me, and I didn't say it back at first because I didn't feel it yet, and he was like, it's OK! You don't have to say it back! But then it dragged on, and I was like… Wow. It's just getting awkward now. He kept saying it to me, and it's weird if I don't say it back! So I lied. I said I loved him but I didn't."

"Oh."

"Yeah. I'm the worst. Fuck."

"And then you broke up with him?"

"I had to. Every time I told him I loved him, he looked so happy. And I really thought at first that it would become true, that we just needed to spend more time together, but nope. My heart was still like, *Ritika, we are not going to melt for this boy.* So I couldn't do it any more. I had to break up with him."

I can't believe that this whole time I thought she adored Jake. I'm upset that she felt she had to deal with this on her own. "What did you say to him?"

"I said that I really like him, and I think he's wonderful, because I do! You saw him: he was always baking me treats, and he paid attention to everything I said. He's the ideal boyfriend, right? But *nooo*, my heart just has impossibly high standards, I guess. Anyway, I told him that he's great, but I just don't think we're going to work out long term, and that I want him to find someone who can really love him the way he deserves, because I am not that person."

"And what did he say?"

"He cried and was like, 'No, Ritika, I love you, we're even going to the same uni, we can stay together.' But then after he stopped crying he was like, 'OK, I have to respect your decision, but can we stay friends?' So I agreed, and he's been texting me a lot, but it just makes me feel bad because I can tell he's really mopey even if he doesn't explicitly say it."

It sounds like a terrible situation. But I know that Ritika acted as she did because she didn't want to hurt Jake. Leo, on the other hand, was never thinking about me, only himself. "So you're ignoring him?"

"Yep."

"Can you tell him that you just need time? That it would be good for him and for you to keep some distance for a while before you try to be friends again?"

Ritika puts her head down and wails. "He's going to be even more gutted. Like, somewhere along the way, I became his best friend! I can't take that away from him too."

"You've got to. It'll be better for him in the long run. He can't get over you properly if you carry on like this."

"That's why I put off replying to his messages. Maybe I can wean him off somehow if I take longer and longer to reply?"

I punch Ritika lightly in the shoulder, and she mumbles a half-hearted *ow*. I say, "It feels to me like it would be better to just be upfront with him about it, but what do I know?" I sigh. "Why didn't you just tell me all of this?"

"Because! I'm a horrible person! Like I said!" She throws her arms up in the air. "And I know how your ex broke up with you, even though you really loved him, and that really hurt you and … I feel like what I did is the same as what he did." She slows down, saying the next words in a smaller voice than I thought possible for her: "I don't want you to hate me."

"I could never hate you, Ritika."

"I broke up with him out of nowhere!"

"Breaking up with him is still a better decision than continuing to lie to him. You did the right thing. You're not a horrible person. And you are not the same as my ex."

Ritika looks at me, imploring me to elaborate with big puppy eyes. And I know, at last, I can tell her about Leo. I know that will be good, for both of us.

"Leo was… At the time, I thought that the break-up was what hurt me. But I think I can see more and more clearly now that it wasn't the break-up. He had been hurting me for a long time before that. He was not a very happy person, and I think the way he dealt with that was by dragging me into his misery with him, even though I didn't really realise it back then."

"Fuck, Elsie. Please tell me he wasn't, like, physically violent with you."

"No, he didn't hit me or anything. But … he was really manipulative, and he made me feel like my sole purpose in life was to make him feel better, and I just… I disappeared into that for a while, and I guess I'm still figuring it out. There are lots of days when I think I could've tried harder to help him, or that he wasn't really so bad. Like maybe I'm blowing things out of proportion in my own head because I'm bitter about our break-up, you know? It's not as if I have a filmed documentary of our relationship that I can show to someone and ask what they think. I know it was bad. I just wish I could have a second opinion from someone who understood it all."

Even as I say this, I feel lighter already, a part of me lifting off and into the clouds, joining the chorus of gulls circling overhead. Just admitting how difficult it is makes it less so.

"Shit," Ritika says.

I wait for her to absorb what I've said. I know it's a lot to take in. People pass by behind us, bits of conversations drifting past, voices I'll never hear again. Distantly a car honks.

Ritika's hand touches my elbow. "Here's a second opinion: he's a dick. I don't need a documentary of your relationship. I can tell just from the way you're talking about it that it was bad. Fuck him."

I feel a surge of warmth at Ritika's ferocity. "I even realised recently that he probably has yellow fever. You know, like he has a fetish for Asian women."

"Ew. Oh no. I hate him so much, and I've never met him."

"I hate him too. But… I do still want him to be OK. I don't think I care about whether he's happy. I did. But it doesn't matter to me what he feels any more. Maybe what I want now is for him to get better, to change, so that he never does this to anyone else again, you know?" I settle my chin on my knees.

Ritika tugs on my arm, and I look at her. Her smile is soft like an old worn jumper, and she puts her hand on my cheek. "I hope he becomes less of an arse too, for the sake of humanity. But what's most important to me is that you're OK."

I manage a shaky smile back. "Yeah, I am. Thanks for listening to me."

"Thanks for telling me."

"Now do you believe me when I say you are not a horrible person, and I don't hate you?"

Her shoulders sag. "I guess. I'm sorry for being so tetchy these last couple of days. The self-loathing was getting a bit much." Ritika stands up. "I'm hungry. Should we get some food?"

She reaches her hand down to me, and I reach up with mine, grasping her fingers to pull myself up.

"I love you," I say.

It's not something my family ever say to each other.

And, since Leo, "I love you" is something I've only typed to people online. But saying it out loud to Ritika now leads me to an oasis of calm inside me I didn't know existed. I thought I had been parched for so long but I have a friend who is as important to me as Leo ever was, if not more, and it isn't frightening to tell her that I love her. It's good.

Leo made me forget that a platonic friendship could run so deep, mean so much, but Ritika made me remember. Joan made me remember.

"I love you too," Ritika says, smiling. "And I really mean it."

We set off up the path to get Joan so we can go for dinner, and we talk about what we want to eat, scrolling on our phones and throwing restaurant suggestions at each other, ruminating on prawns and scallops and burgers as the water murmurs behind us, and the sky stretches above us, and I let go of Leo a little more.

CHAPTER NINETEEN

The remaining three days in Cornwall speed by after that in cliffside walks and picnics by the beach, crab sandwiches and pasties and cream teas and more ice cream, browsing tiny little shops and dozing in the sun in between conversations about movies and music and nothing in particular. At night, we binge episodes of the K-drama that I said I would watch with Ritika and that Joan doesn't mind rewatching, either, and by the end of it Ritika and I are both sobbing while Joan smiles and rolls her eyes at us, but even she tears up at one point, and I throw a crisp at her when she tries to pretend she isn't crying.

On the train ride back to Oxford, the sadness from the end of the K-drama resurfaces, and I realise that I'm thinking about how the three of us will all be off to separate unis after this summer.

"We should do this every year," I say, looking at my friends. "Go on holiday somewhere."

"Oh, you didn't mean we should go on a search for your crush's grandma's long-lost friend every year?" Ritika teases. "Good to know."

"I'm serious. I know we're all going to go to different unis, but we have to keep in touch, OK? This was so nice, and I can't let this be the last holiday we ever go on together."

"It won't," Ritika says seriously. "We'll go on more holidays in the future, I promise."

"And I'll be there as long as you want me there," Joan says, and when I glance away out of the window the sun catches in my eyes, and I have to blink.

It hits me as we get further and further away from Cornwall that we haven't found Theresa. While I was in Padstow, it didn't bother me so much. I was walking round a town that Theresa wrote her letters from, and it still felt so completely possible that she would just appear in front of me, like magic. But now that possibility is fading. There's a really good chance I'll never know what happened to her.

I touch the letters in my bag for reassurance. It's habit by now. Not even looking at them, just reaching into my bag and grasping the sheaf of papers, fiddling with the folded corner of a sheet.

My phone buzzes. It's a text from Ada.

Hey, how are you?

i'm ok! just on the train home to oxford

Oh, already? Wow, that went by quickly

yeah, it really did!

Anyway, I've been working on this fic just like, in my notes app on my phone whenever I have free time

I much prefer writing on my laptop but hey, I am in the middle of the woods right now and surrounded by preteens who are vying for my attention, so

But I'm like mostly done with the fic now. It's super short. I was hoping you could maybe read it through before I post it? I want to gift it to Gracie

And I really want to make sure it's perfect! I'm kinda nervous about it

I think I have a crush on them

Oh.
The world cracks in half around me.

VOLUME II

CHAPTER TWENTY

At home, I'm bombarded with questions about the trip. I show my parents and Po Po a few photos before telling them that I'm too sleepy for all this – and I have work in the morning.

In my bedroom, I stick the postcard from Padstow on the wall, and I kneel on my bed and stare at it. Already the sea seems so far away but, if I concentrate hard enough, I can just about call up the atmosphere of it again, the lullaby of the waves, the salt air in my lungs.

The excuse that I was too sleepy was a lie. I'm already itching to *go* somewhere again, to get out of the house.

I feel so caged in.

Ada never liked me in that way. All this time, I've been hoping. Reading into our interactions something that wasn't there.

I said that I would read through Ada's fic for her. But all I want to do is be as far away from everything as possible.

In my head, I turn over every moment when I thought Ada might like me back. Ada, the Zaria to my Mayumi. I think about how many times I've wanted to reach through my screen to touch her, especially when she laughed, and the sound of her laughter filled my room like a waterfall. What she looked like when she was tired and sad, and how I wanted to kiss the sorrow from her mouth. The way her words made me feel, like all the stars poured down from the sky and gathered in my bed, glowing with other-worldly light.

I was wrong. She doesn't like me like that. What do I do now?

Trying to think of anything that can take my mind off Ada, I remember I said to Joan that I would message Uncle Kevin, so I bring up my conversation with him on WhatsApp. The last time we exchanged messages was back in March on his birthday. And the last time before that was me asking him about the title of a graphic novel he'd said was good when he'd come to visit in February, for the Lunar New Year.

I've always felt this sense of awe around him. My parents are my parents, familiar in a comfortable and dull way, but Uncle Kevin is different. He looks much younger than he is, has a goatee and speaks in a measured voice that's like a magician's. It makes you sit up straight and pay attention.

I type out a message to him:

> hey uncle! how are you? i thought you might like to know i got a job at the local comic book shop recently! i'm really enjoying it. i get a staff discount! so i can definitely read more stuff now if you have any recommendations for me! are you planning to come and visit any time soon? i'm sure po po would like to see you!

After that, I open up my bag and dump everything on to my bed and the floor, shaking it vigorously. And then I get annoyed at myself for making this mess instead of unpacking methodically.

By the time Uncle Kevin replies, I've finally cleared it all away and made my room look passably tidy again.

> Hi Elsie! That's really great to hear that you got a job at the comic book shop! Are you still a fan of Eden Recoiling? Also, has Po Po been saying that she wants to see me?

Po Po *hasn't* said anything. No one has, and that's what's so strange about it.

My weekend shifts at the Speech Balloon pass by in a whirlwind. A local indie creator comes in after seeing our Pride display and wants to know if we would be interested in their – very queer – graphic novel. Nathan has a chat with the creator, Tam, while Felix and I flip through one of the copies of the book that Tam's brought with them.

I'm immediately hooked by the cosy art style and the story of the polyamorous witch coven who have to go on a dangerous journey to gather ingredients for a potion to wake one of their own from a cursed sleep. I'm also awed by Tam themselves – Vietnamese, nonbinary, in their early thirties, with a bi flag pin on their bag.

An hour later, Nathan is talking me through how they organise events at the shop, and by the end of Sunday we've put up an Eventbrite and started advertising Tam's book signing on social media.

With all of that to distract me, I still think about Ada far too much.

On Sunday night, I read the draft of the fic she's written for Gracie. It's very short, but her writing is as beautiful as always. It's like eating my favourite meal in the world, mixed with ash. I can't think of anything to say about it to Ada except *I love it, I'm sure Gracie will too*.

It's Monday morning by the time I remember that I still haven't responded to Uncle Kevin's text.

Why didn't you go to Gung Gung's funeral? I want to ask him.

I scroll back through the photos on my phone to find the ones from our Lunar New Year dinner, when I last saw Uncle Kevin. In them, everyone's wearing something red, and the festive warmth is palpable. I'm in a ruby lace dress, Mum's in a bright scarlet jumper, Dad's wearing a burgundy plaid shirt and Kevin's jacket is a maroon colour. We're all smiling around a table full of food.

When I look at these photos, it becomes even more apparent how much Mum has changed since then. There are shadows living inside her face now, and her grief is incomprehensible to me, both because it's something that I don't personally feel, having only a smudge of Gung Gung on my heart like a blurry fingerprint on the lens of my glasses, and because she hadn't seen him in eight years when he died.

Although eight years is nearly half my life – and the half of my life that I'm actually fully conscious of, at that – I realise that, for Mum, it's only one small portion of hers. I have no idea what that's like. Maybe eight years don't feel like that big a deal to her as they do to me?

The fact that I never really knew Gung Gung saddens me more than his death does. On the street, seeing older Chinese men walking by, I've sometimes thought: *I know almost as much about this man as I do about Gung Gung.* It makes me feel a weird and flimsy tenderness towards these strangers, a translucent, jellyfish-like sadness floating around me as I start to imagine them with granddaughters who know them better.

Had Gung Gung really been so important to Mum? And, if so, why hadn't we gone back to Hong Kong to see him in the past eight years?

I have no answers, and I don't know how to ask the questions out loud. I haven't really known how to deal with Mum since she first received the news that Gung Gung was dying. It's not like she and I were ever that close. As soon as I realised I was queer, I started to distance myself from my parents. I wasn't sure how they would react if they knew, since they acted like they'd never even heard of gay people. And then there was Leo. Somewhere along the way, I've completely lost the map for talking to my parents, and the street signs are all in a foreign language. Or maybe they're just in Chinese, and I can't read Chinese well enough.

Downstairs, Po Po is in the garden, of course. The dahlias started to bloom while I was away, all these brilliant shades of red like in the Lunar New Year photos I've been looking at.

"Good morning, Po Po," I say, as I sit down next to her, handing her a mug filled half with freshly boiled water from the kettle and half with cold tap water so that it's just the right temperature for drinking. In my other hand, I have my breakfast: a bowl of yoghurt and granola.

"Good morning, Yan Yan."

I eat my yoghurt and granola and watch a magpie fly into our garden.

After a week of being in Cornwall, there's a strange

kind of comfort to returning to this routine that I created with Po Po during the weeks before my holiday. I come downstairs later than her every morning, I bring her a mug of warm water, and she takes her medication while I scoff down some cereal or toast. And then we just sit together in the garden. She plays mah-jong on her phone and complains about how easy it is to beat the computer programs. I read comics or scroll through social media on my phone.

Morning wanes into afternoon, and I heat up leftovers for lunch, and then, if it's not too hot to move, I take Po Po out into the town centre, and we have a look at some shops without buying anything, or we go for a walk in a park somewhere. Then it's evening, and my parents come back from work.

Most of the time, when Po Po and I are in the garden, we don't say much to each other. A few times, she's had video calls with her friends on WhatsApp and made me say hi to them.

"My granddaughter!" she says, as I lean into the frame. "Such a gwaai syun. Looking after me every day, helping her mum out in the kitchen."

I'm starting to get used to being a gwaai syun. A good grandchild. Even though I still don't know Po Po that well, hearing the phrase makes me feel close to her. I think I might miss it when she leaves after the summer.

Po Po's friends peer curiously at me from the screen.

"Oh, I remember! She was so little the last time I saw her!" one woman said.

Another: "Ah, what a pretty girl! How old are you now? Going to university yet?"

I still can't keep track of all their names. I told Joan about these conversations, and she teased me about how I couldn't be a gwaai syun if I couldn't remember any of my grandmother's friends' names.

But there was one woman who said, "Oh! I'd forgotten you had a granddaughter! Silly me."

I didn't miss Po Po's wince, even though she laughed it off like it was just a funny joke.

Is an absent granddaughter better than no granddaughter at all? Is an absent *daughter* better than no daughter all? The more I think about it, the more I think that Po Po and Mum probably didn't keep in touch at all over the past eight years. I always assumed that Mum and Po Po were still making phone calls to each other even if Mum wasn't going back to Hong Kong to see her, but the fact that I've never been asked to be present for such a call suggests otherwise.

I have so many things swimming around my mind, the tiny silvery fish of my thoughts darting back and forth.

I can't just sit here in silence any more.

"I wish I'd got to know Gung Gung properly," I say, looking up at the blue sky.

This summer is practically rainless, the sun eternal. Maybe the sun knows that Po Po has come all the way from Hong Kong to be here and is on its best behaviour for her. Even the sun is afraid of Po Po's criticism. She *has* mentioned a few times that England isn't nearly as grey as she was expecting.

Po Po sighs. "It's a pity that our family has been so divided. People have even forgotten that I have a granddaughter. It's so shameful. But Gung Gung was a hard man."

I'm confused. "What do you mean?"

"He was always so stubborn. If he wasn't so stubborn, he wouldn't have produced such stubborn children, and everything would be different."

This is too cryptic for me. "From what I can remember, he was really nice."

"Oh, nice to you! His grandchild! Of course he was nice to you. Grandchildren are everything. It's always a joy to have a grandchild."

'Pou syun.' The Cantonese phrase she used literally means holding your grandchild in your arms. The emotion that this phrase evokes hits me in a surprising way, making my throat close up. I think about being a baby, and Gung Gung rocking me in his arms, cooing over me.

Nice to you. Something only half healed twinges in my gut. "Po Po, did Gung Gung not treat you well?"

Po Po sighs again. "Don't jump to conclusions," she says, folding her hands in her lap.

She doesn't say anything more for a while, and I think maybe that's that, that this is all I'm going to get. Then she says, "Your mum and dad. They seem very happy together."

"Yeah, well, I think so."

My parents just have this sense of ease around each other. They don't argue much. They take care of each other and buy each other little things and smile at each other even when they're tired.

"Hmm. That's good."

And again. Silence. I'm sure this talk of my parents being happy must be related somehow to Gung Gung and Po Po's relationship, but Po Po doesn't elaborate.

"What about Mum?" I press. "Wasn't Gung Gung nice to Mum?"

Po Po frowns. "Your mum didn't like your gung gung very much." Which isn't answering my question exactly, but it's something. It's new information.

I don't know how to reconcile this with my mum's grief.

"What about Uncle Kevin?" I ask.

"Like I said, your gung gung's children are all very stubborn." A bee hovers inquisitively around Po Po's feet. She doesn't appear to notice. "Your uncle's wife was so lovely! He found a good woman, and then…"

I've never thought about Uncle Kevin's divorce much. It happened so long ago. I don't remember his ex-wife at all. "Are you annoyed at him because he got a divorce?"

"Ah… It doesn't matter now, anyway. Do you know if he's going to come and visit soon?"

Aha! "I've asked him but he didn't say."

Immediately, I notice something fragile in Po Po's face, usually so composed. Something that would flake and flutter away like white ash if I breathe near it. It makes me want to reassure her.

"I'm sure he will soon, though, if he knows you want to see him."

"Well, he must be busy."

"When was the last time you saw him?"

"Too long ago. Your po po doesn't even have a good enough memory to remember the last time."

This is a ridiculous answer. Po Po's proud of her memory. Sometimes she tells stories about Mum's childhood at dinner, and, when Mum says she remembers something differently, Po Po always insists that she's right and Mum's wrong. "My memory is impeccable. Better than anyone's." The stories are usually only about Mum and Auntie Susan, not about Uncle Kevin.

But once Po Po said that Mum regularly bullied Kevin into doing school projects for her – Mum hated making posters and that kind of thing, but Kevin was good at it. I could feel the atmosphere around the table stiffen like an old tea towel hung out to dry, as though we were all having to watch a gay kiss on TV again.

Mum refused to admit this had ever happened, but after dinner, when we were doing the dishes, she said to me, "Kevin *liked* doing those posters. I didn't bully him into it."

So Po Po loves reminiscing but she's only interested in

memories from Mum's childhood. Nothing past Mum's adolescence. And she certainly doesn't want to think about the last time she saw Uncle Kevin. But I have no doubt she remembers it and remembers it well.

Po Po lapses into silence after that.

If I can't find out from Po Po what happened, surely I can find out from Uncle Kevin himself. It's something for my brain to fixate on, at least, that isn't just Ada's crush on Gracie.

CHAPTER TWENTY-ONE

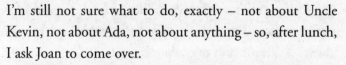

I'm still not sure what to do, exactly – not about Uncle Kevin, not about Ada, not about anything – so, after lunch, I ask Joan to come over.

When she turns up, she waves a USB stick at me, and I blink at her, confused. "I have hundreds of episodes of Chinese dramas on here," she says. "They'll keep your po po entertained."

Joan describes several different Chinese dramas to Po Po, and Po Po chooses one. Joan starts playing it on the TV, and then Joan and I retreat into the kitchen, and I try to make her some coffee.

"You look like you have no idea what you're doing," she says, bemused, as I fumble around with my dad's cafetière.

"Uh, I totally do," I say, looking up instructions on my phone.

She laughs, batting my shoulder aside with a spoon. "No, you really don't. Let me do it."

I watch her. I've seen my dad make coffee lots of times before, but I've never paid that much attention. I try to now but I can't stop thinking about Uncle Kevin.

"Po Po brought up something about Uncle Kevin's ex-wife today," I say. "It sounds like she wishes that he never divorced her."

"That's not uncommon," Joan says. "I know my dad's parents were really upset with him when he and Mum got a divorce. They thought he was in the wrong and should have tried to save the marriage for my sake or something. And now they don't like my dad that much *or* my stepmum. We see them a few times every year, but it's always awkward, and my stepmum hates it."

"But if it's the divorce that's the issue that can't possibly explain it. The divorce happened before I even started going to primary school, I think. It was before you and I became friends. So it was, like, another … six years or so after the divorce that my family stopped going back to Hong Kong. Unless those two things are unrelated? Like my grandparents got angry at Uncle Kevin for one thing, and then my Mum got angry at my grandparents for something else?"

"I guess that could be it."

"Po Po said my mum didn't like Gung Gung very much."

"Maybe he wasn't a good dad? And at some point your

mum just decided she'd had enough and didn't want to deal with him any more?"

Joan pours the steaming coffee from the cafetière into a mug and I think of her alone in this city for the first few days after she fled her family trip in Scotland. "Yeah. Maybe. Po Po said he was a 'hard man', whatever that means. He was so nice to me... I hope he wasn't really awful."

"Maybe it would be better if you stop there," Joan says. "He's gone. You never knew him that well. You can keep it that way and let everything stay in the past."

"But what about Po Po and Uncle Kevin? I still don't know how to reply to Uncle Kevin's text."

"OK, let me see it?"

I open up the chat and put my phone down on the worktop in front of Joan, rereading the text myself.

Hi Elsie! That's really great to hear that you got a job at the comic book shop! Are you still a fan of Eden Recoiling? Also, has Po Po been saying that she wants to see me?

"Er. And did she say that she wants to see him?"

"Not as such, no. But she did ask if he was going to visit soon! Isn't that kind of the same thing?"

"Elsie... No?"

I pick up the spoon and smack her arm lightly with it. "OK, fine. But she *sounded* like she wanted to see him even if she didn't say it out loud. What should I tell my uncle then?"

"I still think maybe it's best not to meddle. We don't know what's going on here. You should just let them deal with whatever happened between them in their own way."

I can't be satisfied with that, though. Not knowing.

I fire off a reply.

> yep, still a huge fan of ER! i've been reading lots of other stuff too but ER is still my fave. po po asked if i know when you might be coming to visit!

"There." I show Joan my phone again. "I didn't lie."

"OK. Well. Let's go and watch some of the court drama that your po po is watching?"

"Yeah, OK."

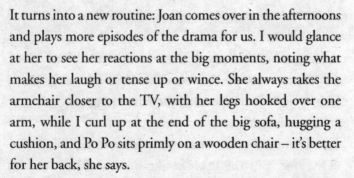

It turns into a new routine: Joan comes over in the afternoons and plays more episodes of the drama for us. I would glance at her to see her reactions at the big moments, noting what makes her laugh or tense up or wince. She always takes the armchair closer to the TV, with her legs hooked over one arm, while I curl up at the end of the big sofa, hugging a cushion, and Po Po sits primly on a wooden chair – it's better for her back, she says.

After spending so much time together on our holiday,

I do miss seeing Ritika, but, between her little cousins coming to visit and her tutoring job, she's got too much going on to hang out.

I don't hear back from Uncle Kevin, and so one night, after dinner, as I'm doing the washing-up and Mum is putting away leftovers in Tupperware into the fridge, I ask, "Why hasn't Uncle Kevin been round recently?"

"He's busy," Mum says.

I rinse out the dish that had contained fried fish in sweetcorn sauce, something Po Po thinks is much better than fish and chips. "Doesn't he want to see Po Po? Isn't that the whole point of bringing her here, so she can be closer to her family for a bit?"

"Yes, and I'm sure he will come at some point."

I pick up a bowl and give it a scrub with the soapy sponge. "Well, maybe Joan and I can go up to visit him?"

The idea was just kind of half formed in my head, but saying it out loud I realise it sounds perfectly reasonable. He always comes to visit us, never the other way round. Mum says that she doesn't like Manchester, that Uncle Kevin loves Oxford. We have a look at a different Oxford college every time he's here, and there's a place in the Covered Market where he likes to get food. But I want to see where he lives.

He's a freelance graphic designer, and he's single and doesn't have children – he got divorced when I was little, maybe five or six years old. When I try to imagine his home, I picture a sleek, trendy flat, mostly monochrome with the occasional splash of colour, well placed and eye-catching, plus cool posters on the walls.

"You and Joan?" Mum says.

"Yeah. We had so much fun in Cornwall, we thought we could have another little trip somewhere, and if we stay with Uncle Kevin it'll save money. I'd ask Ritika to come too, but she's busy. I know you don't like Manchester but I'd like to see it for myself! Maybe I could just take a weekend off work or something? We can even bring Po Po with us so she can see him."

The fridge door shuts decisively behind me. "That's not a good idea."

"Why not?"

"I told you, Kevin's busy. He's got some big project he's working on, deadlines coming up soon. You shouldn't disturb him."

I turn off the tap and look at my mum, who is now wiping down surfaces with a wet dishcloth. "OK," I say.

In my room, I pull out my phone and text Uncle Kevin.

> hi uncle! mum says you're really busy and can't come and see us. i was thinking i could come up to see you? would you mind if a friend and i came to stay with you for a weekend or something?

And I wait again.

On Saturday morning, I'm trying to pick out what to wear for work as usual, cursing myself for not deciding the night before. It's always before I have to rush off to work that I feel truly fed up with every single item of clothing in my wardrobe. I think about the outfits that Joan wears every day, the shirts and the trousers, usually very plain colours – white, black, grey, various quiet shades of blue – but so neatly put together and striking somehow. I don't own anything like that.

The only trousers in my wardrobe are jeans.

After fifteen minutes of deliberating, I throw on a lilac dress with white polka dots. I go downstairs, say good morning to my parents and to Po Po, eat my omelette and run.

But, only an hour later, the door chimes and my mum walks into the Speech Balloon.

"That's my *mum*," I hiss to Felix, but I put on a smile as Mum gets closer. "Hi, Mum. What are you doing here? Is everything OK?"

"Of course everything's OK. If it was an emergency, I would call you, not come here. I said I would try to visit you at work one day, didn't I?"

"OK. Cool. Great. So this is where I work. And this is Felix, my co-worker."

"Hello, Felix."

"Hi, Mrs Lo," Felix says.

"My mum's last name is Pang, actually," I say. "Chinese women don't tend to take their husband's surname."

"Oh cool. Hi, Mrs Pang."

My mum smiles. "This is a nice shop. Elsie said your father owns it?"

"Yeah. My dad's just out the back."

"Mum, I can show you the manga section if you want?"

"Yes, I'd like that."

I lead Mum over. She stands there, just looking at it, for a long time, and then she says, "Wow, I really don't know what any of these are. I'm used to reading manga in Chinese. They have different titles."

I take out my phone and open up the Notes app. "Write down the Chinese titles for me?"

I never have a reason to write Chinese, so my ability to do it is almost non-existent, but my mum uses the Chinese handwriting input to list the titles for me, and I copy and paste each of them into Google to look them up.

Eventually, we figure out together what the English titles are. I can't find all of them on the shelves here, but I do find a couple. Mum flips through them, her face softening, and I recognise the nostalgia in her expression. I probably look at Joan the same way sometimes, with that ache for what we left behind in childhood, remembering simpler things.

"You can use my staff discount if you want to buy

any of these," I say. "But maybe you want to try reading something new? Joan gave me a list of recommendations, but I haven't even started on it yet because there are *so* many other things to read."

"OK, tell me about them."

I pause to consider the titles that Mum used to like when she was younger. I've been reading about different manga genres just to make sure I can keep up if customers ask me questions, and it seems that Mum likes shounen – the high-action stuff.

I take something from the shelf and present it to her. "This is *the* best shounen manga ever, according to Joan. I looked it up – it's super popular – but apparently it's really, really good. And there are also two anime shows of it? But only the second one is actually a proper adaptation..."

"Oh, I think I've heard of this actually, yes," Mum says, leafing through the first few pages. "I'll go for it."

"Cool!"

I turn to go back to the till to ring it up for her, but she puts a hand on my arm. Not for the first time, I think about how thin she is these days, the bones of her wrist too prominent, as if they're about to pierce her skin.

"Yan Yan, I did want to speak to you about something. Uncle Kevin called and said you texted him about going up to visit?"

"Oh. Yeah. I did. Sorry, I know you said he was busy but I thought it couldn't hurt to ask."

"Yes. Well, we talked about it, and he thinks it would be OK for you to visit, but it's probably best not to bring Po Po for now. In fact, you mustn't tell her that you're going up to see him. I'm sure you know that things are a little difficult between her and Uncle Kevin…"

I'm sure you know? It's so bold of my mum to suddenly say that to me when everybody in my family has refused to broach the topic up till now.

"Um. OK. I mean, I don't really know what's going on. Can you not tell me?"

Mum looks down at the book in her hand. "It's better if I leave it to your uncle. You will… It will be good for you to see him. You and Joan." She pats my arm a few times absent-mindedly. "Did he ever meet her?"

"I don't think so. Joan doesn't remember meeting him."

"It's really so lovely to see how much she's grown up," Mum says. "I'm so happy for you that you've found each other again. Sometimes you lose someone important to you, and you never get them back."

After dinner on Sunday, Dad brings up the fact that he's been looking at concert tickets. "How about Thursday?"

"This coming Thursday? Hold on." I bring up the calendar on my phone. "Yeah, no, sorry, Dad. We have an event at the Speech Balloon that evening. I don't have to work then, but I'd like to go to it, anyway." It's Tam's event.

"OK, let's go … Friday then?"

"Yeah, that sounds fine for me. I'll check if Joan and Ritika are free."

Joan replies pretty quickly with a thumbs-up emoji.

Ritika dithers a bit more.

sorry it's just been a lot over here! i have no time to myself these days. conning parents into believing that i can teach their kids maths is taking a lot out of me. WHEW.

you CAN teach their kids maths. you're good at maths!

no i've forgotten all of it already like the moment my exams were over i was like goodbye knowledge, helloooo stupidity.

but i need the £ so

at least my little cousins are gone now so i don't have to deal with children 24/7 any more i LOVE them but they are WAY too energetic

you should come to the concert! i miss you):

i miss you too! what's new in your world?

> got this book-signing event at the speech balloon on thursday with this really cool comic artist called tam! they're nonbinary and vietnamese and i love the sound of their book so much. i'll send you a link to their work

> also i might be going to manchester with joan to see my uncle kevin. would you wanna come?

> nah count me out. manchester's FAR and i'm a busy woman

> ok! but you should definitely come to this concert

> hmm ok yeah i'll have to run over after one of my tutoring sessions but i will be there!

I tell Dad, who says he'll buy the tickets later.

Up in my room, I end up looking at the fic that Ada wrote for Gracie again. She posted it at the beginning of the week, and Gracie was the first to leave a comment, and they had a long conversation right there in the comments thread, throwing I LOVE YOUs at each other like a pillow fight of affection. I didn't leave a long comment like I usually do. Just a quick one: *i already told you how much i loved this and i still do! this is sooo amazing!!*

I haven't really spoken much to Ada since, and she hasn't reached out, either. I know she's probably busy at camp, but I'm guessing her priority now is to message

Gracie whenever she has a spare second.

I have to do something else – anything else – rather than mope over this. So I pull up the family photos on my laptop. Dad moved all of them on to the cloud some years ago, but I've never really looked at them, especially not the ones from years back. They're organised by year, and I'm looking for Uncle Kevin's ex-wife, so I go back to 2008, when I was four. I find some from Lunar New Year, which feels like the obvious time period to look for photos that include my extended family.

I spot Uncle Kevin's ex-wife, a Chinese woman with long hair in a ponytail, wearing a purple fit-and-flare dress. She's pretty.

Me, on the other hand… I really could have easily been mistaken for a boy, with my spiky, short haircut, baggy trousers and polo shirts. *Naam zai tau*.

I look through more of the albums.

There are photos of my ye ye and ma ma – my grandparents on my dad's side. They live on the outskirts of London, and we visit them sometimes. There are photos of trips to Hong Kong. Gung Gung's round face and Po Po's pointier one, younger and smoother. Auntie Susan's there too, with her husband Jeremy and their kids – my cousins.

A few photos of Joan start to crop up here and there throughout my primary school years. Having a picnic in what looks like Port Meadow; queuing for a ride at

Legoland; sledging down the hill in South Park on a snow day. She half hides behind me in nearly every photo, at least one of her pigtails vanishing behind my head.

Eventually she herself vanishes from the photos. There are pictures from a barbecue in our garden the summer Joan moved back to Hong Kong, and she's not there. I'm eating some grilled corn on the cob, and my mum is on one side of me, and Uncle Kevin is on the other, our plates loaded with food. There's a man, half out of frame and blurry, in a green checked shirt. I think he's white – his hair is ginger. I try to remember who he is, but I haven't got a clue. Maybe one of my parents' friends from work?

I keep scrolling. There are no more photos of trips to Hong Kong. My hair gets longer; I get taller. I look awkward and unhappy, fists clenched in the skirt of my dress where there would be pockets on a pair of trousers. The dresses don't suit me, until they do. Until I figured out the trick somehow, with practice. By looking at other girls online where it's safer to do so than in real life, studying their style, thinking about how beautiful they are and trying to crack the code of how to be like them. Asking myself: if I seemed as beautiful as them, would they want to kiss me?

I learned how to smile carefully at the camera, how to angle my face so that it looks best. There are no more artless, toothy grins.

234

I know that Past Me in the photos is about to meet Leo. I close my laptop.

And I lie down and look at the ceiling, and I wonder how adults learn to live with this feeling that the past is always growing bigger, that you're always losing more of yourself to it.

CHAPTER TWENTY-TWO

It's been two weeks since I went to Fields of Food in Truro and left a message, and I still haven't heard anything. I guess this is the universe's way of telling me that finding Theresa was a stupid plan, anyway. There's no use. Ada likes Gracie, and the two of them live in the same city. They have far more chance of working out than Ada and I ever had.

I take Theresa's letters out from my drawer, thinking I'll rip them up, or bury them in the garden the way I've buried other things in the past.

But I'm sentimental, so I can't help but reread the letters.

Becca,
It's been half a year since you left. I haven't been keeping count
of the days, what do you mean?

People still always ask me how you're doing over there in America. I suppose everybody knows how close we are. I tell them what you tell me in your letters. You're good. You're seeing somebody. You found a job that pays well. I wonder when they'll stop asking me. When you'll fade from their minds.

I know you won't fade from mine.

I went out in the boat with my father yesterday. He was surprised I asked to go. He's given up trying to persuade me to carry on the fishing business. But when I'm out at sea I don't miss you so much. I sometimes think that if my dad wasn't a fisherman I might even like fishing.

They're playing your favourite song on the radio. I just want to dance with you again.

Yours,
Tessa

I still find these letters so painfully romantic. I lie down and press the folded sheet of paper over my heart. I wonder what the song was. If it's a fast song or a slow one. Is it sad or happy?

I just want to dance with you again.

I think about that picture of Lily Newham and her wife on Lily's phone. I think about Joan on the pier, dancing with Ritika. The way they laughed together. I didn't think I'd ever get to see Joan laugh again. I didn't think I'd get to see the way Joan has grown without me. All light where she used to be my shadow. I would never have expected this version of Joan, short-haired and surprising, so different from what she was, but so completely what she should be. Sometimes it steals my breath away when she smiles, when her eyes crinkle just so.

I want Theresa and Rebecca to find each other again. I need them to. Some impossible things have to be possible, even if Ada and I aren't. Love has to be real sometimes.

I ring Fields of Food to ask if Isabel – the woman who noted down the message for Catherine Overfield – is in. Thankfully I get passed on to her immediately.

"Hi, Isabel," I say. "This is Elsie. I visited the deli a couple of weeks back, looking for Catherine? Is she back yet?"

"Oh yeah! Sorry, I did mean to pass on your message, but it completely slipped my mind. Catherine's back from her holiday now, though. I'll get her to call you when she has a moment, I promise. I do have your number written down."

"OK, thanks! I really appreciate that."

"Sorry. She'll be in touch."

"Thank you!"

I spend the rest of the day jumpy, thinking that Catherine might call at any moment, but my phone stays still and silent. Joan comes over, and we watch more episodes of the court drama with Po Po, even though

I don't take any of it in because I'm just staring at my phone, willing it to ring. Po Po tells me off for bouncing my leg several times.

After two episodes, Po Po declares that she's going to take a nap, and she goes up to bed. I try to take my mind off whether or not Catherine is going to call by discussing going up to Manchester with Joan. We look at train tickets.

"You seem distracted," Joan says when I keep asking her to repeat things. "Are you all right?"

"Yeah! Yeah. I'm fine. I just… I called Fields of Food to follow up, and Isabel – you remember? – said that Catherine was back from her holiday and would call me soon, so that's all I can really think about."

"OK. Well, why don't we just listen to some music and chill for a bit?"

She puts on a playlist of dreamy classical music and closes her eyes. I sprawl out on the sofa and look at her, remembering afternoons when I would do nothing but listen to her play her bassoon and imagine a world from each piece of music, the notes becoming birds and trees and fountains and people.

Po Po comes back downstairs half an hour later to find us both looking like we're asleep, but we're awake, just carried away on a tide of music. And then my phone rings.

I leap up, running out of the living room as I answer the call. "Hi!"

"Hello. Are you Elsie?"

"Yes! That's me. Hi." I plop myself down on a chair in the garden.

"Hello, Elsie. This is Catherine Overfield. Isabel told me you wanted to talk to me. She said you're looking for a woman named Theresa?"

"Yes, that's right. My friend's grandmother was really good friends with her, but they lost touch."

"Your friend's grandmother. What's her name?"

"Rebecca Lathey, before she got married."

"I see. How on earth did you end up looking for Theresa in my shop?"

"Oh, um. I went to Lily Newham's ice-cream shop, and she told me that the last she knew of Theresa was that she went to stay with you in Plymouth, so I looked you up and saw you'd opened a deli in Truro."

"To be honest with you, love, I don't know how much help I can be. I haven't spoken to Theresa in years."

"Do you still have any contact details for her?"

"Nothing current. She only stayed with me for a few months back in the late seventies before she figured out where she wanted to go next. We were good friends but you know how it is. She wasn't great at keeping in touch and neither was I, to be fair."

"Where did she end up?"

"She went to London for a while, and then I think she was up in Scotland for a bit, and then she moved back down to Birmingham. I didn't hear anything from her after that. That was … in the mid-nineties? She said she'd met somebody, and you know how people get when they're newly in love; they forget everyone else."

That's a long time ago. I was hoping Catherine would have had more recent contact with Theresa. "OK. Do you have an address for where she lived in Birmingham? And do you know the name of the person she fell in love with?"

"I think her name was … Sabina? I can't remember the surname off the top of my head, but I can see if I have it written down anywhere. I used to keep diaries, not very good ones, though, so don't get your hopes up."

"That'd be amazing if you could take a look."

"All right. I'll drop you a note if I manage to find her full name."

"Great, thank you so much."

Before I go back inside, I type 'Sabina Birmingham' into Google. The first thing that comes up is a hair salon. Then there are LinkedIn profiles for people called Sabina who work somewhere in Birmingham, and a nun called Sister Sabina featured in several news articles. I suppose that if Catherine can't find Sabina's full name I'll have to comb through all these.

But I get a text from Catherine much quicker than I thought I might, only half an hour later, when I'm still talking to Joan about the possibility of making a stop in

241

Birmingham on the way to Manchester, which in itself could be easily done. It's what we'd have to do once we were in Birmingham that remains unclear.

> I didn't find Sabina's last name but I did find some other information about her. Apparently she was working in a hotel but was an aspiring artist and Theresa really liked her paintings? Also, she's Indian. Do you think that will help?

This time, I type 'Sabina artist Birmingham' into Google. As I trawl through the results, lying on my front on my bed, Joan also does some searches on her phone.

"I found something!" Joan cries out.

I roll on to my back and sit up straight. "What is it?"

"I was googling art markets in Birmingham, and I found this one called Moseley Arts Market, so I scrolled through their Facebook page. They sometimes list a few of the artists who'll be there, and I found an artist called Sabina Pandey who's exhibited there before. It says here that she does paintings."

"Joan! That's amazing. Are there any contact details for her?"

"Not here. But it does say that the market is on the last Saturday of every month. If we go next Saturday, the market will be on."

I google 'Sabina Pandey artist', but I don't find her website, so I message Moseley Arts Market on Facebook.

> Hi! I'm interested in buying Sabina Pandey's paintings!
> Do you have her contact details?

I look up, and Joan is grinning fiercely at me. "It could be a totally different Sabina," she says. "But this still feels very cool!"

"Yeah. I'm so glad you're doing this with me."

I smile at her, and I think maybe this search is worth it, after all, just for the little moments of shared glee that it's already brought.

"My dad entertained thoughts of being an artist, actually," Joan says quietly.

"Oh."

"Yeah, my mum always told him it wasn't realistic, and she thought it was a waste of time. But my stepmum really likes his art, and she was always encouraging him to keep it up."

"What sort of art does he make?"

Joan shows me photos on her phone. They're very whimsical illustrations, woodland creatures and cluttered cottages. Not very polished, but still pleasing to look at. "Wow. He's actually pretty good."

"I know. He used to make these little books for me when I was tiny. I looked back at some of them, and he was really terrible at trying to write a story to go along with the pictures, but the drawings themselves aren't half bad." Joan sighs.

"Hey," I murmur. "How are you holding up with all that?"

"Sometimes I miss him," Joan says. "But then I remember how we spent our time together disagreeing about everything." She gives me a wry smile. "My stepmum's flying back to Hong Kong at the end of this week, and she wants to see me before she goes."

"And? Are you going to see her?"

"Yeah. I said I'd have lunch with her on Saturday."

"OK. You'll tell me how it goes, yeah?"

"Sure."

We go back downstairs to keep watching the drama with Po Po to distract ourselves as we wait to hear back from the Arts Market. When the episode hits its climax, the wicked conspirator unsheathing his knife to bury it in the chest of somebody who's stumbled upon something he shouldn't have, my phone buzzes in my hands, and I almost scream.

Hello! Sabina hasn't given permission to make her contact details public, but you're welcome to come to the Arts Market if you would like to buy her art! She will have a stall next Saturday!

Well, I know where I'm going next Saturday then.

Joan stays for dinner, and before she leaves we sort out our

244

tickets to Manchester, stopping in Birmingham on the way.

In the hallway, after she finishes tying her shoelaces, I say, "Thanks again. If I manage to find Theresa, it'll be because of you."

Joan makes a face. "I didn't do that much. And it is actually pretty fun. I can't think of a better way to be spending the summer, anyway."

I open the door to let her out. For a moment, I stand in the doorway with her just outside, turning back to look at me. The skyline above the row of houses is almost purple, and Joan's face looks soft, scattered with the pink dusk light. We've been seeing so much of each other, but it doesn't seem enough. Each day with her is like a big bowl of perfectly cooked rice I've scoffed down, herding the fluffy grains straight into my mouth with hasty chopsticks. Every time, I feel sorry that I've eaten it all too quickly. Every time, I want to hold my clean bowl out and ask for seconds.

When I was little, my mum used to tell me that I had to make sure to eat up every last grain of rice in my bowl. If I left any sticking to the ceramic, those grains would represent the warts on the face of the man I was going to marry when I grew up. A clean bowl is the smooth face of my future husband. I've never viewed this as an effective threat or found it as humorous as it's presumably intended to be. As a child, I was possessed by a clear conviction that marriage had nothing to do with me.

I still feel like that now. But Joan is walking backwards off my doorstep, and my heart is an emptied bowl, squeaky clean and cupped in both hands, and I want to hold it out to her and say, "Tim faan."

More rice, please.

I watch her vanish down the darkening street.

The July issue of *Eden Recoiling* comes out on Wednesday, but Ada can't buy it until she gets home from camp at the end of the week, so I promise that I'll wait for her – it's only a few days, anyway. The whole exchange lasts a handful of seconds. She apologises for having been too busy to talk, and I tell her it's OK.

I do buy the issue when I head into the shop on Thursday evening early for Tam's event, but I refrain from even taking a peek at its contents. Felix smiles at me when I ring it up at the till.

"I'll be good and not spoil it for you," he says, making a zipping gesture over his lips.

Then Tam comes in, and the shop starts to fill up with people.

Joan's come with me straight from my house, saying that of course she would love to support a queer Asian indie creator, but Ritika shows up too, which is a surprise. I told her about the event, but she didn't tell me she was coming, and I didn't think she would after all that moaning about how busy she was.

She gives me a big hug. "You were so excited about this, I had to see what all the fuss was about."

It was already wonderful when we had the Pride display in the shop last month, watching for the people coming in whose faces lit up at all the rainbows, but Tam's event is a concentrated dose of joy, having all these people in one room, many of them visibly queer and of colour, all of them excited by this indie comic.

Joan gets several signed copies of Tam's book. "I'm going to send them to my friends in Hong Kong," she says to Tam, and Tam beams. Ritika buys one for herself too.

I soak in the atmosphere of the room, listen to all the chatter around me of people exchanging recommendations. I recognise one of them from my first weekend at work, when Felix and I were putting up the Pride display. The blue-haired girl – although there are multiple people with blue hair present.

She comes up to me, introducing herself as Ellie as I didn't get her name last time, and we chat about *Eden Recoiling*, which she's now all caught up on since I persuaded her to buy the first volume. And I tell her about how I read her favourite graphic novel, the one about a human trans girl who falls in love with a mermaid and becomes a mermaid herself to spend the rest of her life underwater with her love.

At the end of the event, Felix and Joan and Ritika and I go for ice cream, and I can't stop talking about the elation of being in that room, the smile on Tam's face afterwards as they thanked us for giving them this space for their book. I think about how this is the energy that I'd always wanted from the book club at school, this enthusiasm and this understanding of what it means to see yourself, to be seen. Then I think, *Well, why can't I have the book club I've always wanted?*

"Felix," I say, twirling my little wooden spoon in the air, "what do you think about starting a book club?"

CHAPTER TWENTY-THREE

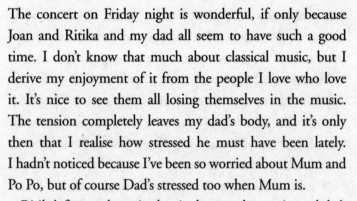

The concert on Friday night is wonderful, if only because Joan and Ritika and my dad all seem to have such a good time. I don't know that much about classical music, but I derive my enjoyment of it from the people I love who love it. It's nice to see them all losing themselves in the music. The tension completely leaves my dad's body, and it's only then that I realise how stressed he must have been lately. I hadn't noticed because I've been so worried about Mum and Po Po, but of course Dad's stressed too when Mum is.

Ritika's fingers dance in the air along to the music, and she's smiling the whole time.

Joan's face is so serene, it makes me feel like I'm standing in the middle of the mountains somewhere, at the edge of a perfectly still lake. When I look at her, I hear something in the music I didn't before. It aches, somewhere between my ribs.

Also, during the interval, she makes a quiet comment to me about how hot one of the cellists is, and I have to agree.

After the concert, Ritika asks me to hang out at hers. It's been a while. When I walk into her room, I say hi to the clay Venus flytrap on her windowsill. Today I decide it's called Ezra.

"How's stuff with Jake?" I ask, perching on the ottoman as she sits down at her desk. "Are you still ignoring him?"

"I told him that I think I need some space this summer," she says, taking a sip of her Diet Coke.

"You did it!"

Ritika puffs out a long breath. "Yeah. I listened to your words of wisdom. We'll be heading to the same uni, so I said we could grab a coffee at the start of term and catch up then and see if we can make this friendship thing work."

"And is he all right with that?"

"Yeah. Hasn't sent me more messages since. It's so weird to have this silence now! I got so used to hearing from him, I find myself wondering if he's OK all the time."

"You'll get used to that too."

"I know." Ritika taps a pen against the desk. "So… I actually went and read a few of Ada's fanfics."

"What?" This is such a strange thing to hear that it feels like I'm dreaming. "You haven't read *Eden Recoiling*!"

"Yeah, I know. But I just wanted to see what her writing was like! You go on about it so much."

People do read fanfics of source material that they

aren't familiar with, but I've just never been one of them. "And what did you think of it?"

"She really is one hell of a writer," Ritika says, scratching at the inside cover of her notebook with her pen. "I get why you've fallen in love with her through her writing."

I wince. Ritika doesn't notice because she's very focused on making a furious scribble that I can't see from here. I want to tell her about the whole Gracie thing, but I get the sense that there's something she isn't saying. I'm trying my best to pay more attention, I guess. I don't want to miss anything important in Ritika's life again.

"Ritika…" I reach out and pull her hand away from the notebook. She drops the pen but she's not looking at me. "You're going to murder that notebook if you're not careful. Is something wrong?"

She takes her hand away. "I don't know. What if I… What does it mean if I…" She stands up, the feet of the chair scraping across the floor. "Ugh!"

She undoes her ponytail and ties it up again, more sloppily than before, a habit of hers when she's stressed. Sitting a few rows behind her in exams, I saw her do this constantly. She flings herself down on to the rug on her floor and sits cross-legged there. Finally she stares up at me defiantly.

I stare back, confused.

"This is so stupid," she mutters. "I don't even know if… Oh, for fuck's sake." She rolls her eyes, and it's clear that she's rolling them at herself. She looks up at the ceiling.

"OK. Elsie. I think… Maybe I like girls."

"Oh. Right." I immediately join her on the floor, kneeling next to her. "How long have you been thinking about this?"

Ritika puts her hands down on the rug, pushing her fingers through the plush faux fur. "Not super long. At first I was going to keep it to myself until I worked it out for sure, but then… I thought it might help to talk about it, you know? You're the expert here."

I laugh a little. "I am *definitely* not an expert. But OK. I'm here. What have you been thinking?"

"I… I don't know. Like, ever since we became friends, right, I've been watching more gay shows and things because of you. And, when I watch those movies with you, and I see girls kissing, a part of me is like, *Oh?* But I was with Jake, so I didn't really think about it. Or maybe it was more that I told myself I didn't have to think about it because I had him. And now I have the time and space to think about it! So I read Ada's fics. You know I read a ton of romance, but it's all straight. When I read those fics, something felt different."

"OK. Have you ever felt attracted to a girl?"

Ritika frowns. "Maybe? I just… This is going to sound terrible. Please don't run away."

"I'm not going to run away."

She worries at her lip. "OK. I think a part of me was annoyed at Joan when we went to Cornwall together because … in the back of my mind, I had this idea that when you and I spent all that time together away from our families, just the two of us, we could… You know. Make out. Or something."

"Oh."

"It's highly possible that I thought I had a crush on you."

"*Oh.*"

"I don't actually! Not really. When we got back from Cornwall, I specifically didn't ask you to hang out much because I just wanted to clear my head a bit. That, and I was also very busy. I wasn't lying about that."

"So… Wait. Your example of being attracted to a girl is … me? But also you're not actually attracted to me?" The shock of Ritika's revelation has been immediately negated – this is pretty funny.

Ritika slaps my arm. "Shut up! They're different things! It's like I *could* make out with you if you were into that. But also … I've had time to think about it, and I don't want to be in a relationship with you. Right now, I think I really just wanna fall in love. I wanna know what that's like. And that's not what I'm looking for from you."

"OK. I think I get it."

"Good. I just mean… I wasn't in love with Jake but I did really like being with him. I miss having that sort of closeness with someone, you know? Kissing is nice. And, you know. Sex." She grins.

I snort.

"But I want that, *and* I want to be in love."

"There'll be lots of queer girls at university," I say. "You'll find someone."

"I hope so." She weaves her arm through the crook of my arm. "It's kind of scary to think about it. All of this has been scary to think about. But, like, in a good way, I guess."

"I love you, and I'm here for you. Welcome to the queer club."

"Thanks. Do I get a T-shirt?"

"I can buy you one."

"Yes! My birthday present this year! Promise!"

"Promise," I say, and I hook my pinkie with hers. "So … speaking of crushes."

Ritika's eyebrows start waggling wildly. "I cannot wait to hear whatever juicy thing you're about to say next."

I push her over, and she laughs, stretching out on the rug. "How do you know it's going to be juicy?" I ask.

"My hot-goss senses are tingling."

"This is not a *fun* piece of hot goss. Ada's got a crush on somebody that isn't me."

"Oh. Who is it?"

"Gracie. They're new to the fandom, and they draw really cool fanart, and they've been chatting with Ada. Oh, *and* they live in New York."

"They? Oh. They use they/them pronouns? Like Tam?"

"Yeah."

"OK. So Ada told you that she has a crush on them?"

"Yeah."

"How are you feeling about it then?"

"Not great." Now that I'm talking about it, I'm realising that I have more feelings about it than I wanted to admit to myself. "I… I think I really did hope that Ada might like me."

"Yeah, of course you did. That's natural, right?"

"Yeah. But… If Ada doesn't like me in that way … maybe there's something wrong with me."

"What?"

I lift my head up. "Maybe there's something wrong with me! Maybe nobody is ever going to look at me and see somebody worthy of love."

Ritika blinks at me for a long time. Then she gets up and walks over to the windowsill and picks up the clay Venus flytrap. "Billy has something very important to say."

"Who's Billy?"

"Right. What did you call him today again?"

"Ezra."

"Oh yeah. You've definitely called him Billy before, though. OK. *Ezra* has something very important to say." She sits back down on the rug and puts Ezra in my lap.

"Hi, Ezra." I nudge one of its prickly clay spikes.

"Ezra says, 'I love you, Elsie. Will you be my girlfriend?'"

I don't laugh. I glare at Ritika. "I'm not going out with a Venus flytrap made out of clay."

"Ezra's very hurt by that. You need to hear him out."

"Sorry, Ezra. Continue."

"You are wonderful. Ada *definitely* loves you."

"How do you know that?"

"I read her fics. I've seen her say I love you to you in the comments. And that time she dedicated a fic to you!"

"It doesn't mean anything. I say I love you to strangers on the internet all the time."

Ritika makes Ezra pretend to bite me. "*I* love you. Elsie. I love you. Do you believe that?"

"Is this Ezra or Ritika speaking?"

"Both."

"OK, yes, I believe that. But I'm talking about love in the romantic sense, Ritika."

Ritika sighs. "Here I am worried that I'll never fall in love, and here you are worried that no one will ever fall in love with you. The thing is, the answer to both of those problems is the same, and you already said it to me."

"I'll find someone?"

"Yep! I can give you the exact same speech that you'd give to me. We're young; we're eighteen; we've got so much ahead of us. Nothing's wrong with you. Also, romance isn't everything, blah-blah-blah."

"Fine. You're right. But it's just hard to see that sometimes when you're a romantic."

Ritika waves at the wall above her bed with all the romance covers. "Yeah. Tell me about it."

She makes Ezra kiss my cheek with its spikes. It feels nice, if sharp.

"But you're still going to keep looking for Theresa?" Ritika asks. I've already told her about my upcoming trip to Birmingham.

"Yeah."

"Why?"

"Well, like we've established, I'm a romantic. You can't expect me to read all those beautiful letters Theresa wrote and then just give up on finding her. I need to know what happened. And having Joan back in my life is so incredible, you know? If I have the ability to let someone experience what it's like to get someone important back, then why not?"

Ritika's eyes glimmer at me, the hint of a smile curving her mouth.

"What?"

"Nothing."

"OK. Stop looking at me so weird then. Anyway. That, plus meeting Lily in Cornwall, was really cool. It was just nice to meet an older queer person. They don't really appear in the media very often. I've never really thought about being old and queer and … happy."

"Yeah, actually, that's another thing I was thinking about too. Before we met Lily, I guess it didn't seem like a very solid thing, you know, the idea that I might like girls? But then we met her, and I thought, wow, one day when I'm old and saggy, I'm *still* going to be into women."

I make Ezra bite Ritika's arm this time. "You're the worst."

"Yeah, I know."

"So… Are you sure you don't want to come with me and Joan to Birmingham? Or even all the way up to Manchester? I'm sure my uncle wouldn't mind if you stayed at his too."

"No, I wouldn't want to impose," Ritika says firmly. "Plus, those train tickets are still expensive! I want to save the money that I've been earning from all the tutoring. I hope you don't mind?"

"No, of course not. I'd love you to come with us, but it's your choice."

"Cool. Let's do a proper holiday next summer, though?"

"Yeah. Proper holiday next summer."

Ritika wiggles Ezra around in the air, and its googly eyes bounce around. "You can bring your boyfriend." She smirks.

"If anything, he's *your* boyfriend. He lives in your room!"

Later, when Ritika's mum is driving me home, I message Ada.

> ritika thinks she's probably queer!! rejoice! also she read YOUR FIC! even though she hasn't read ER! and she said that you're an incredible writer! and it really helped her!

> Ahhhh that's so cool! I'm so happy for her! How are things with you?

good! yeah!! busy! i think i'm gonna start a book club at the speech balloon for people to gather together to read and talk about diverse comics!

Ahhh Elsie that's awesome! I love that!

thanks! it's still just an idea but felix and i are going to figure out the details this weekend

camp ends tomorrow for you, right?

Yep! I love all the campers and I'm gonna miss them, but ngl, I miss my own bed so much! And I've forgotten what it's like to be able to sleep till 11 a.m.!

I'm not gonna miss Kayla and her constant relationship drama, that's for sure.

Also I can't wait to catch up on fandom stuff!

honestly i haven't been keeping up with fandom much either, it's not the same without you and i've just had lots of other stuff going on!

Yeah, sorry it's been ages since we had a good convo, I just never have like more than 5 mins in between stuff to talk to you and the internet here is so patchy!

Once I get home we have to do a video call!

yeah, totally! have fun on the last day of camp!

I will!

Wanna bet how many of these kids are gonna cry when they say goodbye to me? Or make me cry?

what if every single one of them makes you cry

even joshua, your mortal enemy

I think they just might! EVEN JOSHUA, MY MORTAL ENEMY. I'm going to be an emotional wreck!

i'm sure you've been the best camp counsellor ever <3

Aw I love you! <3 Looking forward to Skyping you so I can see your beautiful face!

I look out of the car window at the night sky up above, and I think, yeah, I do know that Ada loves me. And maybe, just maybe, it's OK if that love is purely platonic. Right now, just for a moment, I'm content with that.

CHAPTER TWENTY-FOUR

It's almost closing time on Saturday, and the shop is quietening at last. Felix and I are going to have dinner together again after work, to flesh out our plans for the book club.

I check my phone. I've been texting Joan whenever I have a moment, since she had lunch with her stepmum today. She says she's OK but I've been sending her all the funny tweets I can find, just in case.

There are a couple of new texts from her.

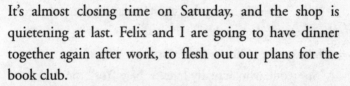

Maybe we could hang out tomorrow after your shift?
I know we don't normally hang out at weekends but it'd be nice to see you.

It's always nice to see you.

"Who are you texting?" Felix asks, leaning his head over my shoulder to peer at my phone screen. "You're smiling. Is it Ada?"

I put my phone down on the counter, feeling caught for some reason. "No. It's Joan. She was asking if I could hang out tomorrow."

"Oh. Hey, she's welcome to come to dinner with us now if she wants."

I text her Felix's suggestion but she says she's busy. I know she found a group of Oxford students who are staying in the city over the summer, and that she meets up with them sometimes.

"Also," I say reluctantly, "Ada has a crush on someone else."

Felix gasps. "Oh my God. No way. Who?"

"Someone who actually lives in New York too."

"No! That's terrible. All your dreams dashed like that!"

"Yeah, I'm trying my best to get over it." I smile and it doesn't feel as fragile as I thought it might. "How's your Spanish boy? Daniel? I hope things are going better with him?"

"Ugh, he's so fit," Felix says in a mock-disgusted tone. "He sent me a selfie earlier from some hipster coffee shop, and I just really wish I could grow a beard like his. Oh, and he's coming to visit."

"Oh my God." I grab Felix's shoulder. "*That's* the headline, surely? Why didn't you say earlier?"

262

Felix plays with the hem of his gold-striped white T-shirt. "I'm nervous! I told him everything I was worried about, like you said. And he was so great about it. I didn't even ask him to visit. He just said he wanted to see me."

"But that's amazing! He must like you so much."

Felix makes an exaggerated sad face. "I guess. I just still feel so... I don't know. What if he *says* he's OK with not having sex, but in reality he just gets bored of me?"

"Then he isn't worth keeping."

It's so easy to say things like this, I know, and then to act in a way completely contrary to your words. So easy to pretend you know how to do the right thing but be unable to do it. The heart is always doing whatever it wants, against all reason.

Felix slumps against the wall. "Maybe it's the gay friends I have but they're all like... Sex! Exclamation mark exclamation mark! Which is extremely wonderful for them – I'm not saying they should be any other way – but. They're good at casual sex. I can't even *imagine* having it. I don't think any of my friends could put up with dating a guy who doesn't want to have sex. It's hard enough feeling like you're an outsider with most people because you're gay! And so you have to work harder to find your people. But you do it, you meet other gay guys, you manage to become friends with some of them, and then it *still* turns out you don't fit in. You're still different. What do you do then?"

I think of myself trying to talk to Cait and Penny,

the two most visible queer girls at school. In sixth form, when we could wear our own clothes, they flaunted their decidedly queer fashion sense: dungarees and Docs and denim jackets, plus glittery rainbow enamel pins. They're nice enough, Cait and Penny, but I got the sense that they never even *considered* I could be queer. I wanted to be like them but I also felt, overwhelmingly, that there was nothing I could ever do to make myself one of them.

The worst thing is that I've never been able to figure out whether this awareness of being set apart from others is something that I've internalised, so that I just *feel* like I'm unwelcome because of my long history of not belonging, or whether it's something that's really happening to me in the actual moment, that I really am being treated differently, in a way I can't articulate but can only feel, because life has made me uniquely sensitive to it.

"I don't really have an answer," I say. "But I hear you."

Felix raises an eyebrow at me, so I point to myself. "I'm queer and not white?"

"Oh. Yeah." Felix looks sheepish.

"But it's not impossible to find your people. People who can understand you – they exist. And the right people – the right person – won't be *putting up* with you. They'll want you exactly as you are."

Felix perks up a little. "You're so cheesy but I love it."

I grin. "So when is Daniel coming?"

"Week after next. He's staying five days."

"Oooh." I rap both fists against the counter to show how thrilled I am for Felix. "I can't wait to hear all about it. Will I get to meet him?"

He hesitates. "This *is* the first time I'm seeing him after we spent, like, two days with each other in Spain, so maybe you can meet him once I'm a bit clearer on where this might be going. For all I know, he could take one look at me, realise he's built up a very different picture of me in the time since we met and run. Turn tail. Change his plane ticket and fly back to Madrid immediately."

I snort. "That's *not* going to happen. Give yourself some credit."

"Oh, I do," Felix says. "*I* think I'm brilliant. But I've never liked someone so much! It's making me all…" He shudders, in lieu of a descriptor. "How do other people cope with having a crush? It's mad!"

"I clearly don't know how to cope, either."

"Oh, Elsie. I'm sorry. Hang on, you're still going up to Birmingham next weekend, though?"

"Yeah, and Manchester, to visit my uncle."

"But you're still looking for Theresa?"

"Yeah. I feel like I'm getting somewhere with it, and I'd hate myself if I just stopped looking. It's … important to me. It's not just about Ada any more. Sorry for abandoning you next weekend."

"It's all right. I'll repay you by abandoning you the weekend after that."

He sticks his tongue out at me, and I pout, which is when Nathan comes out from the back and tells us we can go early, and he'll close up.

I start throwing restaurant suggestions at Felix as we head out, but he just shrugs at every single one of them.

"I *will* make you fall in love with food one day if we're going to stay friends," I say.

"You can try," Felix says, laughing. I shove him, and, in the end, we go for pizza again.

When Ada gets home from camp, we decide to read the July issue of *Eden Recoiling* together on Skype.

She arrives on my screen with a big grin. "Oh my God, it is *so* good to be home," she says. "I am so full right now. Mom made a mountain of jollof rice and pepper stew and all this other food. And look, puff puff!" She shows me her plate, balls of golden fried dough goodness rolling around on it.

"Oh, I want one!"

We talk a bit about her last day of camp – Ada did cry lots. "Some of them made me really cute thank-you cards! Including Joshua! Would you believe it!" She gestures to the cards, all lined up on the windowsill behind her.

After Ada's told me more stories from camp, we start reading the issue. It turns out that Neff feels guilty – *Neff!* –

that Mayumi's gone off on her own to search for the apple tree. He heads out after her, and then Zaria finds that Neff and Mayumi are both gone, and she goes too, but she ends up ambushed in this ghost town by some malicious plants – who turn out to be people-plant hybrids.

"Shit, what if Mayumi comes and saves Zaria instead?" Ada says.

"Oh my God. That's a *game-changer*."

We speculate about this at length, until it gets really late for me, and I have to go to bed since I still have work tomorrow.

Before I sign off, Ada says, "Oh man, Elsie, it's been so good to see your face again."

And my heart does still swell, just a little, with that habitual hope. Ada didn't even mention Gracie *once*. What if I still have a chance?

But I remember how I felt last night, in the car, as Ritika's mum drove me home. How I was beginning to accept, with warmth, the idea that Ada's love for me is simply platonic and no less beautiful for that. It's better to hold on to that clarity than to keep deluding myself.

I really have to let this go.

The bubble-tea shop is quiet on Sunday evening when I pop in with Joan after work. This time, I decide against rose-milk tea. It's time for a new drink that doesn't remind me of being sad.

"How does this compare to the stuff in Hong Kong?" I ask, taking a sip of my passion-fruit tea.

Joan has ordered an oolong milk tea. "This isn't bad," she says. At the sceptical look on my face, she insists, "No, really. It's pretty good. You think it's good too, right? Or you wouldn't come here?"

"Yeah, I think it's good but it's been so long since I've been to Hong Kong that I'm, like, maybe I've forgotten what it should actually taste like?"

"Well, be reassured that it tastes as it should."

I laugh. "So. How are you? How was your stepmum?"

"She's OK. She thinks I should try officially coming out to my dad. Even though he knows. We know he knows. But I've never told him in my own words."

"You think you will?"

"Yeah." Joan chews on a tapioca pearl. "Yeah. I'll try it."

"When?"

"Not sure. I'll let you know when I do."

"OK."

"The good news is, I got my exam results, so my place at Oxford is confirmed, and I can definitely stay here."

"*What?*" I half shriek. I can feel the staff staring at me, but I don't care. I grab Joan's hand. "Congrats!"

She glances down at our hands. At the weight of her gaze, a strange panic sputters in my chest. Like not realising that something's burning until you finally smell the smoke. A line of flame suddenly scorches where our hands overlap.

I pull my hand away. Joan looks up at me, her dark eyes oddly intense for a moment, like things left blackened by fire. "Thanks," she says.

"You should've told me earlier," I say quickly. "I would have paid for your drink!"

She smiles, her eyes quiet, crinkling in that way that makes her whole face as sweet as the tea I'm drinking.

"Now I can extort something more expensive from you," she says.

CHAPTER TWENTY-FIVE

It's the night before Joan and I go up to Birmingham and then Manchester, and Gracie's asked Ada out on a date.

HOLY SHIT ELSIE!!

GRACIE ASKED ME OUT

LIKE ON A FOR REAL DATE

I can't reply. I can't think of what to say. I'm in my room, and the sky is bruise-dark outside. It's late but not so late that everybody's asleep. I've been trying to be content with Ada's love just the way it is, but this still *sucks*.

I'm seized with this hysterical urge to go and talk to my mum about it. I've told her about Ada before – "a friend

I met online" – but not that I have a crush on her or anything, seeing as I'm not out to my family.

And I'm still not ready for them to know I'm queer just yet.

My bedroom windows are wide open but the room still feels alive with heat, the air like a warm animal curled against my body.

I text Ritika:

> gracie asked ada out on a date):

shit): i'm sorry

although now that that ship has sailed is it a good time to tell you that i haven't been team ada for a while

> ??? what is that supposed to mean??

it means joan tse is RIGHT THERE, she is super cute and you two obviously care about each other deeply. i am team joan

I have to put my phone down on my bedside table for a moment. Team Joan? The confusion swims through me. Yes, I care about Joan a lot. And, while I had been worried that because she'd been the one to cut off contact with me all those years ago it might mean that she didn't care about me, that worry has long since been banished.

She does care. Every day she's there, like a sturdy tree in the garden, something I can lean against, something that can shade me from the melting heat. Quiet and gentle and strong.

But she's my *best friend*. I can't possibly be interested in her romantically.

Is she super cute? I wouldn't exactly use the word 'cute' to describe her. Joan as a child was cute, with those pigtails. Whereas I was a tomboy. She's the butch one now, though. She's … handsome, I guess. Hard to look away from. Everything she wears suits her so perfectly. My eyes are always drawn to her. I think about her sleeves, rolled up. I think about her undercut, the nape of her neck. I think about her dancing on the pier in Padstow. I think about her face during the concert, the way looking at it made the music sound different to me. I think about last Sunday in the bubble-tea shop, my hand on hers, how it felt too warm. Her eyes on me, even warmer.

I snatch up my phone again and type angrily.

> RITIKA THIS IS MY LOVE LIFE WE'RE TALKING ABOUT NOT A TV SHOW

> i know! but JOAN THOUGH

> hang on… did you not want to come with me and joan next weekend because you want us to be alone together?

> maaaaaybe. i don't want to third-wheel

> you're not going to third-wheel! joan and i are friends,
> just like you and i are friends

> let's agree to disagree

I put my phone on charge, switch off the lights and go to bed, thinking about Ritika's messages.

Thinking about Joan.

In the morning, I check my phone and realise that Ritika's texts made me completely forget how upset I was about Ada's date, and I never actually replied to Ada's message.

I scroll through Tumblr and see that Ada's posted a pre-date selfie. She looks amazing. She's shaved her head again recently, and she's wearing a pale pink chequered button-down with an emerald-green bow tie and just a little bit of make-up: eyeliner and something that makes her cheeks glow even more than usual.

The selfie was posted just after I went to bed. Now it's about 3 a.m. in New York; Ada ought to be asleep. Or maybe... Maybe she's still with Gracie, having fun.

If she and Gracie work out, Ada would have somebody who could be there for her, as present as Joan is for me right now. I want that for her. She's never dated anyone but she's a romantic deep down to her core, the writer of the most convincing love stories I've ever read. She always talks about how she wants that kind of love for herself, the kind of love she writes about, and how she feels insecure about her writing because how does she know what romance really is? I've always told her that she knows it better than anyone, that her vision of love is more earnest and moving than any other I've come across in any piece of writing, fan-made or otherwise.

I want someone to sweep her off her feet and all the other clichés. She deserves the love she dreams of, something big and bounding, like a goofy dog chasing a bird across a field, joy and infectious energy in its every leap.

I finally reply to her message:

> happy for you! hope the date went well. i wanna know all the details!

Another train ride, this time in the rain.

It's chucking it down. Big droplets of it smashing against the windows of the train. But it isn't any less hot – it's muggy now, and the air is like the inside of a leather glove that's been worn all day.

I'm in the window seat, Joan next to me. I can't stop thinking about Ritika's messages.

She's wearing a short-sleeved grey herringbone button-down shirt and blue denim shorts that come down to her knees. When the train conductor came round to check our tickets, he called her "sir". It wasn't the first time I'd heard someone mistake Joan for a guy. She often looks like she could be a male K-pop idol.

"So, I got up early and called my dad today," she says.

"Oh my God, you came out to him? What was it like?"

"Not the best," Joan says. "But, at the same time, not as bad as I was expecting."

"What were you expecting?"

"He's definitely not shy about making homophobic comments, so I thought he would make those to my face, but all he said was, 'This is why you left, isn't it?' I said yes. And he said, 'Do you think you'll come back?' And I said, 'Do you think you'll change your mind about gay people?'"

"And what did he say?"

"He said he hoped I would change *my* mind about being gay, and I told him that was not going to happen. He asked if I had a girlfriend. I told him I'd had one but not any more. Then he said he would call me again, and that he wanted to know if I ever got a girlfriend or a boyfriend. I told him that I'm never going to have a boyfriend, and he said, 'I'll call you again next month. Good job on your exam results by the way.'"

"Maybe he's working on changing his mind?"

"Maybe. We'll see."

"So you'll answer his next call?"

"I think so. At least I know I can just hang up if it gets bad."

"What about your stepmum? Did you tell her you spoke to him?"

"Yeah, we had a quick call. She thinks that it'll take some time but he'll come round. There was a pop star who came out recently in Hong Kong, and Dad apparently just pointed out the news and then didn't make any sort of negative comment about it."

"I guess that's a start."

"Do you have any plans to come out to your family?" Joan asks.

"Not at the moment. I think it'll be easier once I actually have a girlfriend, maybe. I realised I didn't even know the Cantonese word for 'bisexual'. I had to look it up."

Joan says the word: soeng sing lyun.

"Yeah. That. I could come out to them in English, obviously, but they prefer having serious conversations in Cantonese. It's all a bit weird, though. Imagining myself saying that out loud to them. If I have a girlfriend, I can just say, look, I have a girlfriend!"

And now my brain is stuck on the whole Team Joan thing again. I can't look at her when I'm saying the word 'girlfriend'.

"You don't have to come out to them if you don't want to. You know that, right?"

"I know. I do want to come out to them at some point. I just think it's too difficult right now. But then I feel like I'm a useless coward because it seems like everyone else is out to their family."

"You're doing fine," Joan says.

But Joan is *Joan*. She's living exactly the way she wants to, dressing in a way that proclaims her identity to the world, distancing herself from her family because they can't love her the way she deserves to be loved. There's so much courage and confidence in everything she does and everything she is. I'm a flickering shadow next to her, shape-shifting with each subtle change in the light.

"What about your friends? Are they out to their families?"

"My ex-girlfriend isn't. I have other friends who aren't out, either."

"But some of them are? How did their families react?"

"Well, Michael's parents basically pretend he never came out. Cordelia's parents are completely fine with it. Veronica's dad makes some very strange comments sometimes but he mostly means well."

"Oh, OK. And how does Michael feel about that situation with his parents?"

"He thinks he'll wear them down eventually." Joan looks at her watch, tapping at its face. "Has Ada come out to her family?"

"Only to her brother. She thinks her parents will probably be fine with it but she wants to wait till college, just to have that distance, if she needs it."

"See, not everyone's out to their family! How is she, anyway?"

"She's doing OK."

"You still haven't told her that you're looking for Theresa?" Joan asks.

"No. I… It's not really just about her any more. She's… She's into someone else."

"Oh."

"Yeah."

"How are you feeling about that?"

"Not wonderful, to be honest. But I'm happy for Ada, really."

"But why are you still looking for Theresa then?"

"That feeling of having you back in my life," I say, watching Joan closely. "I want to give that feeling to someone else, if I can."

Joan blinks rapidly, and then she ducks her head and looks away at the seats across the aisle, a man asleep and alone, drooling on to an open book in his lap. When she looks back at me, it's with a half-smile, her eyes only just beginning to crinkle.

There's a break in the rain when the train pulls into Birmingham. We get a bus from the station to where the Moseley Arts Market is, and we realise after we get off the bus and start looking at the stalls that there's a farmers' market here too.

We're both thirsty, so Joan grabs an iced coffee from a stall while I get a carrot juice. "Iced?" I comment, as she's handed her drink. "How unlike you."

I've never seen her drink a coffee with ice in. Besides, it's much cooler since the sky has wrung itself out. A breeze picks up the hem of my dress, and I can feel the goosebumps on my bare calves. I'm regretting not wearing tights.

She smirks. "Good to change things up once in a while. Also, I'm an iced-coffee-in-winter, hot-coffee-in-summer kind of person."

This is a revelation to me. There's still so much to learn about Joan. I only know Joan-in-summer. Well, I knew Joan all through the turning of the year when we were children, but back then she definitely didn't drink coffee. I don't know what she's like now, in other seasons. What clothes does she wear in the winter? "It *is* still summer."

"Yes, but I wanted to celebrate the relief and joy I feel at the drop in temperature."

"I thought the hot weather didn't really bother you. Isn't it hotter in Hong Kong?"

"We have air conditioning there. My room here has been boiling all summer. That's why I go to your house so much, to be honest. Because it's cooler."

I skip over a large puddle; Joan just splashes right through it in her Timberland boots.

"Not because you want to see me," I ask, before thinking to add: "and watch dramas with my po po?"

"No, I'm really just there for the powerful fan in your living room," Joan says, shrugging carelessly, before she grins at me.

I'm absurdly conscious of the impulse to knock my shoulder into hers. If she was anybody else, Ritika or Felix, I would have just shoved her without thinking about it. But with her, in this moment, the impulse seems to ricochet round my body, from my brain down to my arms down to my legs and back up, into my shoulders, and I finally tilt my body towards Joan's, falling like a bowling pin against her. She grunts as my shoulder collides with hers, and she pushes me away with her hands, laughing.

We look through all the stalls until we find it. Sabina Pandey's.

I pick up a business card from a stack on the table to confirm that it's really her.

Sabina herself stands behind the table, her long greying

hair pulled back into a bun. Her face is full of life, her cheeks plump and her brown eyes warm with humour. She's wearing heavy jewellery: a necklace of gleaming black stones, chunky gold rings on both hands and a shimmering bracelet that looks like honey hardened into a solid band round her wrist.

Laid out on the table are paintings of the seaside. They're all quite small, none of them bigger than an A4 piece of paper. Distant sails on the water; a golden stretch of sand. There's even one that could be an Instagram photo: an ice-cream cone held out against the blue, blue sea in the background. I think of all the photos I took while I was in Cornwall with Joan and Ritika.

"I love your art, Ms Pandey," I say.

"Thank you. Please call me Sabina."

There are some paintings of a white cat too, curled on a step, dozing in the sun, making funny faces. "Is that your cat?" Joan asks.

Sabina nods.

"It's beautiful," Joan says.

"She's a terror. Her name is Tapioca."

"Um…" I say, not sure how to broach the topic of what I came here for except to just dive right into it. "This is going to sound really weird… But is there any chance you know a person called Theresa Bennett?"

Sabina's eyes widen. "That *is* a strange question. Why are you asking?"

"I'm looking for her. My friend's grandmother knew her once, and I'm just trying to see if I can put them back in touch."

"And how did you know to come and ask *me*?"

"We found another of Theresa's friends. I don't know if you know her. Her name is Catherine Overfield? She remembered that Theresa moved here and then ... met someone called Sabina. We had to do a little digging after that."

"Wow, that's some impressive detective work," Sabina says, clasping her hands together. "I am the Sabina you're looking for. I painted these in Theresa's hometown, in fact." She gestures to the paintings of the sea.

"Oh, we were there too just earlier this month!" I almost shout.

Sabina smiles. "I was there in April. Avoiding the peak season, you know. I visit every few years; it's become a ritual of mine."

"You visit it? With Theresa?"

"No, no. Just by myself, usually, but I took my partner with me this year."

"But you go there *because* of Theresa?"

"Well, yes, in a way. She had such a love-hate relationship with the place. She talked about it all the time, and I would ask her if she ever wanted to go back, and she'd look at me like it was the worst thing she'd ever heard. After she ... ended things with me, I went there on my own, just to see what it was that Theresa had wanted to escape so badly. And I liked it a lot. It was good to paint there, so I kept returning. I've lived in Birmingham all my life, and have no intention of living anywhere else, but I must say the sea does have its attraction, doesn't it?"

"Yeah. These paintings really capture it."

"What's your friend's grandmother's name?"

"Rebecca Lathey."

"Ah," Sabina says knowingly.

"Did Theresa talk about her?"

"Yes, but I got the sense it was a thorny subject for her."

"Do you and Theresa still talk?"

"Not as much as we used to but I still consider her a friend. She doesn't live near here any more."

"Do you know where she is now?"

"In Brighton, I believe, unless she's moved again," Sabina says. "I wouldn't put that past her. But she missed the sea too much, in the end. I think I have her address written down in my address book…"

"An address book?"

"Yes, an actual book, would you believe?"

Sabina takes out a small notebook with a purple leather cover from her bag and flips through it. She dictates the address to me as I type it into the Notes app on my phone. And then I remember how little luck I've had with addresses in the past, so I ask if she has Theresa's number, which she does. She gives it to me with a warning that

Theresa isn't the best at picking up her phone.

I have so many more questions but I don't want to pry too much, either. "Were you and Theresa together for a long time?"

"We were together for several years," Sabina says. "But we're much better off as friends. I'm a person who likes to stay put, and she isn't. I have a wonderful partner called Mo now, though."

She looks down fondly at a painting of a person in a suit playing with the same white cat as in the other paintings.

"Is that Mo?" Joan asks.

"Yes, that's Mo and Tapioca. Who was actually Mo's cat, at first, before she moved in with me."

"Is that painting for sale?"

"You'd like to buy it?" Sabina says.

"Yeah. I don't often see butch women in paintings. This is really cool. Is she Asian too?"

Sabina smiles at that. "She's Korean-American. She moved to the UK about a decade ago. I paint her a lot but most of the paintings aren't for sale. I don't think many people would want to buy them, anyway. I'm happy to sell this one to you."

Sabina shows Joan photos of some of her other paintings of Mo, since Joan seems so interested. There's a gorgeous portrait of Mo, grey-haired in a dapper waistcoat. Joan's face goes slack with awe. "Where can I get that *waistcoat*?" she whispers.

Sabina laughs. "Oh, I should put you in touch with Mo. Anyway, you'll be getting this painting?"

"Yeah, I love it. And I might get one of the paintings of Cornwall too. They're lovely."

Joan asks me which one she should get. I point to the one with the ice-cream cone, and I watch as Joan pays for her paintings, and Sabina packs them up carefully for her.

As we leave the stall, I try the phone number that Sabina gave me but, just as she warned, nobody answers. But it doesn't matter. I can try again later.

I actually have Theresa's number.

CHAPTER TWENTY-SIX

We head back into the city centre on the bus to find somewhere to eat. We end up in the Bullring, a huge shopping centre next to the train station, where we have sushi for lunch. Joan keeps putting the last slice of sashimi – whatever it is: salmon, tuna, squid – on to my plate, even when I protest. I keep wondering – is it possible? Does she like me? What if I just ask her? Each slice of sashimi melts silently into my mouth, and the words are held there, on the tip of my tongue.

After we've eaten lunch, we still have time to kill before we need to catch the train up to Manchester, so we wander round the Bullring mall for a bit, dipping in and out of shops.

My phone buzzes while we're looking through some clothes racks, and I see it's a text from Ada.

AHHH the date was awesome! I was worried it was going to be awkward meeting Gracie in person but it wasn't at all. It was like we'd known each other forever. I didn't think things like this really happened! Also Gracie is so cool oh my god I like them so much. They were wearing ORANGE LIPSTICK.

I ended up with some of it on my own lips, haha!

I *knew* Ada would be into the orange lipstick.

"This would look good on you, I think," Joan says, interrupting my thoughts. She's holding up a white strappy dress with a low back.

It's cute. Definitely something that would fit right into my wardrobe. But that's the problem, maybe. The niggling sense that there's something wrong with the outfits I currently own has been growing.

"Oh, you think so?" I say. "I'm not gonna buy anything, though. I don't really have much spare money to spend on clothes right now." I try to redirect the focus of the conversation. "Do you shop in the men's section?"

"Yeah, mostly. It's easier to find things that fit me in Hong Kong. I've tried looking at clothes here, but I've given up."

"When did you start dressing like this?"

"Oh well, in Hong Kong, a lot of lesbians do. There were girls who wore stuff like this at school. I looked to the TBs, and I thought that I needed to start dressing like them, to broadcast the signal that I'm interested in girls. And it turned out that I actually felt so much more comfortable in these clothes than I ever did in a skirt or a dress, so that was great."

"TBs?"

"Tomboys."

"Oh. Like butches?"

"Yeah, I guess. I'm not sure if these identities exactly map on to, well, Western identities. But yeah, that's probably close. I really look up to butches too, as you can probably tell."

I flick through hangers without really paying much attention to what's on them. My heart is deep in this conversation, like it's taken root in it and is absorbing all the nutrients it needs from Joan's words. The other day, Joan showed me a picture of her group of friends and pointed out her ex, who was wearing a black lace dress in the photo.

"So your ex-girlfriend, what is she?"

"I think some people would call her a TBG. A tomboy's girl."

I giggle. I can't help it. It just sounds so strange to my ears. But, if I'd grown up in Hong Kong, this would be how *I* would understand queer women too. Tomboys and their girls.

Joan frowns at me, and I stop laughing. "There are also girls who identify as 'pure', so they're feminine and they're attracted to other feminine girls."

"Wait, so TBGs only date TBs and 'pures' only date other 'pures'?"

"Yeah."

"And TBs? They only date TBGs?"

"Yeah, strictly speaking. But, to be honest, a lot of people I know don't really fully identify with any of these labels. They feel a bit old-fashioned. 'No label' has become another label that a lot of us use instead."

At first I think I understand. That this is the equivalent of those people who are, like, "No, I don't want to label myself – I'm just *human*," and have inevitably created a category of their own. I respect their choice not to label themselves, and I would be delighted if one day there's no need for labels at all but, as long as I'm marginalised for being queer, I'm always going to find comfort and strength from knowing that there's a word for who I am, and people out there who share the same identity. Bisexuality has a history and a community, and that inspires me.

But I suppose this is different to what Joan's talking about. 'No label' seems more like how Ada chooses to identify as queer because she doesn't wholly vibe with other words in the queer vocabulary, and she likes how the word 'queer' celebrates being different and outside the norm, outside the definitions of society.

If all I could choose to identify as was TB, TBG or pure, I would definitely sidestep those and go for 'no label' too.

Joan continues. "Personally, I like TB just because

something about it resonates with me, and it's what I started out identifying as because I was dressing like the TBs that I knew at school. But it's not as if I'm only attracted to girls with long hair who wear make-up and dresses."

"You're not?"

My heart feels suddenly as weightless as a moonbeam. What if I don't want to be so feminine any more? Is it possible that Joan likes me, and would it be possible that she'd still like me if I didn't have long hair, didn't wear dresses?

"No," Joan says, scratching the back of her neck as her shoulders hunch in embarrassment. "I was very into one of the other TBs at school. But she's mostly only interested in TBGs."

"Is she the one in the picture you showed me the other day?"

Joan ducks behind a different rack of clothes before answering. "Yeah."

I make Joan show me the picture again and point out the girl, and I tease her about it. Joan smiles and hides her face behind her hands.

"Her loss," I say, shrugging.

Joan turns away, feeling the fabric of a blue-and-white striped shirt, rubbing it between her thumb and forefinger.

"Hey, do you remember when we were little, and I was

such a … naam zai tau?" I ask.

"How could I forget? You were a little style icon."

"What? Really?"

Joan laughs. "Yeah. I was like… Wow, I wished I'd dressed like Elsie back then. What stopped me from doing that? I guess my parents just really liked buying all this girly stuff for me to wear, and I never really expressed my own opinion much. Whereas you were probably a tyrant."

This makes me feel light-headed, like I've drunk too much cold, fizzy Coke. It's a rush of pleasure, I realise, that Joan used to admire me in this way.

"I wasn't a *tyrant*."

But, in truth, I don't really remember. Until this summer, I'd completely forgotten about being a naam zai tau as a child. I don't remember telling my parents that I wanted all those boys' clothes. But I must have. Surely they hadn't dressed me like that of their own accord. I remember how unrecognisable I was in the old family photos I looked through the other day. I honestly would have thought the child in them was a boy if I didn't know better. The short hair, the mischievous grins and most of all the *posture* – I had such arrogantly boyish stances in the photos, feet planted firmly apart and arms crossed, in my baggy cargo shorts and white muscle tee. Honestly, tiny me had some *swagger*.

"But you recognised me," I say to Joan. "I must look *so* different."

"You recognised me too," Joan says.

"Yeah. Well. You… I still thought about you a lot. I never imagined you'd grow up to become a butch lesbian – sorry, a TB – but somehow, the moment I saw you, some part of my brain knew, and it seemed instantly right that you should look like this. Sorry, that sounds ridiculous, but… I'm just so glad you are who you are now. You just seem so completely … self-assured. It's amazing."

Joan shakes her head, bending down to check out a pair of lemon-yellow trainers. "I… Actually, I searched for you on social media. That's how I knew what you looked like now. I was thinking about you too. Like I said, I wanted to see you again. I was planning to get in touch."

"Oh."

So Joan didn't recognise me by some magical intuition. Of course not. But she had been thinking about me. I knew that already but I hadn't really allowed myself to think much about it.

Now I'm picturing her scrolling through photos of me on the internet.

She checks her watch. "Maybe we should think about heading over to the train station?"

I check my watch too. "Oh yeah. Sure. Let's get going."

And the whole way to the train station, and on the train, I still can't stop wondering – does she like me in that way?

Do *I* like her in that way?

CHAPTER TWENTY-SEVEN

It's evening by the time we arrive at Uncle Kevin's place.

It isn't Uncle Kevin who opens the door, though.

The man in the doorway is tall, white and ginger.

He looks just a little familiar. And then I think, *Oh. It's the stranger in the photos I found of that barbecue years ago in our garden. The summer Joan moved back to Hong Kong.*

"Hello! Elsie! And Joan! Hello, hello. Welcome. Oh, Elsie, it is so good to see you again. Do you remember me at all?" His Scottish accent takes me just as much by surprise as his presence.

He spreads his arms, ready to envelope me in a hug, just as Uncle Kevin, in an apron with a photo of a golden retriever on it, steps into view behind this stranger.

"David, I *told* you to let me answer the door."

Kevin's Hong Kong accent has always been a little more

pronounced than my parents'. I smile to hear it, even though I'm still confused.

"You were busy with the ... salmon or something," David says. "I wasn't going to keep our guests waiting."

Kevin comes forward. "Sorry, sorry. Elsie, so nice to see you. And Joan, lovely to meet you. Elsie, I'm not sure if you remember David?"

David. His Scottish accent... A memory, long buried, unearths itself. *This is David, your uncle's friend.* Somebody had said that to me. My mum? The barbecue was so many years ago. I was only eleven. "Um. Kind of? Just a little?"

"Right. Well. David is my ... partner."

Kevin clears his throat but, even before he clarifies his statement, the meaning of it slides through me, a sugar cube dropped into a cup of tea, dissolving into every part of me. There isn't a cell in my body that thinks David is Kevin's *business* partner. But Kevin clarifies, anyway. "My husband." He bobs his head nervously as he flips my world like a pancake.

Uncle Kevin is *married to a man*.

Joan's hand presses against my back. It's the only thing holding me up, a lone, sturdy pillar supporting a collapsing roof. "Nice to meet you too, Uncle," she says. "Thank you for letting us stay over."

"I hope you two haven't eaten." Kevin rubs his hands together and cracks his knuckles. He's still nervous. Because I haven't said anything yet. "I've been cooking."

"Yes, quite a feast," David says, also rubbing his hands together. "You girls better be hungry."

"I'm starving," Joan says, her voice too cheery and about an octave higher than normal. She pushes me gently. I need it because, without that pressure propelling me, I'm going nowhere, a car with its back wheels stuck in a ditch.

I move beyond the doorway mechanically, nudging my feet out of my soggy black canvas shoes. I'm not taking anything in. David's freckled and bearded face is superimposed upon everything else in my vision.

Kevin follows me into the living room. Joan's probably still unlacing her boots, and David's with her. But Kevin is hovering round me and running his hand up and down his arm with frenetic energy. "Elsie. Hey. I know it's probably a bit of a surprise…"

"Why did nobody ever say anything to me?" I say.

It's possible that I'm actually shouting. I don't know how to control the volume of my voice. I'm not here. I'm enveloped inside my shock, the exploding star of it pulsing and white.

"Your parents didn't want me to," Kevin says quietly. "Anyway, we haven't been married long. Only a year."

"But you must have been going out with him before that."

"Yes. We've been together for many years. But your mum and dad thought it was best if we didn't tell you."

All this time. I hadn't known. My *parents* kept it from me.

"You're upset," Kevin says.

It occurs to me finally that he probably thinks I'm upset because he's gay. But of course that's not why at all. I grapple for the words to tell him this but none come to me, so instead I say, "I'm not upset. Can I please have some water?"

"Of course." Kevin disappears and reappears with a glass.

I sit down at the table and down the water in one go, suddenly desperately thirsty. I wasn't intending to slam the glass on the table, but that's what it sounds like. Slamming.

Joan comes into the living room and carefully sits down next to me, and I manage to say, at last, "I just wish I'd known earlier. I'm happy for you and David. I don't understand why I couldn't have been told about this. I should've come to the *wedding*. Wait – did you not invite my parents?"

"We didn't really have one," Kevin says. "Just a simple ceremony with a few friends. We're not the wedding type. I've been married before and… Well, you know. But your mum was there."

I'm shaking. My mum was there but she barred me from something that would've meant so much to me. "I would've loved to have been there. If I wasn't told about it before, why am I allowed to know about it now?"

"I've always wanted to tell you," Kevin says, putting his hand on my arm. "And you're old enough now. You're eighteen; you're heading off to uni soon. We shouldn't be hiding this from you any more. When you messaged me to ask if you could come up here and stay with us, I thought this was the perfect opportunity to tell you everything. I had a chat with your mum, and she agreed that it was time."

I want to retreat to a dark room and lie down and process this alone. But there are still so many questions in my head.

Joan has acquired a bowl of pistachios from somewhere, and she offers it to me. I take a handful just as David walks in with a steaming mug and sets it down in front of her. He goes to stand behind Kevin, his hands on Kevin's shoulders, and he looks like a giant.

He's my uncle too.

I prise a pistachio shell apart. "Does Po Po know?"

"She doesn't know we're married," Kevin says slowly. "But she does know I'm in a relationship with David. I haven't talked to her in a long time."

A long time? How long?

I feel the world expanding and contracting around me, like one big beating heart, squeezing, releasing.

"Eight years?" I ask.

"Eight years," Kevin confirms.

Kevin and David have gone back into the kitchen to put the finishing touches to dinner. I look round the living room, finally taking it all in. The framed photos of Kevin and David and their friends, the modern-art prints, the shelf of books and comics. The walls are painted forest green, their shade matched by the leafy potted plants next to the TV. There's an abstract steel sculpture in a corner of the room, about half my height, the swirling curves of it turbulent and angry somehow.

Eight years. Eight years ago, we stopped going back to Hong Kong to see Po Po and Gung Gung. Because Kevin came out to them, tried to introduce David to them, but they couldn't accept him. They disowned him.

And Mum had sided with her brother, not her parents.

"Did you really have no idea?" Joan asks.

I shake my head. "If my mum was OK with it – if she could go as far as taking a stand against her parents, if she went to Kevin and David's wedding ceremony and everything – why couldn't she just tell me about it? Why did she have to keep it a secret from me?"

"She probably thought you were too young to be exposed to all this family drama."

"Or to the fact that my uncle is gay."

"Or that." Joan sighs. "I'm sorry."

I think of Po Po sitting next to me in the garden. Po Po, who disowned her son for being gay. There beside me, with her hands folded in her lap. Her jade bracelet, her liver-spotted skin. Telling her son she never wanted to see him again.

But she does want him to visit, right? She didn't say so explicitly but I think she does. Doesn't she?

Dinner is indeed a feast. Sweet chilli salmon, grilled pork chops, stir-fried choy sum with garlic, and soy-sauce chicken wings.

As Kevin places that last dish in the centre of the table, I stare at him. Soy-sauce chicken wings are Po Po's favourite. Does Kevin remember that? Does he associate them with her at all?

He seems to notice me staring and says, "I hope you like the food! I'm not much of a cook. Not like your mum."

David puts bowls heaped with rice in front of me and Joan and sits down. "That's nonsense," he says, picking up and pointing his chopsticks at Kevin, and I notice the ease with which he holds them – though my parents would always tell me off when I used to gesticulate with my chopsticks at the dinner table, until I stopped doing it. They think it's rude, but Kevin doesn't seem to mind. "You could go on *MasterChef*."

"So what have you girls been up to today?" David asks.

Joan's eyes flicker to mine. "We actually stopped in Birmingham and had a wander around," she says. "I bought some stuff at an arts market."

"Ooh, how lovely. Do you have time to explore Manchester tomorrow? We can show you around."

"Yeah," I say. "I think we have a bit of time."

David and Kevin start to reel off attractions in Manchester, sharing their memories of the various places. "We had a really good lunch somewhere around there... Do you remember?" Kevin says of one of the museums.

"Oh yeah, it was Spanish, wasn't it? Tapas?"

Eventually Joan asks David and Kevin how they met.

"At university," Kevin says.

"Wait... You've been together *that* long?" I ask. "What about your ex-wife?"

"No, no. David and I *were* together when we were at university, but we broke up when I went back to Hong Kong. I was in Hong Kong for a while, trying a few different jobs. Then I came back to England and did a graphic-design course, which is where I met Nicole, my ex-wife. I really liked her, and I thought we could be happy – that I could make my family happy. But then I found a new job, and, when I showed up on the first day, it turned out that David was also working there."

"It was fate," David says, picking up Kevin's hand and kissing his fingers.

"Yeah. I made an effort to avoid it for a long time. David and I tried to be friends. But I couldn't deny it in the end. I told Nicole, and it was hard at first, but we're still on good terms now."

"What do you do?" Joan asks David.

"I'm a software developer," David says. "Back then, we were both working for a video-game company."

"That's cool," Joan says, and asks them about the games they worked on.

I busy myself with a chicken wing, biting into the juicy skin and meat and tearing it from the bone. The flavour of it, darkly sweet and intensely savoury, clings to my tongue.

After we finish the food – or as much of it as we can – Kevin brings out pudding, which, incongruous with the rest of the meal, turns out to be banoffee pie. He explains that he doesn't really know how to make any Chinese desserts.

"Well, Mum's never made any, either," I say. I have no complaints about the banoffee pie. It's one of my favourites.

"And actually David normally does the baking around here, so…"

David's hand, which was on the back of Kevin's chair, comes up to ruffle Kevin's hair. "You're a good baker too."

They touch each other so often and so naturally, just two people in love. Watching them as I eat the banoffee pie, the crunchy biscuit base of it crumbling in my mouth, the cream as light as sunshine, my resentment that I'd been kept in the dark fades away. At least I know about them now.

At least they're happy.

Kevin refuses to let me and Joan help with the washing-up. "We have a dishwasher," David says.

"Against my wishes," says Kevin, piling up the plates.

I laugh. We don't have a dishwasher at home. Mum thinks it's a waste of water and electricity. As I understand it, they aren't a very common appliance in Hong Kong.

Joan asks about having a shower, and David shows her the bathroom. I hear the noise of the dishwasher starting up, and Kevin comes out of the kitchen.

"You're not going to come and see Po Po then," I say softly.

"Your mum's been trying to persuade me. She says Po Po feels differently now. But I don't know what I'm going to do yet." He sits down on the sofa, slumping against the cushions.

I turn round in my chair to face him. His neon-yellow glasses are new to me; his last pair had brown frames. Behind those slightly smudged lenses, his eyes are pensive and sad. His goatee is the same as ever. His grey Henley shirt has a stain on it, probably soy sauce, despite the apron he was wearing earlier. He looks younger than my dad, even though he's several years older.

He's my uncle, and he's married to a man.

One time, when he came to our house last year, I spent all of dinner rambling on at him about *Eden Recoiling*, and then I showed him the bookshelf in my room, and he read the first few issues right then and there. I asked him who his favourite character was so far.

"Nefarious Warthorn is very impressive," he said.

I frowned at him. At that point, I was going through a bit of an anti-Neff phase. I was just so sick of how everyone in fandom fawned over him and didn't pay any attention to Zaria and Mayumi.

"Zaria's *my* favourite," I said, incredibly conscious of

the fact that, in the issue he'd just read, Zaria had kissed a woman.

"She is pretty cool," he agreed.

That page where Zaria was first shown to be queer flashes across my mind.

"Uncle…" I say, thinking about how strong Zaria is, how fearless, "I'm bi."

Kevin sits up straight, his eyes wide. "Oh, Elsie! That's…" He reaches out with his hands. "Come here."

I stand up, hesitantly, and Kevin stands up too. He hugs me.

Hugs don't happen often in my family. But Kevin is hugging me, and I think of his parents disowning him, the price he paid to be with David, to live with this man who would kiss his fingers and ruffle his hair every day, and I hug him back, as tightly as I can.

"I'm proud of you," he says.

CHAPTER TWENTY-EIGHT

There's a spare bedroom, which Kevin uses as his office since he works from home. Besides a desk with two outrageously large monitors, an office chair, a printer and stacks of folders, it also contains a double bed that looks pristine. "Are you both OK to sleep in here?" Kevin asks. "Or one of you could have the sofa in the living room. It's very comfy."

Joan and I glance at each other. Her hair, wet from the shower, drips into her eyes, and she blinks. "I can sleep on the sofa," she offers.

"I'm sure we could both take the bed," I say.

"Wait." Kevin narrows his eyes at me. "I'm thinking your mum wouldn't be too pleased with me if I let you sleep in the same bed as a boy, and, since it turns out that you're not only attracted to boys, maybe I should rethink this."

"Uncle!" I hiss. "There's nothing going on between me and Joan."

"All right." Kevin holds his hands up. "I'll take your word for it as long as your mum doesn't find out. Goodnight!"

As he strolls down the corridor to the room that he and David share, I give Joan an embarrassed smile, but she's not looking at me.

"Maybe I *should* take the sofa," she says, her eyes on the wall. She thumbs a small chip in the paint.

"Why? The bed is big enough."

Joan says nothing. Something buzzes beneath my skin. It's like hearing the whine of a mosquito by your ear and feeling a bite – whether real or imagined – begin to itch, but not being able to see the culprit and close your fist round it. It flies past, eluding me. My body tingles, alert and watchful. I can see the muscles of Joan's throat move as she swallows. Her eyes remain fixed on the wall.

"I think—" she finally says, just as I also open my mouth to speak, the question that I've held back all day finally too loud to be contained.

"Do you like me?" I ask, trying to hide my terror behind a smile that I hope is teasing. It slips away as soon as she reacts.

"What?" she splutters.

The calm breaks on her face, as though I've dropped a pebble into a still pond. The effect is startling. Getting to know her again this summer, I keep feeling that she's older than me even though we're the same age. Like she's done so much more growing when all I've managed is to stagger round my teenage years in confusion, uncovering more wounds every time I think I've healed, becoming smaller instead of bigger. It's not like she doesn't carry around her own baggage, all that stuff with her dad, but even when she's talking about that to me she seems like an adult, living an adult life. On the grown-up side of eighteen rather than the child side.

But now she looks … *young*, like me. Wide-eyed and fumbling, as though she's lost the script for her life and, like everybody else, is forced to make it up as she goes along.

The panic in her eyes shrinks her down to my size. I start to understand that it's possible that I can become as grown-up as she always seems, that there isn't such an unbridgeable chasm between me and this confidence I covet in her, because it isn't something innate, but something practised.

"Do you like me?" I repeat. "Do you… Do you have *feelings* for me?"

"No." She shakes her head, as if saying the word isn't enough. "I don't. You're my best friend. I *don't* –" her voice rips through her like a letter opener tearing an envelope, the letter within bearing the worst possible news – "I don't think of you in that way."

Whatever knife cut through her cuts through me too. We

stare at each other. Her hair is still dripping, one clear drop of water beading at the tip of a clump of hair, gathering volume in the silence. Suddenly that drop of water is all I can focus on. I feel like I'm inside it as it swells, knowing that the fall is inevitable but clinging, anyway.

It falls, and my gaze darts down with it. It joins the crowd of its kin, little dots of water on the wood-tiled floor around Joan's bare feet.

"I'm taking the sofa," she says, and I don't protest.

it's all your fault

I send this text to Ritika before realising that it sounds a bit too alarming without context. I send another one.

joan DOESN'T like me!! and now i might have ruined everything

BITCH WHAT

I stand in Kevin's office with the door closed and type furiously, explaining to Ritika what just happened.

OH SHIT. i'm so sorry!

> **but, like, you don't even have feelings for her like that, right? it was only two days ago you were telling me you two are JUST FRIENDS like me and you are just friends, remember?? just scroll up if you have the memory of a goldfish bcos it's right there**

I don't have to scroll up. I remember it well.
I knock my head back against the door.

I lie on the double bed with my arm draped over my face. I can't remember the last time I slept in a double bed, if ever. It seems horribly enormous, like an open field. I can't sleep like this. I wish for a tent, a sleeping bag, something to help me feel more enclosed and less exposed. A cocoon, to take away my tremendous awareness of the space around me.

It's raining again. I can hear it pelting against the window, an army of ghosts trying to get in.

Joan could have been in this bed with me. If I hadn't asked her such a stupid question. But then maybe the whole reason why she didn't want to sleep in the same bed as me is because she's worried about *my* feelings for her. Because she deduced them, somehow, before I even really figured them out myself.

But I've been figuring them out today.

I've spent all day with Joan. Every second I haven't been talking to her, I have been thinking about her. About the possibility of us.

The first time I had a crush on a girl, it was Chloe Godby in my class. She was white, with soft brown hair and a mouth that made me think of the first syllable of her last name. She played football, and so did one of my friends from the book club at the time, so I used to watch them play, but really I was watching Chloe.

In the months before that, I'd become obsessed with a certain actress and devoured every single movie – as well as every interview on YouTube – she'd ever been in. After replaying a particular sex scene over and over, hypnotised by her bra strap sliding off her shoulder, the camera lovingly swooping down the length of her naked back, I admitted to myself that perhaps I wasn't straight.

This actress was also white.

When I started to dream of having a girlfriend, the girlfriend of my imagination was always white. In nearly every movie, TV show and book I consumed, the romantic heroine was always white. White women are beautiful and worthy of love. Mainstream media taught me that. White women are attractive, and women who aren't white are as good as invisible.

I was fourteen, and I wasn't fully aware of any of this. But the message was burrowing deep into my brain.

What I *was* aware of was my own sense that I was

undesirable. Around me, girls were talking about boys they'd kissed, but when I looked in the mirror I didn't see somebody any boy would want to kiss. My face was flat and round, my eyes small and my eyelashes non-existent. It was as if everything remotely interesting or appealing had been pressed out of my face. I wasn't attractive, and I knew it.

And then Leo happened.

The moment he showed interest in me, I felt like I'd won the lottery. A boy liked me. A *white* boy liked *me*.

After Leo, when I first found Ada's fanfic and started looking at her blog, I didn't know she was Black, that her mum was from Nigeria. I assumed she was white, like the majority of people I came across in fandom. She didn't use to post selfies then because she struggled with body-image issues and low self-esteem. She talked about how great it was to see a queer Black female character like Zaria, but it didn't make me think, *Oh, Ada's Black.*

I didn't know what she looked like but already thoughts of her had become part of my daily routine. *Wake up, think about Ada. Brush teeth, think about Ada. Walk to school, think about Ada.*

Then we Skyped for the first time, and it hit me how messed up it was that, when I fantasised about flying to New York and meeting her, I'd imagined her as a white girl.

She's gorgeous just the way she is and always has been. At that point, she had an Afro, and the first time we

Skyped she was wearing a yellow shirt with a navy bow tie – her first-ever bow tie, the beginning of her collection. She'd bought it just for the Skype call, wanting to try something new and feeling that it was safe for her to do so with me, and I kept telling her how cute she was, but she kept shrugging off my compliments and making self-deprecating comments.

After we ended the call, I spent the whole night thinking about how we both believed in our undesirability.

And, as we talked more in the days and weeks that followed, I started to become conscious of how I'd been infected with the idea that whiteness was more desirable and attractive than any other option.

I thought I was working on eradicating this notion from my mind. But I haven't got rid of it. It still subtly colours my way of thinking.

I knew I liked Joan a lot. I knew that I liked being with her, just sitting watching TV or eating dinner or having the most mundane conversations. I knew that I liked how she was wholeheartedly herself, someone honest and brave and unashamed. I knew that I liked her sense of style, that I found the way she dressed attractive. But I didn't realise that it wasn't just her clothes or her hair: it's *her* I'm attracted to. Joan in her entirety. I didn't know that because some part of me still doesn't think that Chinese people can be attractive.

Deep down, I'm still convinced of my own ugliness and

the ugliness of anyone who looks like me.

Worse – Joan isn't feminine, and all my life I've been taught that the only way to be desirable is to strive for femininity. The further you fall from it, the uglier you are.

It's even in that offhand remark my mother made about Joan: *She used to be such a pretty child.*

But I realised, in that corridor outside this room – just as Joan told me she didn't think of me in that way and gutted me – that *I* think of her in that way.

I see it at last. Joan is beautiful, handsome, *hot* in a way that makes everything inside me glow like the moon. Looking at her makes me forget that the world tried to teach me what its definition of ugliness is. I want Joan. Her eyes and her mouth and her collarbones, her fingers and her wrists and the hairs on her arms.

What if she knows that and is afraid of me?

But she can't be. She's *Joan*. Surely she'd understand what it's like for a girl to have a crush on another girl, even if she can't like me back. I think of all the times I averted my eyes in the changing room at school before and after PE lessons, terrified that someone might think I'd looked at them a second too long and work out that I was queer.

Joan wouldn't be afraid of me – she'd know that I'm the one who's afraid.

I clutch that thought to me and hope that our friendship is still intact in the morning. Just when it's dawned on me at last that *we* might be possible, it turns out that we aren't. *I don't think of you in that way*. But that doesn't mean that we can't still be best friends. Keeping her in my life is all that matters.

The rain sounds more comforting now, more like nature's lullaby.

I close my eyes and let myself imagine her in this bed with me. I let myself imagine how, in my sleep, I might unconsciously drift closer and closer to her.

I let myself imagine her hip against mine, an unbearable warmth.

CHAPTER TWENTY-NINE

Morning, when it comes, is still grey, but it smells like scrambled eggs.

I'm not sure if I actually slept or not. I probably did but it feels like one of those nights where I stayed up reading a fifty-chapter fanfic only for it to end badly, without warning, in a beloved character's death.

I tiptoe into the living room but Joan is already awake, sitting on the sofa with her knees drawn up to her chest and a cream blanket rumpled beside her like the frothy foam on a cappuccino. She's watching the news on TV, the volume low. Her hair is a mess, without any product in it yet, and the shadows under her eyes are deep. She looks up at me and smiles. "Morning."

"Hey," I reply, and now I feel guilty. Guilty for thinking of her the way I did last night, imagining the heat of her skin. She doesn't think of me in that way. The panic on her face last night returns to me, but there's no sign of it now. Her smile has all the smoothness that her hair does not. But it doesn't reach her eyes. "Had your morning coffee yet?"

"Just about to." She springs up from the sofa and heads towards the kitchen. "I think your uncle's making some kind of luxury breakfast in there."

I follow her. "Did you sleep well?"

"The sofa was very comfy, as your uncle said."

"That's not what I asked."

Joan shrugs, slipping into the kitchen where Kevin is just plating up the scrambled eggs, and I can see the pink flakes of smoked salmon he's added to it. In another pan, he's also frying pancakes. There are punnets of gleaming strawberries and plump blueberries laid out on the kitchen worktop, and a squeezy bottle of honey, presumably all to go with the pancakes.

"Wow, Uncle Kevin, you didn't have to make all this," I say, though I'm salivating. Barely sleeping has made me *really* hungry.

"It's not every day my niece comes to see me and also comes out to me!" Kevin flings his arm out with dramatic flourish, spatula in hand. "It's an occasion worthy of celebration."

"So this is a coming-out breakfast."

That should've been a little absurd but instead it makes me feel luminous with a kind of whirling joy, like I'm arriving at a theme park, all its whizzing colours spread out before me. I've never needed pancakes as much as I do in this moment.

"Yes, a coming-out breakfast!" Kevin says. "I wish I'd got to have one."

"This is *your* coming-out breakfast too," I say. "You came out to me."

"I can't make my own coming-out breakfast." He retrieves the toast that's just popped up from the toaster and puts a slice on each plate with the scrambled eggs. "Now, if I come to visit you next time, and *you* make me breakfast in return…"

"So you're going to come and see Po Po?" I ask.

The idea of it makes me feel conflicted. I'm angry at her on Kevin's behalf, but it's his choice ultimately. And I do get the sense that Po Po wants to see him. I'd like to hope that they can reconcile.

Kevin sighs, flipping a pancake. "I don't know. I'm still thinking about it. But, either way, she's going back to Hong Kong soon, and I'll definitely come and see you after that."

"I'll be off to uni in October."

"Christmas then, at the latest." He jerks his shoulder at the plates. "Go and eat the scrambled eggs before they get cold."

Joan is fiddling around with the Nespresso machine. I take the plates into the dining room, and a minute later she sits down opposite me at the table with her coffee.

Silences with Joan have never been awkward in the past, but this one hangs between us like a wet shower curtain, as though one of us has burst in on the other naked behind the filmy fabric, and that mental image only makes everything worse.

"I'm sorry about last night," I say, after both of us have spent too long just chewing. "I don't know what made me ask that question."

Joan's face is unreadable but at this point David comes into the room, yawning and stretching, and I look up at him gratefully.

"How did you sleep, girls?" he asks.

"Really well, thanks," I say automatically.

"Not bad," Joan says. "I love your sofa."

I glance at Joan out of the corner of my eye. Do I look as tired as she does? Does she know I'm lying, just as she is?

David is perky enough to make up for our collective lack of energy. "Yeah, it's a darn good sofa." He sniffs the buttery air, oblivious to the limp atmosphere between me and Joan. "Is he making pancakes too? God, he's really gone all out, hasn't he?"

He gazes in the direction of the kitchen with adoration in his sleep-soft eyes, an expression that crushes me. That he can still look so obviously, happily in love with Kevin when they've known each other for nearly twenty years seems like a miracle I'll never get to experience.

We spend the morning pottering round a museum. I don't take anything in, and as soon as we leave I don't even really remember what it's the museum *of*. But pretending to focus on the exhibits at least meant that I could avoid talking to Joan.

All of us are still too full from breakfast to have a proper lunch, so we just sit down for a cup of tea, and I let Uncle Kevin and David's chatter drift round me. They're so *warm*. I always liked Uncle Kevin's upbeat vibe but this feels like it's on a whole new level. He and David keep getting lost in tangent upon tangent, and I'm content to just let the conversation unspool around me.

I meet Joan's eyes across the table, and she looks away.

Before we head to the train station, Uncle Kevin says, "Oh, it's actually Nicole's birthday soon. I should get her something. There's this really quirky gift shop that I like. Mind if we stop by there?"

Joan checks her watch. "Sounds good. We have time."

The gift shop is so colourful and has lots of cool stuff. Uncle Kevin enlists me to help him find a present for Nicole but I come across Joan looking at a cute ceramic figurine of a yawning white tiger. "Are they still your favourite animal?"

She jolts at my presence. "Oh. Yeah. I love them."

"Me too," I say. "Though I probably like snakes more

now because of *Eden Recoiling*."

Joan picks up the figurine and plays with it. "How do you remember that they're my favourite animal?"

"I dug up the card that you gave me when you left. It had a tiger on it. It made me remember how we both liked tigers when we were little."

"Oh. Yeah. You like them because they have stripes?"

I laugh. "Yeah. And you know what? Turns out lots of *snakes* have stripes too."

Joan laughs as well, just a little. She puts the figurine down and bends down to study a pile of woven rugs. I go back to trying to find a gift for Nicole.

As we exit the shop, Uncle Kevin shows David the vase that I helped to pick out, and I hold out to Joan the tiger figurine that I just bought.

"I got this for you. You never did extort something more expensive from me to celebrate your exam results, so I thought you might like this."

The wonder on Joan's face makes me feel like we might still be OK. She takes the tiger and cups it in both hands, more gingerly than she did in the shop. "Thank you, Elsie," she says softly. Just as softly, she strokes the tiger's head.

Desperately, I think about how I want her to touch me just like that.

When we get back to Oxford after a quiet three-hour train ride where Joan and I focused all our attention on our own phones, Joan heads back to her flat. I tell her that I'm going home but I don't want to yet. My parents are going to be there. My parents, who kept Uncle Kevin's relationship with David a secret from me for so long. And my po po. Who wasn't able to accept her own son.

I go to Ritika's house instead. When she opens the door, I can hear her brothers shouting somewhere. They often seem to be having a fight, usually over some video game. I asked Ritika about it once, and she said it was pretty much an eternal argument that never died and carried on when I wasn't around.

"Why didn't you tell me you were coming?" she asks, as I take off my shoes. "Are you staying for dinner? Dad's making lamb curry."

I can smell it, the spices heavy in the air and delicious. I didn't think I was hungry but I am now immediately. "Yes, please!"

I take out my phone to message my parents that I've gone to Ritika's for dinner.

We pop into the kitchen to say hi to her dad before we go up to Ritika's room. I flop down on her bed.

"I've had a *weekend*," I say.

"Apart from what happened with Joan?"

"Yeah. I have Theresa's current phone number. Also, my uncle is gay! He's married to a man! And nobody told me!"

"Holy shit. Wow. That's a lot! Wow."

I groan, rolling over and planting my face in the bed. "I know. And I don't even want to think about what happened with Joan."

"*Noooo*, you have to tell me what happened properly. You were kind of incoherent in your texts."

I grab one of Ritika's pillows and pull it down over my head like a shield against my despair. After giving me a few moments to wallow, Ritika yanks the pillow away.

"It can't be that bad," she says.

"It's bad. I do like Joan, OK! You were right! I actually really like her but she doesn't like me!" I recount my conversation from the night before as accurately as I can.

Ritika gently places the pillow back on my head. "OK. Well. That's … pretty bad. But you didn't say anything about how *you* feel to her."

"What?"

"You only asked her how she feels. Maybe you should let her know your feelings. It's good to make yourself clear. She might change her mind or whatever."

"I don't know if there's any point. Won't it just make her uncomfortable?"

"I honestly think you're kind of really bad at telling people you like them."

"Ugh, it's not like *you've* ever done it before, either."

Ritika thinks about this. Jake was the one who asked her out. "Yeah. You're right. But I think I definitely could if I had to. You, on the other hand… I don't understand why you didn't just tell Ada."

"I don't know! I just couldn't do it!"

"Have you ever really sat down and thought about why you couldn't?"

I turn my head to glare at her, the pillow sliding off me, but a sadness touches her face the way the golden light at dusk changes a room, transports it to a softer realm.

I close my eyes. Maybe I do know. Maybe I know that what I've been clinging on to is that perfect glass dome my heart lives in when I'm crushing on somebody, when I get to linger in the sweetness of how I feel about them at a distance. If I don't tell people I like them, I don't give them the power to hurt me. If the glass dome is cracked even a fraction, who knows what could get in?

Part of me felt safe liking Ada because I didn't truly believe that things were ever going to work out with her. Of course my feelings for her were genuine but they were also a sanctuary for my heart. It was beautiful to imagine us getting together because it didn't seem like something that would happen. But Joan's *here*. I see her every day. And the idea of a romantic relationship with her seemed so much more inaccessible to me *because* it was so much more real. My heart wouldn't let itself be vulnerable enough to reach for it.

"I just don't want to be hurt again," I say. Tears leak from my eyes. I open them, but it's hard to look at Ritika's face, her kindness and affection too bright. "I'm afraid of what comes after I tell someone I like them. I don't even mean rejection. But being in a relationship – that's the part that scares me the most."

Ritika's hand presses against my cheek. "It'll be OK. I know it's scary but I'm always going to be here for you. You can count on me to have your back."

I open my eyes. She brushes away my tears.

"Thanks," I say, though it doesn't feel adequate. "I love you."

CHAPTER THIRTY

Once I've stuffed myself with lamb curry and a mountain of rice – that's what Ritika and I bond over the most, I reckon, our shared love of rice, that purest and most beautiful of carbohydrates and food staples – Ritika's mum drives me home, as she always does after dark. She drops me off, and I stand at the front door of my house like I'm about to walk into an exam. An insect buzzes as it flies past me, and I flinch.

I unlock the door and slip inside. The sounds of a movie greet me, roaring engines and screeching tyres and booming collisions. A car chase. I initially can't tell whether it's an English movie or a Chinese one, but a deep voice shouts, "Turn left!" in Cantonese just as I walk into the living room.

Mum is on her laptop at the dinner table – she doesn't

like action movies, which is weird because I now know that she likes action-filled manga. Po Po, on the other hand, loves them. She's – unexpectedly? – a huge fan of explosions, and she and Dad are on the sofa, both of them avid.

"Hi, Mum," I say.

She looks up at me with a tense smile. "Hi. How was Joan?"

The official story – the one we gave Po Po – is that I'd gone for a sleepover at Joan's. Now I'm thinking about how I *still* haven't seen where Joan is staying, even though she's been to my house nearly every day this summer. I know that it's an impermanent home, a sublet that would probably contain nothing of Joan's personality, that in less than two months' time she's going to move into her uni accommodation, but I want to see it nonetheless. If I'd really gone for a sleepover at Joan's, would I still have made such a mess of our friendship?

I'm so tired. It's been a really full weekend, and so much has happened. And now I have to deal with my family, who don't know that I'm queer, who have no idea about this part of me that's not just essential but dear. This whole weekend has revolved so completely around the radiant sun of my queerness, something the rest of me depends upon to flourish and *live*.

I don't have the energy to even interact with my parents and my grandmother right now if I have to keep shutting away the part of myself that brings me the fiercest light, the warmest strength.

325

"Mum, why didn't you tell me that Uncle Kevin was married? And you went to the wedding?"

I say this in Cantonese. Horror engulfs Mum's face. I can feel Dad and Po Po looking at me, all their attention pointing at me like a knife.

"You promised you wouldn't tell Po Po you went to see him!" Mum says in English.

I also switch to English, just because it's an easier language for me to be emotional in. "Why did you think I couldn't know? There's nothing wrong with being gay. And clearly you agree because you sided with Kevin! You went to their wedding. Why didn't you take me?"

I fling my overnight bag down, and it skids some way across the floor. I'm running on pure exasperation right now. I just wish everybody in my family would *talk* to each other for once.

Behind me, I can hear Dad murmuring to Po Po in Cantonese – though it isn't a very soft murmur, given that Po Po's hearing isn't optimal – saying that they should go into the kitchen and leave me and Mum to talk in private. But she stays put and asks, "Yan Yan, you went to see your uncle?"

I turn. Her face is tremulous and vulnerable in a way I've never seen before, like a trill held in a songbird's throat. "Yes, Po Po, I did. And … he told me you disowned him." I use the plural of 'you' in Cantonese, meaning her and my dead gung gung.

"How is he?"

I wasn't expecting this question, which is as gentle as a leaf touching the ground. Some of my indignation fizzles out, and what's beneath is profound exhaustion. "He's ... good."

"And his ... friend?" Po Po says distantly.

"You mean his husband."

She makes a small noise, which could be affirmative or just her clearing her throat, and says nothing.

"David's really nice. They seem happy together."

Po Po nods, folding her hands neatly in her lap. "Did he say anything about coming to see me?"

"I don't know. I think... Well, I think if he wants to see you he will. I can't speak for him."

"Is he still angry at me?"

"I ... I really can't say."

I don't think anger is the right word. If my parents disowned me for being queer, anger would definitely feature, but eight years on surely it would be more sadness than anything.

I turn back to Mum, carrying on in English. "I just don't understand why you couldn't have told me before. I can't believe you kept me from something so ... wonderful."

She winces. "Maybe we can go upstairs and talk?"

I don't know why we have to but I suppose talking in English in front of Po Po is rude, or maybe Mum doesn't want Dad to be involved, either. I follow her upstairs, and she picks the master bedroom, not mine. The muted tones of the room, compared to the bright colours in mine, always make me feel more grown up, but also a little sombre.

We both sit on the very beige bed.

"It's been a strange eight years," she says. In Cantonese now because it's a language she feels more comfortable in.

I personally prefer English but I answer in Cantonese because I can't have this conversation if we're fundamentally disconnected on some level. "Yeah, I'm now finally getting that. All I felt before was a bit confused as to why we hadn't been back to Hong Kong in so long."

"Yes… Well, eight years ago, your uncle went to Hong Kong with his friend."

God, even Mum was still pulling this shit. "His *husband*."

Mum puts her hand on my knee. "His husband," she amends. "But David wasn't his husband then. He was his … boyfriend."

She says this as carefully as one would pick up a xiaolongbao with chopsticks pinched round the tip of the dumpling, so as not to break the thin wrapper and let all the hot, flavourful broth inside leak out. She glances at me as if seeking my approval but I'm not going to congratulate her just for this minimal effort.

"We… In Cantonese, we have a habit of calling these people friends. Even if you had a boyfriend, I would probably sometimes call him your friend."

I didn't know that. "OK."

"So… Kevin and David went to Hong Kong, and they tried to go for yum cha with Po Po and Gung Gung. And Gung Gung walked out when it became clear who this white man was to Kevin. Po Po apparently stayed behind just to finish her dim sum and then left. The only time Gung Gung spoke to Kevin after that was a phone call to say that he didn't ever want to see him again. No word from Po Po at all. Kevin came back and told me what happened, and I … I was so upset. I had known this about him since we were teenagers. He's my brother. He's… It was clear to me that my parents were wrong. I thought that if *I* stopped speaking to them and if your Auntie Susan also stopped…"

"So Auntie Susan hadn't been to Hong Kong in eight years, either?"

"Yes. Like me, she returned for Ah Gung's last few days and for his funeral." Mum sighs. "But yes. That was our tactic. For eight years, we never visited, never called, never messaged. Apart from in the first few weeks after they disowned Kevin, when Susan and I both rang to tell them that we weren't happy with how they had treated him. And, after that, no contact at all. We thought that we could change their minds. If none of their children were talking to them, maybe they'd soften. Surely they'd get lonely."

"But they didn't."

"They didn't. Your gung gung was always disastrously stubborn."

"And what about Po Po? How does she feel about all this now?"

"I'm not sure. I know she has her regrets but we haven't delved too deeply into the subject. It turns out that, when you don't speak to somebody for eight years, it's not easy to start again, especially about the one issue that divided you for so long. All I know is that I don't want her to be alone right now."

"So why didn't you tell me any of this?"

"It was a difficult situation. I wasn't sure you'd understand it. You were only ten."

"And Kevin being in a relationship with a man? That wouldn't have been hard for a ten-year-old to grasp. Plenty of ten-year-olds understand that just fine."

I'm getting frustrated. Joan said she'd known she was a lesbian when she was only eleven.

"Yes. I know. But you were... You were. You know. You were such a naam zai tau. Everyone thought you were a little boy. I wanted to wait until you were older. When you were more settled in your own identity."

"Wait, what?" There's some kind of twisted logic behind my mum's words that isn't easy to piece together, intellectually or emotionally. "You didn't want me to know about Uncle Kevin because I was a naam zai tau? You thought that if I knew about him I would... I would *become* gay."

Before today, I don't think I'd ever said the word 'gay'

330

to my mum. This one word feels like an emergency siren wailing through the streets, all other traffic parting frantically before it. Flashing lights above me and underneath the word GAY emblazoned in bold capital letters on my forehead.

"No… Not. Not that. I just didn't want to put any ideas in your head that weren't already there."

This is absolutely infuriating. I cover my face with my hands. "Oh my God. Mum. That's…"

I don't even know what to say. It seems like the perfect opportunity to come out and say, *Well, I did* turn out to be queer, *despite your best efforts at keeping the whole concept of being gay under wraps.* But I can't do it.

"And now I'm old enough to find out?"

"You're too old for me to keep things from you. And then there's Joan…"

"What about her?"

"Ah, your mum went to secondary school in Hong Kong! I've known girls like her. There have always been girls like her. I thought, if she's your best friend, then you already have those ideas in your head."

Mum and I are fast veering into very weird territory. Not that this whole conversation isn't totally bizarre. Two days ago, I never would have expected to be talking about my *gay uncle* with my mum.

"Oh my God. OK. Well, I'm glad you've told me everything now. Please don't say you're keeping any more massive family secrets from me because I will not be able to handle it."

"No. I'm all out of secrets."

"Great."

I get up to finally, *finally* retreat to the sanctuary of my own bedroom after what feels like a whole month away from it, but my mum touches my arm.

"Wait. I have more to say."

"What is it?"

"I … I don't regret picking my brother's side. But it was still a very hard eight years. And it's been especially hard this year. My father dying… I know Kevin couldn't do it; he still couldn't bring himself to see the man who had so completely rejected him. But Susan and I had to see your Ah Gung one last time before he died. And, when I saw him fading in front of my own eyes, I … I wished everything could have been different."

Mum pauses to stroke a photo on her bedside table, of her and her siblings and her parents. The picture is probably older than me. But I don't think it's always been there. Mum must have been going through photo albums. The frame is pristine, and they're all together, at some sort of celebratory banquet – the wall in the background is tomato-red. Maybe it had been one of Gung Gung's birthdays. He's in the centre, as jolly as I remember him.

"I miss him," Mum continues. "The side of him that was gentle and fed pigeons and crooned along to love songs on the radio. I wish he'd never given me a reason to hate him. And I … I don't want that for us, Yan Yan. Do you hear me? I don't want our relationship to ever fall apart so badly that we don't speak for the rest of my life. I will try my best to listen to you and understand you, no matter what."

She clasps one of my hands between both of hers and starts to cry.

I hate seeing her like this, the desolation on her face like a brick thrown through the glass walls of my heart. I imagine her sitting beside Gung Gung's hospital bed, looking exactly like this, holding his withered hand as it grew cold.

Her own hands are bony too, but they're as warm as the air in the kitchen whenever it's white with steam from her cooking.

"I hear you," I say.

Now that I know that she's so supportive of Uncle Kevin, I'm slightly more confident that she would be OK with me being bi, but I still don't feel like coming out to her right now.

"Thanks, Mum. I'll never disown you, either."

Mum looks startled by my terrible attempt at a joke but she's no longer crying, and she might even be smiling, just a little. "Promise, little onion?"

Little onion. She hasn't called me that since I was a child. I can't even remember where the nickname comes from. "Promise, Mum."

As I leave the room, I try very hard to believe that my mum will always love me unconditionally, an exercise that I've made myself do repeatedly ever since I realised I was queer, and in this moment it seems just a little less impossible than it ever had before.

CHAPTER THIRTY-ONE

For the umpteenth time this summer, with the morning light streaming through my window, I examine my wardrobe. It isn't helping with my frustration at all.

I'm avoiding leaving my room. I can't bring myself to confront my po po yet. If Mum can't broach the subject with Po Po, I'm going to do it for her. But I'm trying to put it off a little longer.

So I'm thinking about my clothes. Really thinking about them.

Dresses, miniskirts, fitted tops. Nothing so short or tight that my parents would disapprove. I mostly prefer things that look pretty. Lace and softness, florals everywhere. I like opening my wardrobe and seeing a garden in bloom.

When I started secondary school, without Joan, I was suddenly so much more aware of how wrong I looked compared to other girls. There was the school uniform that we all wore, of course, but when I bumped into anyone I knew from school at the weekends, when I was out and about with my parents, I could practically hear the laughter as soon as I turned my back.

So I made myself more like all the girls in pretty dresses, to fit in. By the time Leo came along, there was no trace of the girl I used to be, with her short hair and cargo shorts and her distaste of anything girly. I had erased her.

And Leo was clear about what he liked me to wear. Which outfits he thought I looked best in. The way it cut through his breath when he saw me wearing something that turned him on still makes me shiver to recall.

And my parents, too, had an image they wanted me to fit into. Mum's eyes lighting up when she saw me in a pretty dress, Dad's face smoothing over with approval. *My daughter is so beautiful.*

If it hadn't been for Joan, I would have forgotten about the girl I was entirely. I would have lost her forever, just as I'd lost Joan.

But I have Joan back.

It's not that I hate these feminine clothes now. I don't. I like how they look; I even like how they look *on me*. But more and more I think liking something because it's pretty and liking something because it truly expresses who I am are two different things. I wonder if I would feel more comfortable in something else. If the girl I was before still lives inside me;

if I can draw out the ghost of her and colour her in again.

But I don't know where to start. It would be weird if I suddenly started dressing like Joan. *Joan* would find that weird, wouldn't she? First that terrible conversation I got us into about her non-existent feelings for me, and now, if I was seen to be … *copying* her style, that wouldn't help the situation at all.

I nudge the wardrobe doors shut. Maybe if I wait until I start uni, then she wouldn't be around, and isn't uni the perfect opportunity to reinvent myself, anyway?

But this train of thought only conveys me to a yet more unpleasant destination, because now I'm thinking about being away from Joan again, for months at a time.

She hasn't said anything about whether she'd be coming over to watch TV with me and my po po today. Given that I'm planning to talk to Po Po about her homophobia, and I have no idea how that's going to go, it seems best if I wait until I've done that to ask Joan over.

I message her.

> i'm gonna talk to my po po about kevin

> Hope it goes well, let me know if I should drop in after.

So at least that means she still wants to see me, right?

I can think about all of this later. There's an old woman downstairs I have to talk to.

The temperature has dropped a little after the rain over the weekend, and there's a fresh breeze coming from outside, cold and sweet. Po Po isn't in the garden but standing in the kitchen, looking at the family photos on the fridge door, held there by an assortment of magnets including some from Disneyland Paris just last summer, where the most adventurous ride my mum was willing to go on had been Dumbo the Flying Elephant. Most of the photos are recent, and they're of me and Mum and Dad. A couple include Auntie Susan and her family, and some feature Kevin too.

I wonder if there might be photos with David in them soon, now that I know about him.

There were probably photos of Po Po and Gung Gung on this fridge door once upon a time, but I can't recall. Maybe Mum took them down because it hurt her too much to be reminded daily of her stubborn parents.

"Could I make you some tea?" I ask Po Po. Weird how I can still be civil to someone who disowned her son for being gay.

"No need, thank you," she says. "Let's talk about your uncle."

I'm a little surprised that she's raising the topic first, but this makes it easier for me. We go into the living room, where I sit down cross-legged on the armchair that I've come to think of as Joan's seat this summer.

"Did he say anything about me?" she asks.

"I think he preferred not to talk about you."

She sighs. "But he's doing well."

"Yes." Bitterness, like a bowlful of Chinese medicine, laces my voice.

"You probably have no experience of this." Po Po rubs one of her hands over the other, twisting her jade bracelet round and round her wrist. "But sometimes you fall in love with someone, and over time they... They either become, or they turn out to be, a completely different person. And, by the time you see it, it's too late."

I have so much more experience of this than Po Po assumes. "Are you talking about Gung Gung?"

"When I first met him, he was the sunniest person I'd ever known. But, as I would learn, a life together with him was not easy. He had to be right all the time. He couldn't compromise. So I shed more and more of myself in order to keep our marriage running smoothly. This didn't feel like a problem at first. I could have flaked away into nothing and it wouldn't have bothered me. I loved him that much."

Po Po stares down at her hands. They're wrinkled like creased silk.

It's strange hearing Po Po talk about love. Not that I think she's incapable of it or anything, but really it isn't a subject my family is comfortable with. Love is something that happens silently. When Dad takes my empty bowl and refills it with rice without me having to ask for more; when Mum cooks my favourite dish, beef with sha cha sauce, and keeps picking up pieces of beef with her chopsticks and dropping them in my bowl even though I insist I've had enough; when Mum plays Dad's favourite classical music tracks to wake him up on Sunday mornings so that the whole house fills with orchestral swells, gentle and vibrant at once, and brings him breakfast in bed; when Dad brings home a box of Mum's favourite cookies, gooey and warm with half-melted chocolate.

So much of what I understand of love in my family seems to revolve around food.

When I look at Po Po, it's with the taste of soy-sauce chicken wings in my mouth.

I feel a new kind of sympathy for her, knowing that we share the experience of making ourselves smaller and smaller for love. How much more do we have in common? I remembered so little of her before this summer but I know how insubstantial a person can become when they're drained by the wrong kind of love. To me now, Po Po is as vivid as an autumn afternoon, ablaze with colour.

"Po Po… You don't blame yourself for the way you loved him, do you?"

"I'm too busy blaming myself for other things."

"Po Po…"

Her shoulders sag a little. "It got harder when we had children. When they grew up, I started to daydream about leaving him sometimes. But … in the end, your po po is an old-fashioned woman. A divorce seemed out of the question." She winces. "And all my children wanted to head off into different parts of the world. I couldn't bear being left alone, so I stayed with your gung gung."

I hadn't thought about that. The fear of loneliness. And I hate how much I understand it. I hadn't been the one to break up with Leo. If it had been up to me, we might have stayed together forever, and some days that's the thought that frightens me more than anything: how much of myself I was willing to sacrifice to an undeserving love.

"It must have been hard when all your children moved away, and you were alone with him. I'm sorry."

"If I had been a better parent, maybe at least one of them would have stayed."

"I think a lot of children want independence from their parents. It's not necessarily your fault if their paths take them elsewhere. And especially… I guess Kevin especially. It would have been a lot easier for him to have that space for himself."

"I always felt like I had an inkling… About your uncle."

Po Po looks down at her feet, which are clad in fluffy slippers, incongruous with the rest of her elegant outfit, her satin blouse and sleek trousers. She always dresses flawlessly even if all she's going to do is lounge around the house.

"But then he married a woman. When he got divorced, I hoped he would just quietly live his life in England, and your gung gung would never have to find out. But your uncle came to see us and, as soon as he walked into the restaurant with his friend, I knew it would all go wrong. Your gung gung left in a rage, and I kept sitting there, and we all had shrimp dumplings and cheung fun."

"So you were OK with it?"

"No. I was just better at controlling my temper than your gung gung. I was *angry* at my son. We already didn't know what to tell people about his divorce. He could've had a normal life. Instead he chose to upset his parents."

"He wasn't doing it to upset you. He wanted you to be happy for him."

"At the time, I could only hate him for being so selfish."

I feel riled by this comment. "He wasn't selfish!"

"I know many people who would agree with me."

"That doesn't mean you're right."

"I understand that a little better now. But your gung gung never wanted to see your uncle again. I was that way too, at first. I didn't want anybody I knew to find out that my son was … like that."

"Gay."

"Yes. But then all our children stopped speaking to us, and my life felt so empty. I thought I could pretend to be

OK with your uncle's friend if it meant my children would talk to me again. But your gung gung still wouldn't relent."

"Why didn't you reach out to Uncle Kevin then? You didn't have to wait for Gung Gung's cue. You could've just done it."

"I could have. But I disappeared into my sadness. I'd lost too much of myself to your gung gung. Besides, I had always been the stricter parent. I had to be – he wouldn't put any of the work in. He only liked to play with his children, give them sweets and pocket money, and send them on their way. Would they believe me if I said that it was your gung gung, and not me, who had a problem with your uncle?"

"So you didn't even try?"

"The truth is, as time went on, I got angrier at your uncle again. It was his fault, I thought. Why couldn't he have just kept quiet? Then our family would still be all right."

Po Po is crying now, tears rolling down her cheeks. It's horrible to witness. I'm not on her side; I'm on Kevin's side. Coming out to his parents must have taken so much courage and strength. For Po Po to dismiss that is like a fishbone piercing the tender flesh in my mouth. And yet.

I do feel sorry for her. I hand her some tissues from the box on the coffee table, and she dabs at her face. "And you feel differently about it now?"

"I don't know, Yan Yan."

"I thought…"

"In eight years, I have seen things change around me. It's easier now, to think about your uncle being with his friend."

"But you're still angry at him for something?"

"I didn't think that I had given birth to such a hard-hearted son, who would refuse to come to the side of his dying father. That is something I don't know how to forgive."

My heart feels so bruised by every moment of this conversation. "Have you thought about how hard it must have been for Uncle Kevin? I don't think it was a straightforward decision for him."

Po Po looks ahead with steely eyes. "Perhaps. But the decision he made is one I cannot agree with."

"Do you even want to see him then?"

"Of course."

"Even though you're still angry at him?"

"Yes. Because, as angry as I am at him, I'm even angrier at myself." Her eyes turn to me, watery and fathomless, the dark of a stormy night.

"Oh."

She reaches for my hand and clasps it tight. "Please, will you talk to your uncle? Tell him I want to see him. I miss him so much. I want to see him and his friend. I want to cook for them. Please."

Seeing an old woman this miserable, and begging to see her own son, kills me. The misery feels contagious; my stomach roils with it. I ask myself what I would do if I was in Kevin's shoes but it's unimaginable to me, the thought of cutting off contact with my mum for eight whole years.

"I can't promise anything but I'll try to talk to him."

Po Po gasps, her face wet with fresh tears. "Thank you."

"Are you sure you don't want some tea?"

I'm conscious of how English this nervous habit is, offering people tea as comfort. Tea doesn't, as far as I know, serve that function in Hong Kong.

"Yes, OK. Thank you."

I go into the kitchen, grateful to escape the living room for a bit, and put the kettle on. I also make myself a cheese sandwich because I haven't had breakfast yet, and I'm abruptly starving. I stand by the kettle as the water starts to bubble noisily, and I look out of the kitchen window at the garden, my mouth full of soft bread and grated cheddar. A gleaming bird swoops down. A cloud, gauzy as something you would use to dress a wound, drifts past. I press one hand down on the cool surface of the kitchen worktop and try not to cry.

CHAPTER THIRTY-TWO

When Po Po has her cup of Iron Buddha tea, I retreat to my room.

I scroll through the photos I took over the weekend. Sabina Pandey's stall. The bronze bull statue at the Bullring in Birmingham. The dinner table in Kevin's flat laden with dishes. The exterior of Manchester Town Hall.

I call the number for Theresa Bennett that Sabina gave me. Not really thinking about it, not letting myself think about it, but just pressing the call button casually, almost accidentally, a careless brush of my thumb against the screen. She probably won't pick up, anyway.

I hug a pillow close to me as the phone rings and rings.

I'm not expecting it when a voice answers, strong and clear, "Hello?"

My heart stumbles. "Hi, I'm looking for Theresa Bennett."

"Yeah, that's me." The voice is rumbly, thick like a dollop of chunky peanut butter. "Who's looking for me?"

I can't believe I'm speaking to Theresa on the phone. "M-my name is Elsie but really I'm looking for you on Rebecca Hobbs's behalf. Well, you would've known her as Rebecca Lathey—"

"Becca?" Her voice shifts, turns from something that was part solid, part liquid, to something entirely gaseous, thin and insubstantial. "Oh. Jesus. Becca Lathey? Is she… Is she there?"

"No. She's not. But I know where she is. I could get her contact info for you."

"You can? Who are you?"

"I'm friends with her granddaughter."

"She has a *granddaughter*?" Theresa splutters. "Oh my word. Fancy that."

"Maybe I could give your number to her? Then she can call you…"

"She told you to find me?"

I panic. I didn't think this far ahead. "Not exactly… I just know she's missed you all these years, and I thought I would find you for her, as a surprise."

"So she doesn't know you're looking for me?" she asks.

"No?"

Theresa makes a noise low in her throat as though she's been struck. "Hell, then how do you know she actually wants to speak to me?"

"She talks about you," I say desperately, wishing I'd gone

to meet her in person because this is no conversation to have over the phone. I don't know how to reassure her from this distance. "She still thinks about you a lot."

"That isn't the same thing as wanting to speak to me, darling," Theresa growls, and for the first time I consider whether Rebecca really *does* want to see Theresa again, whether I'm meddling in things I have no right to. Theresa's right. Thinking about someone often isn't the same as wanting to interact with them again.

"I think she does, though," I say weakly.

"I'd rather not suffer another heartbreak in my old age," Theresa says, now making her voice airy and light, as though then she wouldn't be vulnerable to something that I can tell has already hurt her. "Bye, darling. Have a good day."

The line goes dead, and with its lifeless drone everything around me seems to wither too. There's only one way forward I can see. I have to tell Ada, so she can ask her grandma whether she does want to see Theresa.

It's still early, though. Ada won't be awake yet. But I write a quick message to her, anyway.

> hey, i need to talk to you about something. skype when you're up and available?

Then I remember about Ada's anxiety, and how she hates it when people are ominously vague, not making it explicit what it is they want to talk about, so I add:

> it's nothing bad, don't worry. it's about that thing you told me about your grandma and her long-lost friend

With all this going on, I can't ask Joan to come over yet. I flick through my phone aimlessly, opening various apps and seeing nothing of note. I told Po Po I would talk to Uncle Kevin. I don't want to disrupt his day by dredging up such depressing things. But it's something he needs time to think about, and he might as well start now.

> hey uncle, thanks so much again for having me and joan over. it was so nice to meet david (properly). i can't tell you how much it means to me to see the two of you so happy. i've been talking to po po though and she's sorry for what happened. i understand it if you still want to keep your distance but i'm just letting you know. she has a lot to say to you and i think you should hear her out. she'd like to see you and david. she wants to cook for both of you

I switch to my conversation with Joan.

> i talked to po po. it went well but i have a lot to deal with today. maybe come over tomorrow?

Her reply is instantaneous.

> Of course.

I sit at my desk and open my laptop, and go through my daily routine of checking my Tumblr dashboard and liking and reblogging posts. The mindlessness of it is calming, like watching waves come into the shore.

For lunch, I heat up some stir-fried udon I find in the fridge for me and Po Po. "No Joan today?" she asks.

"She's busy," I say. "She'll be here tomorrow."

I leave Po Po watching a Cantonese soap on her iPad and go upstairs to Skype Ada.

When she appears, Ada is smiling. I'm not sure if it's just my imagination or whether she really does look more … *more* than usual, her brown skin lit by something golden underneath, her warm brown eyes like the crackling kindling of a campfire.

"Have you been hanging out with Gracie again?" I ask.

"Yeah. We were both like, oh, maybe we should take things slow, and then we kinda just spent the entire weekend with each other." Ada hides her face with one hand. "Oh, I don't know, Elsie. It's like nothing I've ever felt."

She's wearing a hot-pink shirt. It isn't a colour I've ever tried to wear, but it looks good on her. And, of course, she's never without a bow tie.

"That's great," I say, but my voice sounds wooden to my own ears. I've figured out that I'm into Joan but that doesn't mean that I don't still feel a soft yearning for Ada, like the ache in your muscles after running at full speed, chasing something that wouldn't wait for you to catch up.

Ada cocks her head. "You said you wanted to talk about G-ma?"

"I've been looking for Theresa Bennett," I say. "And I found her."

"Hold up," Ada says, raising her hands like she's physically trying to stop me. "What?"

I repeat what I just said.

Ada blinks. "You went looking for her without telling me? That's... That's kinda weird. It feels pretty invasive, to be honest. And ... we tell each other everything! Why did you keep this from me?"

This is not the reaction I was hoping for but, if I'm being honest, it's not entirely unexpected. Looking back, especially now that I don't have such wild romantic notions about Ada any more, I can see clearly that it was not a good idea to do this behind her back, to meddle in someone else's family history without telling them.

"I wanted to surprise you if I found her. The chances of it happening seemed small, so I didn't want to tell you until anything was certain."

"I would've liked to know, anyway. Like this is *my* grandma's friend, and you were just over there... How long have you been doing this?"

"Since you told me about them."

Ada's face is like a broken doorway, ineffectually closed, beyond which she curls away from me.

"I sort of had a crush on you," I blurt. This is probably, absolutely, the wrong time to start taking Ritika and Felix's advice about telling people how I feel to heart, but it's the only thing I can think of to explain my irrational behaviour because it's the truth.

Ada's face collapses completely. "Oh. Elsie, I... Um. I don't really know what to say. How is that related?"

"I wanted to do something nice for you. It was going to be some kind of grand gesture. I was in Cornwall, anyway, so I thought why not? But I didn't find her there."

And now I can't stop myself from blabbering on.

"It's a long story but I ended up going to Birmingham and meeting this woman who'd dated Theresa, and she gave me Theresa's number. And then I also found out that my uncle is gay and married to a man? And my grandparents disowned him? And I came back and had this whole conversation with my grandma about it, and she fully cried. It was a lot. There's so much about my family I didn't know. Oh, and I figured out that I'm actually in love with Joan. So. You don't really have to worry about me having a crush on you because that's all in the past now."

I take a deep breath. I had no idea all that was going to come out of my mouth. But these past few days have just been way too much.

Ada looks wide-eyed and frazzled. "Wow. That's intense.

Um. Can you just send me Theresa's number? I'll give it to my grandma, and she can decide what to do with it. I know you had good intentions but it's super overwhelming for me right now. I just … This is all making me very anxious, and I need you to give me some space. Is that OK?"

She's so small on my screen, a girl I've never seen in her real-life size, just a handful of blurry pixels in a video that freezes now and again and lags behind the sound.

"OK."

She watches as I message her the number on my phone, as well as Theresa's address. I imagine that I can just about hear the buzz of Ada's phone on the other side of the world as it receives my message, and she gives me the tiniest of smiles, nothing like the one she greeted me with at the beginning of the call. This smile could be blown away by a whispering draught.

"Take care," she says, and the image of her winks out into darkness.

I lie down on my bed. I've spent most of my summer so far looking for Theresa Bennett, and, now that I've found her, I don't know if I'll be allowed a part in the conclusion of the story. I may never find out how it's going to end. The imagined reunion between Theresa and Rebecca that I've been nurturing in my head is like a potted plant that I may never get to see bloom.

And, not only that, I might've scared one of my best friends away.

CHAPTER THIRTY-THREE

The day wilts. The whole *week* wilts. Things between Joan and I are still slightly awkward, and there's a chill hanging in my house as though all the windows have been left wide open through a bitterly cold night.

One evening, I talk to my parents about my conversation with Po Po while Dad is brushing his teeth and Mum's reading in bed.

"Wasn't it difficult, Mum? To decide to let Po Po stay here."

"It was," Mum says. "But, in the end, I just couldn't let her be on her own over there. It really feels so different now that I've lost a parent. I want to try to have a better relationship with the one I still have."

"Did Po Po ever apologise to you for everything?"

"She did. But she didn't say much beyond that she wished

she could go back to the past and do it over. You've managed to get more out of her than I have in months. Why is that?"

"Maybe because Yan Yan doesn't have the same history with her," Dad suggests, poking his head out of the bathroom, wiping his chin with a face towel. "It's easier to clear the air when there isn't so much emotional baggage in the way."

"I guess so," Mum says.

"Did you ask Uncle Kevin how he felt about it before you brought Po Po over to stay?"

"Yes. He said it was up to me but that he wasn't sure if he would come to see her."

"Do you think he did the right thing, not going over to Hong Kong to see Gung Gung before he died?"

"I think there is no right thing." Mum squeezes my shoulder. "Kevin probably asks himself the same thing all the time too."

Working at the Speech Balloon over the weekend isn't particularly fun without Felix's company. He's taken the weekend off since Daniel is flying back to Madrid on Sunday night. Clearly things between them are going well.

I have to put up with this other guy instead, the one with the scruffy beard, apparently called Matt. He acts like I'm not even there, and he's not the only one who'd rather I wasn't in the shop. A customer quizzes me about my knowledge of comics as though he doesn't think I'm enough of an expert to work here.

I text Felix:

> work is not the same without you!

It's not until I get home later that he replies.

Don't act like you didn't abandon me last weekend!

What did i miss?

> oh, just some annoying dudes. i can't believe i have to do this all over again tomorrow

Oh no, I'm sorry): Tell me who to punch

> you couldn't punch anybody if you tried, but thanks. how's daniel?

He's wonderful! Tell you all about it soon xoxo

On the way home, I stop by the Chinese supermarket and buy myself a bag of Vitasoy. I thought it would cheer me up but, once I get home, I realise I only want to drink it if Joan is there to race me.

I put away the Vitasoy in a kitchen cupboard and glance

through my WhatsApp. The only thing I've heard from Uncle Kevin since Monday is this:

> Yes, it was really good to see you! And Joan! I will think about this.

My thumb hovers above the button for the Tumblr app, but I don't open it. It doesn't have any notifications, so I know that Ada hasn't messaged me. I have to stay away from Tumblr. I have to give Ada some space, as she asked.

As soon as Joan steps through the front door on Monday after my weekend working with surly Matt, I brandish the Vitasoy cartons at her, beaming brightly.

Her eyes glitter. "You want a race?"

"Absolutely."

"OK, let me catch my breath first."

As she crouches down to unlace her shoes, I think about how her hair is getting longer, the undercut no longer visible as such.

"You still haven't heard from Ada?" she asks, putting her boots on the rack, where Mum cleared a spot weeks ago just for her.

I shake my head. "And my weekend sucked. How was yours?"

Joan winces. "Not the best. I talked to my stepmum. She asked my dad if he would come and have dinner with her friend – the one who's gay – and her friend's partner. And Dad just kind of shut down, so they had a huge fight. She's gone to stay with her parents for a bit. She was crying on the phone to me. I still feel like it's all my fault."

"It's not, though."

I'm not brave enough to touch Joan, not really, not when *I don't think of you in that way* is always echoing in my head, so I hand her a Vitasoy carton instead, and our fingers brushing has to be enough.

"You're just trying to be yourself, which is right and true and amazing, and your dad and your stepmum are making their own choices."

Joan sighs. "I wanted her to pick my side but I didn't want this. So I could definitely do with a Vitasoy right now."

We go into the living room and ask Po Po to adjudicate the race. If memory serves, sometimes it was a close enough competition that the presence of a referee would have been appreciated. Po Po seems slightly bemused but she entertains our silliness.

We rip the straws out, puncture the little foil openings with them and ready ourselves.

Po Po counts down from three: "Saam, yi, yat."

I drink, sucking big mouthfuls of soymilk from the carton, feeling it shrink in my hand, watching Joan's cheeks hollow out with each drag on her straw.

She's staring at me too. It seems OK for me to focus on her with this degree of intensity as my world narrows down to me and her and our deep, frenzied gulps. It's never taken either of us longer than forty seconds but right now this moment stretches on forever.

She finishes first. I let her; I slowed down because I want to see her win.

She raises the carton in the air and spins round on the spot, yelling, "I win!", more effervescent in victory now than she ever was as a child, and performs such a weird jiggly dance, more arms than hips, that it makes me snort and swallow the soymilk I still had in my mouth entirely the wrong way.

I cough, ugly and spitting, and Joan springs closer with an expression of alarm and puts her hand on my back soothingly. "You OK?"

"Y-yeah," I gasp. "Ha. Yeah."

I cough some more. My throat is stinging but perhaps I'm coughing more to keep Joan's hand rubbing my back than anything else.

Somewhere along the way, my wheezing brims over into laughter. Just the stupid way Joan danced, and me choking on Vitasoy, and Po Po spectating the whole while, looking extremely unimpressed.

I can't stop laughing. Joan's gaze meets mine, and she cracks up too, eyes crinkling, her hand still on my back and her forehead falling on to my shoulder as her whole body shakes with laughter. I feel it reverberate in my bones, the soymilk's sweetness still lingering in my mouth.

After that, we're back to normal. The awkwardness is dispelled but the way I feel about her, around her – my heart a jellyfish in a dark aquarium, floating, blooming, glowing – that feeling remains. I don't know how such an intense emotion isn't transparent and on display to everybody, but she doesn't seem to notice, or if she does she says nothing.

She still comes over every day and stays for dinner most nights. Mum's been reading more and more volumes of that shounen manga that Joan recommended, and so have I, and so we talk about that at the dinner table a lot, enough that Dad has also now declared that he's going to read it just so he knows what we're all going on about. Po Po has no interest in reading it but she does seem to enjoy it when we're all talking over each other at the dinner table. It's much better than what was happening before, which was mostly long silences punctuated by stilted conversation.

It's strange to finally feel like I have something in common with my mum, something we both love that we can chat about. And it's all thanks to Joan.

In the midst of this week, I get my A-level results. All A*s, which means that I'm going to Cambridge.

I message my parents the results while they're at work, and for a second I think they're going to take the day off and come home and give me a hug.

My dad writes:

So proud of u!!! Knew u could do it!

Followed by a million celebratory gifs and stickers.
My mum writes:

OH YOU AMAZING LITTLE ONION, WE CAN GO TO WHATEVER RESTAURANT YOU WANT OK. GOOD!

I go into the garden and tell Po Po, and she leaps up from the chair like I've just stolen fifty years from her and made her young again. "Ah, you are such a clever girl! Wonderful! Wonderful!" She claps her hand against my cheek several times. "Oh, your po po could dance with happiness right now! Like your friend."

Thinking about Joan's noodly dancing fills me with even more delight than my results do, and I hate – hate – this giddy feeling of having a crush, especially one that I know isn't reciprocated. And Ada... If we were still talking to each other, she would probably already be writing a fic to congratulate me.

I message Auntie Susan as well because Mum says that she'd want to know, and Uncle Kevin because I want him to know.

When Uncle Kevin writes back to congratulate me, I reply:

> i think we're probably going to have a celebratory family meal soon and i would love to see you both there

> but no pressure. it's ok if you don't want to

> Still mulling it over. Thanks for understanding.

> of course. i love you uncle kevin

> You're my favourite niece :)

I'm Uncle Kevin's *only* niece but this sentiment still warms me, especially knowing that we understand each other in a way no one else in our family would. I check in with Ritika, who tells me that she's got the results she needs to secure her offer from Warwick, and then I message Joan about it too.

She shows up an hour later with a huge poster of Zaria Zero that I've been coveting at the Speech Balloon, and a smile more precious than anything because to me everything about her is precious now. Having a crush is honestly just about the most moronic feeling on earth, the way it turns ordinary gestures and moments to pure honeyed light. I've never told her that I want the poster but somehow she just knew, and that's a special feeling too, sparkling and sun-warm.

The weekend that follows results day, I finally get to see Felix, whose golden hair is more halo-like than ever before as he swans into the shop as though he has a chorus of angels around him hymning his joy, and I envy him.

"So," I say, when we open up, "Daniel."

"Oh, I took him around; we did all the touristy stuff. We went punting with a picnic and everything."

"Ooooh, *romantic*."

"Yeah, it really was. It was a dream. And he'd booked this Airbnb room, and we just cuddled and kissed, and it was brilliant. I didn't feel like I wanted to have sex, and he never pushed. I think I might be ace, and I really think there's a good chance we might work. Oh, it was all just so ridiculously perfect."

I put my hand over my heart. "Oh, you guys are killing me. That is so cute. I've got to say, I'm pretty jealous."

"You should be," he says with a smirk. "How are things with you?"

I bring him up to speed on everything that's been happening.

"Well, you lead a much more exciting life," Felix remarks.

"I don't want it to be *exciting*. I just want to be content, like you," I say dolefully. "I like Joan so much. How do I get over it?"

"You should do something about it," Felix says. "Just … express your feelings, in any case. I know you said she told you she doesn't like you in that way, but she doesn't know how you feel. You need an answer for *you*. You need closure."

"Closure," I repeat.

"Yeah," Felix says. "You don't want to go around with this permanent sense of something unresolved."

It's the same advice Ritika offered but, given how disastrous it was to tell Ada about my crush on her, I'm even more hesitant than before. It's terrifying, the possibility that I might sour my friendship with Joan too, and the notion of simply opening my heart like a door Joan could choose to walk through or not as she pleases. I only told Ada because my crush on her was in the past tense, not something wholly alive and breathing with a pulse inextricable from my own. Not like how I feel about Joan.

But Felix and Ritika are right. I know they're right. I just don't want to listen.

It's not till a queer couple walks in, holding hands and exchanging adorable little kisses as they flick through concept art books, and I tear up while surreptitiously sneaking glances at them, that I realise that: one, my period is probably about to start; and two, I really, *really* need to do something about my crush on Joan.

When I get home in the evening, the smell of garlic and ginger sizzling in a hot wok draws me towards the kitchen.

"What are you making?" I ask.

"Mapo tofu," Mum says.

Ritika loves mapo tofu, so I text her to invite her over. While I'm waiting for dinner to be ready, I head up to my room. Now that I don't go on Tumblr any more, so much of my day seems to have been freed up. I've been spending it reading more comics, but it also leaves me extra time with my thoughts. I still haven't heard from Ada, and I keep wondering whether her grandma has contacted Theresa yet. The search for Theresa had become so important to me. I constantly feel bereft of something.

I take out Theresa's letters again and look through them.

Every letter from you is like Christmas come early. I hold your words in my hands, and it's as if I can touch more than that. Do you take as long deliberating over what to write as I do? I always want to tell you more than I can get down on the page. But occasionally something too honest slips out, and I have to let it stay on paper.

I wonder, then, if this might be the best solution. To write down my feelings for Joan. Maybe it'll be easier than saying it all out loud. Maybe I'll be able to express myself more clearly and truthfully that way.

I'm still scared. Scared of what it means to be inseparable. Scared of what it means to be with anybody so intimately that they could turn our love into a knife and hold it against my throat at any moment, and that, worst of all, I would let them without even making a sound.

But I trust myself to trust Joan, and that is stronger than my fear.

I start to draft a letter on my phone.

Dear Joan,
You never replied to the letters I sent you when we were eleven. So I'm writing you another one, and you'd better reply to this. I won't forgive you otherwise.

I sometimes feel that seven years ago I knew who I was better than I do now. I've changed so much, I don't understand who I am most of the time, and the person I have sometimes been in those past seven years baffles me. But you came back into my life, and you still care about me, and being friends with you still feels like the most magical and best part of my life. I know that you only recognised me that day because you looked me up on social media beforehand, but still. I like to think there's something deeper than that. If you still recognise me, I must be doing something right. It means I haven't changed so much that I'm no longer myself, after all.

I kept thinking whenever I looked at you that I wished I was more like you. I thought that I wanted to be you because you are the coolest, the bravest, the kindest. I wished I could be as sure of who I am as you. And, of course, that's all true. But I didn't realise that I could want to be you and also want you at the same time.

I do now.

I want you. I want to kiss you, be your girlfriend, hold your hand.

I know you said you don't think of me in that way, but I think of you like that. I just wanted to tell you. I love being your friend, Joan, and I'm OK with it if that's all we can be because it's already the whole world to me. Knowing you is an adventure in itself. It's the only adventure I want. It doesn't matter in what way I know you as long as you're in my life.

Please just don't disappear for seven years again. Don't disappear at all.

Yours,

Elsie

I slip into my parents' room to print out a series of pictures: a bassoon; stir-fried egg with shrimp; brown Timberland boots; two hands touching fingertips against a backdrop of foamy jade-hued sea; a screenshot from the Chinese drama we've been watching with my Po Po, featuring the actress that Joan and I both agreed was extremely hot; a majestic tiger, curled up and sleeping; a black bomber jacket; an iced coffee in the rain, droplets clinging to the side of the cup; two packets of Vitasoy, side by side.

I fold a piece of A4 in half to make a card, gluing the nine pictures on to the front in a grid, and I copy the letter on to the paper by hand from my phone. Beside my name at the end, I draw, badly, Joan's favourite manga character from the series that my mum and I have been reading, picking a copy of it off my bookshelf for reference. I am definitely not an artist, and I'm not a writer, either, but I hope that I'm enough of one that this letter adequately conveys what I feel to Joan.

At least the front of the card looks pretty.

CHAPTER THIRTY-FOUR

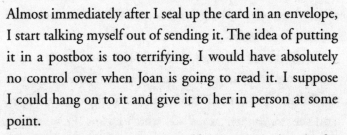

Almost immediately after I seal up the card in an envelope, I start talking myself out of sending it. The idea of putting it in a postbox is too terrifying. I would have absolutely no control over when Joan is going to read it. I suppose I could hang on to it and give it to her in person at some point.

Or I could just keep it to myself. It was a good outlet for my feelings to write everything down. But I don't *need* her to read it, do I?

The doorbell rings. It must be Ritika arriving for dinner. I give the letter one last exasperated shake and put it in my bag before running downstairs to get the door.

As Ritika steps into the living room, she waves at my po po. I realise that she hasn't been over to my house yet all summer, and this is the first time they've met each other.

Po Po says to me, "Your friend is very pretty."

I translate that for Ritika, who preens.

After dinner, Ritika and I go up to my room, and she's using my laptop to show me this K-pop video that she's newly obsessed with when my phone buzzes on my desk, not just the fleeting buzz of a notification, but the continuous buzz of a call.

Nobody ever calls me except my immediate family, and they're all here in this house.

The caller ID shows Ada's name.

My heart skydives. "It's Ada," I hiss at Ritika.

"Pick up!" she shouts.

I manage to hit the green button and put my phone to my ear. "Hey. Ada?"

"Yeah. It's me. I've just landed in London."

I almost drop the phone. Ada is in the same country as me for the first time since our online acquaintance began, and she's *calling me to tell me*, which means she wants me to know, which means she hasn't cut me out of her life completely. "Seriously?"

"Seriously. I'm with my grandma. We're going to go to Brighton first thing tomorrow morning, but first we're staying in a hotel in London."

"Does Theresa know that you're coming?"

"Yeah. As soon as I told G-ma you'd found her, she was ecstatic. Just knowing Theresa's still out there. But it took her over a week to work up the courage to call, and, when she finally did, they talked briefly, but G-ma was just like, 'I *have* to go see her right now!' So my parents scraped together some savings, and we bought plane tickets, and we're *here*."

Ada's here in England, I mouth at Ritika, who frowns, clearly not able to read my lips. "That's incredible," I say to Ada.

"Yeah, it is. You should've seen how happy you made G-ma with this news. I'm sorry I haven't been in touch till now. It was all a lot to process."

"No, that's OK. I'm just glad to hear from you. I was kind of worried that maybe you never wanted to speak to me again."

"Really? There's no way that would happen. I just needed more time to absorb our whole conversation. You did something amazing, Elsie. I wish you would've told me about it from the beginning, that's all."

"Yeah. I'm so sorry I didn't."

"Do you think you could come? Tomorrow? I mean, we've been friends for two years, and we've never met in person, and this seems like the perfect opportunity. And you should get to meet G-ma and Theresa."

"You really want me to?"

"Of course."

It's all I can do not to jump up and down on the spot, screaming. "Then I'll definitely be there. There's no way I'm going to miss this."

"Awesome. I'll send you the details."

"Thanks, Ada," I say, keeping my voice as steady as possible. "I'll see you tomorrow."

I put my phone down, and Ritika pounces, squeezing her arms round me. "You're seeing her tomorrow? What is going on? Oh my God, Elsie, tell me!"

I do, rushing, breathless.

"I'm coming with you," Ritika says firmly, and hits me with a pillow, punctuating her exclamations with it. "This is completely batshit! She's here! You actually found the person you were looking for, and your internet best friend is here!"

I grab another pillow and hurl it at Ritika in retaliation, shrieking with an emotion too great to name, and we fight until my dad comes in to see if everything's all right, and we fall on the bed, panting, our faces red, our hair rumpled and our hearts full.

So I find myself on a train yet again with Ritika and Joan.

Last night, the first thing I did after the pillow fight was text Joan and tell her about Ada's arrival.

will you come?

Do you have to ask? You know I will.

Then this morning I sent a message to Felix, apologising for the fact that I can't make it to work.

> it's a (good) emergency, ada is HERE, i'm going to meet her and her grandma and theresa bennett!! pls tell your dad i'm sick or something!

He grumbled at me but wished me luck. And now Ritika and Joan and I are on a train, though my parents believe that I'm at work, and I'm bursting with energy. I know that it's going to run out long before midday, but I can't tamp it down. I'm just as excited as I was on the journey to Cornwall, but so much has changed since then.

I think about my letter to Joan burning a hole in my bag. I think about finally seeing Ada in real life soon. I think about meeting Theresa Bennett, almost a figure of legend to me by now.

The landscape speeds by in a blur, swathes of green and blue, and with it I feel this summer, the best summer of my life so far, hurtling past me, too quickly for me to beg it to stay.

We play cards and, when the refreshment cart trundles past, Joan gets us all chocolate bars. She's still nursing the dregs of her coffee, and she keeps losing every game we're playing, even though I thought *I* would surely be the most distracted one. I don't point this out, just nibble at my chocolate bar and consider the cards in my hand.

Eventually, we get into London, and we have to take the tube to Victoria Station to get another train from there. On the second train, I'm too restless to concentrate on cards at all. Ritika and Joan talk about university, what they imagine or hope it will be like, what clubs and societies they want to join.

"Maybe I'll find the perfect Indian husband like my parents want me to," Ritika says. "I wonder how they'd react if I found a wife instead…"

"Your parents are pretty chill, though, aren't they?" I ask. "They're always giving food to that gay couple next door. Your mum and dad love them."

"I'm just worried they'll feel differently when it comes to their own daughter."

I lean against Ritika to comfort her. "We'll be here for you, no matter what."

I ask Joan whether she has any updates from her stepmum. Last I heard, her stepmum had moved back in with her dad again.

"She found a support group for parents with LGBT kids," Joan says. "She asked my dad if he'd think about going. And he's actually said that he would."

"Wow, that's incredible."

"Yeah, it seems positive. I just hope he doesn't back out at the last minute."

"Me too."

"Is there much queer representation in the media in

Hong Kong?" Ritika asks. "Like does your dad ever get to see queer people on TV in a positive way?"

"That's a good question," Joan says. "It's better than it used to be. There have been one or two shows recently but he did *not* watch them. We do have a few good queer movies but they aren't very mainstream at all." She starts listing some films.

I want to pay attention to the conversation but, as we get closer and closer to Brighton, I'm feeling more and more anxious because so much of my summer has been building up to this. So I put on my headphones and listen to a folk-song playlist on Spotify.

The jauntiness of the music seems to help, somewhat.

And then we're here.

The journey, nearly three hours in total, has felt like eternity and also no time at all, and it makes me more afraid of the slippery nature of time. The noon heat feels unbearable after the air-conditioned carriage. We walk to the café where Ada is waiting for me. It isn't hard to spot her.

She's wearing orange lipstick and a fantastic mint-green shirt with a taupe bow tie. She looks amazing. I walk over to her but I don't feel like I'm moving my own limbs; something carries me over to her, a tidal wave surging and taking me along with it.

"Ada," I say, surprised at my own voice. "Oh my God. You're really here."

Without saying a word, she stands up and hugs me.

We've talked about this before. Hugging. I know she isn't much of a hugger, and she would recoil from most hugs, but sometimes she wished she could reach through the screen and hug me. And now she's here, hugging me, and everything in me loosens, like a ribbon fluttering in the wind.

"You're the biggest weirdo I know, but I'm so grateful I know you," she says, as she draws back. "Just *tell* me if you're going to do something this wild next time, OK?" Her voice sounds a little different in person. Warmer.

"OK," I say. "I definitely will."

"Aight, so when you gonna introduce me to your friends?"

I turn round. "Ada, this is Joan and Ritika. Joan and Ritika, Ada."

Ada's grandma is at Theresa's house right this moment, a few streets away. Ada is giving them some time to be alone and talk, so we all order sandwiches. Ritika and I get milkshakes, and Joan, predictably, has a coffee. While Joan is ordering and talking to the waiter, Ada tilts her head towards Joan and smirks at me knowingly.

I roll my eyes, embarrassed. "I love the lipstick," I say to her.

"Gracie let me borrow it," Ada says. "I never really liked the idea of wearing such bold make-up before but this just looked so good on them, I had to try it."

"So things are going well between you two?"

"Super well." Ada shimmies in her seat. "Now tell me

376

about how you found Theresa!"

We eat our sandwiches, and we tell her, all three of us, a summarised version of the search, and I feel how lucky we've been in trying to find Theresa, my whole summer imbued with a cosmic sheen of queer magic.

"My friends kind of found the whole idea a bit ridiculous at first," I say.

"Yeah, we did," Ritika chirps.

"It was a pretty dumb-ass move," Ada agrees softly, her eyes glimmering. "Only you would've done it. But you damn well did it. Now let's get the check and see how it's going over there."

The lemon milkshake is velvety and cold in my mouth. I did it. My success hits me, really hits me, for the first time. I actually did it.

CHAPTER THIRTY-FIVE

Theresa Bennett's house is clean and tidy, and the interior is a haven of gentle colours, the walls painted soothing lavender or salmon pink or cornflower blue. She herself is a stocky, handsome woman, short sandy curls fading into grey, and she's wearing a black button-down and blue jeans. The house doesn't exactly seem to match her, but what do I know?

"Isn't this house lovely?" Ada's grandma says to me, as I'm probably looking around too much. "It's a dream. This is exactly the kind of place I would want to live in. Sad to think she's been here all alone for years."

Perhaps that's why this house seems so unlike Theresa, because she'd been thinking of someone else.

Rebecca Hobbs looks the same as the glimpses of her I've seen on screen when she pops into Ada's room to say hi. She's wearing a blue shirt dress that's nearly the same shade as the wall behind her, with a chunky necklace of white shells.

"Thank you so much for finding Tessa," she says, clasping my hands.

Theresa is hobbling round the kitchen, making tea for everyone except Joan, who has declined. Theresa doesn't seem able to sit still – either this restlessness is a character trait of hers, which, given what I know of her, seems likely, or she's just overwhelmed by the day, which is completely understandable. Or both.

"I really thought I'd never see you again," she says to Rebecca.

"I thought *you'd* had enough of me!"

"And I thought the same of you!"

"So what happened?" I ask. "Can you tell us?"

"Yes," Rebecca says, sitting down at the table next to me. "This woman sent me a love letter that I never received. I don't know how. Maybe it got lost in the post—"

"I'm telling you, it was your old man. He must have intercepted it!" Theresa says emphatically, her hands flailing. "He was always *suspicious* of me, and you told me you thought he'd been opening your post! And you'd just got engaged, you said. Your father must have taken my letter so you'd marry Howard, according to plan."

"Well, maybe," Rebecca concedes. "We'll never know now, and I don't like to speak ill of the dead. In any case, Theresa confessed that she was in love with me in this letter, except I *never* received it so I never learned of this, and, because I never received it, I couldn't respond. Then I got married, and the last letter I wrote to her was to tell her that news. I heard nothing from her after that. Now I know she moved away from Cornwall a few months later."

Theresa thumps two mugs of builder's brew in front of me and Ritika. "To get away from the place where I still saw you everywhere. And I always wanted a life outside Cornwall, anyway."

"And you got it."

"I did. I never wanted a life without you, though."

"Oh, Tessa," Rebecca murmurs, reaching for Theresa's arm as she passes by on her way to get the third mug for Ada. "At least I found you again, thanks to these sweet teenagers."

"And thanks to the fact that you kept all of my letters, apparently!" Theresa says.

"Oh, and you expect me to believe you haven't kept all of mine?"

Theresa gives Rebecca a helpless look, and Rebecca just smiles winningly.

"So you two weren't…" I begin, and I'm not sure how to finish. *Dating? Girlfriends? Lovers?* "I mean, you didn't know about her feelings for you at all until now, Rebecca?"

"I might have *thought* there was something before I

moved to the States, but I never... Nothing was said – it was only an undercurrent – and I moved away and thought maybe I'd imagined it."

"You weren't imagining anything." Theresa bobs about, energetically wiping down surfaces that are already spotless. "It was only when you'd gone over to America, and you wrote to me about ... about *Howard*, that I thought I had to tell you. I had nothing left to lose. You were on the other side of the ocean, anyway, and you were going to marry this man, and I had to tell you."

I've been wondering about what their reunion might be like for so long, and it's glorious to watch them move round each other in the same room together. My heart aches for all those years they lost, but here they are now, at least. Breathing the same air.

"I wish I could've read that letter," Rebecca says. "Do you remember what it said?"

Theresa waves her hand vaguely. "I remember how it felt. I can write you a dozen better ones now."

"Will you?" Rebecca asks earnestly.

In answer, Theresa stills completely, her shoulders relaxed. It makes me think of butter melting in a pan, the golden aroma of it. She looks like she would catch a falling star for Rebecca if that's what Rebecca wanted.

"What are you going to do now?" I ask.

"I'm not sure," Rebecca says and sips her tea. "We've just spent the past couple of hours catching up on each other's lives! We haven't even had a chance to speak about what comes next. I hadn't been ... thinking of the future for a while. After Howard died, it was frightening to imagine the lonely road ahead of me, just me on my own. But I suppose the future may be brighter than I thought."

"You think you might want to come and live here?" Theresa asks, back to her jittery self, wringing a tea towel over the sink.

I feel like we're intruding, that this is surely a discussion they would want to have in private, and I clutch the handle of my mug nervously but Rebecca only thinks for a moment before she gets up and stands behind Theresa at the sink. She runs her fingers through Theresa's hair and says, "Yes. Yes. Oh, my dear, yes. I don't want to waste another second."

Theresa turns, her face wrinkled in anguish. She rubs a tentative thumb against Rebecca's cheek. "What about the rest of your family? You'll be the only one here. I don't want to steal you from them."

"They can come and visit me. You will, won't you, Ada?"

Ada squeaks, "Duh!"

"Right. So that's settled then. You'll be my family here, Tessa. Isn't that what you want? It's what I want."

"Of course it's what I want. It's what I've always wanted."

Theresa still looks like this is hurting her, incredulous of the possible happiness that awaits her, fearful that it's a mirage, trapped in a love she's thought unrequited for *decades*. She caresses Rebecca's jaw, tilts Rebecca's face up towards hers and—

I look away. This is the moment that my summer's work has brought me towards, and I should let them have their privacy. But, even though I'm not watching it happen, I can feel it unfolding in the room. Like origami in reverse, a dainty crane magically unbecoming, every fold peeling back until it smooths out into one flat square of paper, pristine and unmarked, with limitless possibility.

It's the most beautiful thing I've ever felt.

I meet Joan's gaze in that moment, and it's—

I could *swear* that it's warm with longing.

I'm so sure, right this second, that there's something between us. There has to be.

But then it's gone. She glances away, and I do too, and I'm not sure any more.

But it's OK. I'm still … content.

In this room, the colours are like a lullaby, like a sunset or sunrise at sea. I think of these two women living together in this house, sharing a bed, sleeping next to each other, waking up next to each other. I've played a part in making that happen.

Other people I know from school are spending their summers in other countries, finding themselves, getting involved in big meaningful projects. And that's great for them, it really is, but here I am, just sitting in somebody's kitchen in a corner of England, and somehow it holds the whole world, and so many mirrors to tell me who I might be, and how I might *live*.

It's enough.

Ada and I walk along Brighton beach. We're here by the seaside together, after all.

She and her grandma are planning to stay on a little longer. Ada said that she wanted to talk to me one-to-one before I went back to Oxford, and I was glad. We do have some stuff to discuss, I know.

The sea sparkles under the sun, spreading out into the distance. There are things in this world that do go on forever. Things that stay. I get why Theresa had to come back to the sea.

"I really missed you," Ada says, hands in her pockets.

"I missed you too."

"Thanks for finding Theresa. She and G-ma really look like they belong together."

"Yeah. I'm so happy for them." I kick a stone at my feet. "So, we're still friends, right? I know I said that I had a crush on you but I don't any more, so I hope that doesn't make things weird?"

"Elsie…" Ada stops in front of a bench and sits down. "People get crushes on their friends sometimes. It's normal. I've had crushes on friends who didn't like me back, and it's been chill. And I love you, you know? We'll be fine."

"I love you too." I sit down as well and gaze at the sea in front of us and all the people lying on blankets sunbathing, chatting, reading. "This is … probably awkward to ask now, but did you ever like me? In that way?"

Ada takes a deep breath. "Honestly? I don't think so. You're amazing, Elsie, and you're gorgeous, and I could talk to you all day. You're so important to me, and I want you to be in my life. But there's just … something that I feel with Gracie, that I felt the instant I met them, that I don't think I've ever really felt with you. But that doesn't change the fact that I think our friendship is one of the best things that's ever happened to me."

"Same," I say. "It kind of hurts a little, though, to know that I was reading things wrong."

Ada sighs. "Sorry. It's hard to be… If my messages were flirty, it was kind of just … fun. To be that way with someone without any expectations. It felt like we both needed the confidence boost."

I turn and smile at her. "Yeah, actually, you're probably right. It did help me a lot, you know, the way we talked to each other. It really gave me the feeling that I could go out there into the world and do something, be someone."

"Yeah. I needed that too. But … you could've tried to tell me, you know? That you had a crush. When it was still a thing. I wouldn't have let that ruin our friendship. It's always better to tell someone because you never know."

"Yeah. I'm trying to get better at that. Telling people I like them."

Ada's eyes light up. "You said you have a crush on Joan! You're gonna tell her?"

I put my face down in my lap. "Yeah."

"Oh, Elsie! I hope it goes well. I have a good feeling about this. But, if not, you have to remember that it's not the end of the world." She pats my knee. "Hey, look at me."

I lift my head.

"You'll be fine. No matter what the outcome, you will feel better for having told her than if you keep it to yourself. And I'll always be here. OK?"

"OK."

She hugs me, and it hits me again how incredible this is, that she's here in person, that she can physically give me a hug. "Can we take a selfie?" she asks.

"Yeah."

She fishes out her phone. We get up from the bench and turn round so we can have the sea in the background. I'm too emotionally overwhelmed to smile for the first few shots but eventually we get some photos where I don't look so dazed, and she sends them to me. I set one of them as my lock screen immediately.

Ada and I, in the same photo. I'll need this as proof that today happened, or it'll feel like a dream within a few days.

We start walking again, back in the direction we came, where Joan and Ritika are waiting, and we talk about what

Ada's planning to do while she's here in England. Pebbles crunch under our feet.

"We're here for the next week or so," Ada says. "So maybe I can actually come to Oxford?"

"Oh! We have our first book-club meeting at the Speech Balloon this Friday. Do you think you'll be able to make it?"

"Oh, are you kidding? I *have* to be there. That's awesome."

I give her the details. I imagine Ada, at the Speech Balloon, with Felix – and Joan and Ritika told me they were going to come too. And Ellie will be there, the blue-haired girl, and I reached out to Tam, who said they would love to come along too, and there are more people who have expressed interest, more people I'll get to meet. I can't wait.

"Also, I think I'll be visiting England regularly, now that my grandma's gonna live here and all," Ada says. "So, next time I'm over, I'll come prepared with a costume so we can do a Zaria/Mayumi cosplay shoot, OK?"

My heart bursts like a canon of confetti. "Yeah, that sounds perfect."

I say bye to Ada at the train station, and she gives me another hug, but I know I'll see her again in just a few days when she comes to Oxford for the book club.

Joan had seemed rather subdued and silent all day but after we get on the train, as we wait for it to leave the station, she says, "That was... Wow. Imagine not seeing the person you love for forty years and then reuniting with them and finding out that they loved you too, all along."

"Yeah. Imagine."

She sinks back into her pensive state. Ritika and I talk about how we would decorate our dream house, but I'm so tired, all I can think about is my own bedroom, the mattress that knows my shape, the wall I've made into a shrine of my favourite ship. I can't believe I'll have to travel another three hours to get there, but I don't have to believe it: I just have to get through it.

The train pulls out of the station, and I realise that it's freezing. The air conditioning is far too functional. I thought I would appreciate it after the heat but soon I'm shivering, goosebumps on my bare arms. I have my eyes closed, trying to nap, but it's impossible in this fridge of a carriage. I wrap my arms round myself and curl up as much as I can on the seat.

There's a rustling noise and something soft and quilted falls across my body, blanketing me. I crack my eyes open just a little and glimpse Joan's hands, tucking the black bomber jacket she seems to always carry in her backpack under my shoulders.

I open my eyes all the way and catch hers, the tenderness

in them, the protectiveness.

It cuts my breath short.

I want so badly to kiss her. But what if she recoils? And we're on a train, in public, and I don't want to have to worry about other people's reactions too.

"Thanks," I mumble, closing my eyes again.

The jacket smells so much like her. I think of the picture of the bomber jacket I included on the card, more meaningful now than before, and I decide in this moment that I'll give the letter to Joan as soon as we're alone.

I don't actually manage to sleep, after all.

CHAPTER THIRTY-SIX

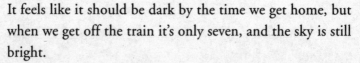

It feels like it should be dark by the time we get home, but when we get off the train it's only seven, and the sky is still bright.

"Thanks for coming along," I say to Ritika as we walk down the steps from the station, my smile probably sloppy with exhaustion. I have a mind to go straight to bed without even having dinner.

"Of course," she says. "I'm kinda sad I missed your visit to your uncle's now. I mean, Sabina Pandey sounded cool as hell."

"She *is* cool as hell."

We pause for a little while under the clear sky, breathing in the summer air, sweet and golden in our lungs.

"Right, I've got to get myself home asap," Ritika says cheerfully. "Dad says he's made biryani, and I'm *not* going to be late for that."

I exchange a glance with Ritika and see the hint of a smirk forming on her face. But I don't dare hope. I don't.

"See ya both." Ritika winks at me and walks backwards for a few paces before turning round, and we watch her go.

"Elsie," Joan says.

I look at her. She's so, so cute, it continues to devastate me each time I hear in my head, *I don't think of you in that way.*

"What's up?" I say, as casually as I can.

"Do you want to come back to my flat? I know your parents are probably waiting for you for dinner, but … I've got to talk to you. Somewhere private."

"Oh."

Don't hope, don't hope, don't hope.

"Yeah. Sure." I take my phone out from my bag, my hands shaking so much I'm surprised it doesn't slip from my fingers and shatter on the ground. I type out a message to my mum.

going to joan's for dinner! sorry, please eat without me

I let Joan take the lead. I have a vague idea where her flat is but I'm not completely certain. We're quiet, saying nothing. She's saving her words for when we're alone, and I'm freaking out. Every single person on the street we walk past, I wonder whether they can see what I'm feeling, this sun of hope burning in my chest.

I try to ground myself in each step, each thud of my foot

hitting the pavement, so I won't rocket into outer space with this hope fuelling me. Eventually, it feels like I'm climbing a mountain rather than walking on a flat surface, sweating with the effort of not combusting.

But we get there in the end. Her key in the front door of the block, then up the stairs, up, up. Another key in the door to the flat. Click.

She steps in. The flat is neat, which is what I expected. It's a small studio. Kitchenette, a door to what must be the bathroom, a table with a couple of chairs and a double bed. There's a big bassoon case beside the bed. The paintings Joan bought from Sabina are hung up on the wall: Mo in a suit playing with Tapioca the cat and an ice-cream cone against the Cornish seascape. The tiger figurine I bought her is sitting on the bedside table, where it might be the first thing Joan sees every morning. All of this sets me aglow with feeling, my hope sparking brighter and brighter.

On a noticeboard, Joan has pinned a handful of photos: one of her family, one of her group of friends in Hong Kong and one of—

Me and her.

Tiny little me and tiny little her.

Me a naam zai tau. Joan with pigtails and ribbons.

Not for the first time I wish I could be as brave and true as I had been as a child, as heedless of the way other people perceive me, completely comfortable in my own skin, not constantly questioning who I am and how I should be and why my heart is such a mess. But then I remember where my heart has led me: to this moment right now. And, for the first time in a long time, I don't find fault with it. I'm grateful for my silly, quivering heart, as hopelessly frail and terrifyingly defenceless as it is. I'm grateful for it in all its messiness.

"Want some food?" Joan asks.

"I'm not hungry," I say quickly. *Get on with what you want to say. Please. I can't stand this.*

"I'll make you something, anyway. Trust me, it's good. It'll only take a few minutes."

I fill up two glasses of tap water, sit down and let her start cooking. She puts the kettle on, chops up a bunch of spring onions from the fridge, pours the boiled water into a pan with a high flame underneath and drops two nests of dried egg noodles into it. "Time three minutes," she says.

I set the timer on my phone. She takes a small blue-and-white porcelain bowl – we have lots of those at home – lines up the condiments and starts mixing a sauce. Light soy sauce, dark soy sauce, sesame oil, Shaoxing rice wine, white pepper, salt and sugar. She places a small wok on the other hob, drizzles it with vegetable oil, turns the heat on high. The white parts of the spring onions go into the wok. It sizzles, smokes. My timer goes off and Joan lifts the pan of cooked noodles, dumping its contents into a colander to drain, before sliding the noodles into the wok.

She tosses the noodles, stands and waits.

The sauce is next; it smells divine as it hits the wok, followed by the rest of the spring onion and a packet of beansprouts. A few more tosses and it's done.

She divides the noodles between two plates, puts one in front of me and sits down with the other. Passes me a pair of chopsticks. I hadn't been hungry but now I'm salivating.

It's a simple dish and also sublime. I inhale those noodles more quickly than I would finish a carton of Vitasoy in a race, and I'm angry when they're all gone. I want seconds, thirds. I want this to be my dinner every night. I want always to eat food that Joan has cooked for me, and to watch her cook, moving in that way she does.

"Wow," I say.

Joan smiles and refills our two empty glasses of tap water from the sink. "Soy sauce noodles are good, aren't they?"

"Yeah." I take another sip of water. "So what did you want to say?"

No matter what this conversation turns out to be about, I'm going to give her the letter. My bag is at my feet – I could reach down and grab the envelope any second. I'm not going to back out of it.

Joan sits up straight, gripping her glass, looking at me with a deep frown, like she wants to shield her eyes from me, but she perseveres, anyway.

"I was thinking. Seeing Rebecca and Theresa finally find each other again after all those years… I don't want to miss my chance. The other day you asked me if I had feelings for you. I said no. I lied. I'm sorry."

I don't know what my heart is doing. Somersaults, flying trapeze, *something* wild and in defiance of gravity. "You're sorry."

"You keep saying I'm brave, but I'm not. I was too scared to tell you. I just don't want to make things awkward. We'd only just become friends again after so long. And I know you really liked Ada and probably still do. But the truth is, Elsie, you were the reason I realised I was a lesbian. You were the first girl I ever had a crush on. I never wanted to cut off contact with you. It was my dad. You were such a naam zai tau. He was worried you were a bad influence on me. I listened to him. What else could I do? I was eleven. But now I know better. You were the best influence. I am who I am only because I knew you, and I thought of you all the time, all these years. It's why I decided to go to Oxford, so I could have a chance to be close to you again. I'm sorry if this makes you feel uncomfortable, but—"

"Joan. What?"

I've never heard anything so completely outlandish in my life. I was the first girl she liked. *She still likes me.*

"Was that why you were so tense and … off all day? Because you thought I liked Ada, and I was going to see her, and you were … jealous?"

Joan scowls. "I know you said she's seeing someone else now but you've been talking about how you have a crush on her all summer! Ugh, I'm sorry, I told myself I would be a supportive friend, but really—"

I stand up, unable to bear this any longer without *moving*. "Joan. Oh my God. Joan. Don't be sorry – *you're* the one I have a crush on."

I lean over and grab the collar of her stupidly cute button-down. She rises to meet me, disbelief in her blinking eyes, and I kiss her stupidly cute face at last, her mouth the answer I've been seeking, but it isn't closure, it's an opening, a door flung wide to all the possibilities of my future, *our* future.

I laugh into our kiss, delighted by the sheer fact of it, her soft lips and my palms cupping her cheeks. Our teeth knock together because I'm laughing, and she sighs, her hands in my hair.

"Why are you laughing?" she mutters.

"I'm so happy," I say.

"*I'm* so happy," she says. "I love your hair. You don't know how much—"

I freeze. I've been thinking, for a while, about wearing it short again like I used to when I was a child, like Joan's. What if Joan only likes me because I'm feminine, like her ex?

As if she can read my mind, she whispers, "I loved it when we were little, and you had that terrible bowl cut. I'd love it no matter what it looks like. I'd love *you*."

Of course. She liked me even when I was boyish. She liked me first and always.

Wait – she *loves* me.

I need this table out of the way.

"Maybe we should try kissing on the bed," I say.

"Good idea."

As I pull away, I nearly trip over my own chair, my exhilaration getting the better of me. Joan falls against me, giggling, and we stumble on to the bed in a pile of uncoordinated limbs, and I think, hysterically, *She loves me*.

I straddle her hips. Her body below me is a miracle, a festival of warmth and sound as I touch her, move against her.

"I love you," I say, like they're the only words I know, and I let myself look and look and look my fill, until I finally take my glasses off, and hers too, and set them on the bedside table, and kiss her the way I devoured those soy-sauce noodles she made for me: like I would always, always be hungry for more.

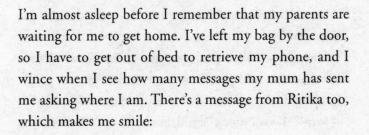

I'm almost asleep before I remember that my parents are waiting for me to get home. I've left my bag by the door, so I have to get out of bed to retrieve my phone, and I wince when I see how many messages my mum has sent me asking where I am. There's a message from Ritika too, which makes me smile:

> **is something HAPPENING with joan i am ON THE EDGE OF MY SEAT elsie please**

> **i'll tell you all about it later!**

I call my mum, and, as soon as she picks up, I rush through my speech. "Hey, I'm so sorry. I completely lost track of time. Can I stay at Joan's tonight? I don't want to have to try to get home now, this late."

The line is silent for such a long time that I wonder if my mum is even there at the other end, but then she says, "OK. Just this once. Don't be back home too late tomorrow morning, OK?"

"Yeah, sure. Goodnight."

"Goodnight." I toss my phone in my bag and throw myself back into bed, snuggling against Joan, wrapping my arm round her waist, tucking my chin on to her shoulder.

"Do you think your mum knows?" she asks.

I kiss Joan's neck before letting myself consider the question. "Oh God, I think she probably does."

"I can't believe she's letting you get away with this."

"I can't believe it, either. I guess my mum's all for gay rights now."

Joan snorts. "She's probably just guilty about all that stuff she never told you about your uncle and your po po. You should take advantage of it while you can."

"Joan!" I say, mock scandalised. "I can't believe you

would suggest such a thing. What about filial piety and all that?"

"I have no idea what that is," she says, laughing, and rolls over so that we're facing each other. She gathers me in her arms, smushes her cheek against my breastbone, and, if I thought I knew before tonight what it is to feel so safe, so known, so seen and loved and accepted in someone's embrace, she proves me wrong. What I had known before was only the tiniest fraction of this.

In the morning, there's Joan's naked back under the sunlight, her shoulder blades visible to me – and only me in this wide world – mappable by my fingers, little ridges with shadowed valleys. I look for a long time. I touch for even longer, simply because I can. Joan shifts under my hands and grunts, still half asleep.

I get out of bed and feel new, remade. I don't want to put on yesterday's clothes, yet another one of my floral sundresses. I open Joan's wardrobe carefully so as not to make too much noise, and I look through her shirts, trousers, shorts. I put on one of the button-downs – the herringbone one. I like that one a lot on Joan. And chinos, grey ones, ankle-length.

I take my time with each button on the shirt, noting that they're on the right, not the left as I'm used to with women's shirts. Still, the buttons are pearly and small, delicate things, really. Then I look at myself in the mirror, appraising.

I'm … different.

I like it.

I stand up straighter, put my hands in my pockets. Pockets! I could get used to dressing like this. I'm not sure what my parents would think but there will be uni, away from their eyes, to experiment…

I twirl this way and that for a little while, until Joan says, "Elsie?"

I hear her sitting up in bed. "I'm here," I say.

"You're … you're wearing my clothes?"

I turn to face her. "Yeah. Do you mind?"

"Do I mind? Oh Jesus." She groans, putting her head down in her lap. "Elsie, you're killing me. You look so good. You're wearing *my clothes*, and you look better than I do in them. Please come over here right now."

"I do *not* look better than you. You're so hot in them."

But it feels amazing to hear those words from Joan, the affirmation I didn't know I was craving. I saunter over, kneel on the bed, and Joan tugs on my shirt, unbuttoning it from the bottom up, her hand slipping underneath impatiently as she kisses me, shuddering and biting my lip when she realises I'm not wearing a bra.

I hear a snuffling noise behind me. "What's that?" I ask, drawing back.

"Post coming through the door," Joan replies.

I'm obsessed with her tousled hair, and I mess it up some more, revelling in the fact that this is something I can do now.

Then I remember the letter I resolved to give to her.

"I actually wrote you something," I say hurriedly before I lose my nerve, brushing my thumb against her knuckles. "I was all prepared to give it to you, and then you surprised me with your own speech last night, and I completely forgot about it."

"What is it?" Joan asks. "Can I read it now?"

"Yeah. I'll get it."

I find the letter in my bag, one corner a little bent. I hand it to Joan and immediately feel too embarrassed to even look at her, so I burrow my head beneath one of her pillows while I wait.

The tearing of an envelope, the sigh of paper.

Even *knowing* that Joan loves me, it still seems like too much.

I feel as if I'm waiting for a very long time.

But eventually Joan kisses my hair, her hand stroking the small of my back, up and down, up and down, and she says, her voice light as silk, "See? You're just as brave as I am. You're incredible. You're my incredible girlfriend. I won't disappear again, Elsie. I won't."

CHAPTER THIRTY-SEVEN

It's the last Saturday of August, and I've taken the day off work.

We're having lunch outside in the garden today. Special occasion, to celebrate my A-level results. Mum even bought a gold tablecloth, which Po Po curled her lip at like it was too over the top. I kind of agree with Po Po, for once, but I appreciate Mum's enthusiasm.

My family are inside the house, busy getting all the food ready, but Mum said there were already too many people in the kitchen, so I'm sitting with Joan on the steps leading down to the garden, calling Uncle Kevin.

"Hi, Uncle," I say when he picks up.

"Hi, Elsie," he says.

"I wish you could've come today." I pluck a fistful of grass.

"Well, I think that if I'd been there today it's very

possible that your po po and I would both have ended up in tears, and I didn't want to ruin this day for you like that."

"Do you think you will come down? At some point?"

"I'd like to think so, yes. I'll try to visit before you're off to uni, OK?"

"Will you really?"

"I can't promise but I'd like to."

I scatter the grass back on to the ground. "Joan says hi too, by the way." Joan grins beside me.

"Oh, wonderful. Say hi to her back. How are you two?"

"We're… She's my girlfriend now."

"Aw! I knew you two were good together. Are you planning to come out to the family?"

"I don't know yet. Maybe. I think Mum might kind of already know, anyway."

"Oh, does she? Well, good luck if you do come out. You know your uncle has your back."

"Yeah. I know. Thanks, Uncle."

"So what's on the menu for today? What food am I missing out on?"

I try to tell him, but I keep forgetting dishes, and Joan has to remind me. Po Po is doing the cooking today and she's making *way* too much food.

"Soy-sauce chicken wings?" Uncle Kevin sighs. "My favourite. Oh man, I'm missing out. Nothing compares to the way she makes them."

"They're *your* favourite?"

"Yeah. Since childhood."

"I thought they were Po Po's favourite."

"That's news to me. I used to have to beg her to make them! Beg! 'We already ate it last month. If you eat it so often, you'll be bored of it, ai yah.' I only wanted to eat it more than once a month! Was that too excessive? I didn't think so."

"Oh."

There's silence for a little while. I wonder if it's sinking in, how the dish that Uncle Kevin loves the most has become Po Po's own favourite in the eight years that she didn't hear a word from him.

"Well," he says, "I suppose I'd better leave you to get on with eating all that food. Congrats again, Elsie. You make your uncle so proud."

He hangs up, and I see that while I was on the call Ada messaged me. She's back in New York now, has been for a week.

OH MY GOD ELSIE!!! I've been so busy this week hanging out with Gracie and getting some stuff ready for college that I haven't managed to read the new issue of ER till now! Have you read it yet?

no? i've been really busy this week too! i haven't been on tumblr or twitter in days!

> **AHHHHH ELSIE. YOU HAVE TO READ IT AND THEN MESSAGE ME IMMEDIATELY. I DON'T WANT TO SPOIL IT FOR YOU BUT!!!!**

I'm not sure from this message whether something good or bad has happened, but *something* must have. I dread that perhaps they've killed off Zaria, given her capture in the last issue, but nothing about Ada's message seems angry to me. Did Zaria and Mayumi kiss? That's the only thing I can think of that would provoke such a strong reaction.

> **ADA IF THEY KISSED YOU NEED TO JUST TELL ME NOW**

> **JUST READ IT GODDAMMIT ELSIE**

I text Felix.

> **felix??? HAVE YOU READ THE LATEST ISSUE OF ER AND IF SO DO ZARIA AND MAYUMI KISS???**

> You abandoned me at work again so I'm not going to tell you):

I send him a bunch of knife emojis, just as Mum comes out and tells me to set the table.

"Can I help?" Joan asks.

"No, that's all right," Mum says, smiling. "Food's almost ready!"

I get up and follow Mum into the kitchen, glad for a methodical task to occupy myself with, but the air is hot and thick with smoke from the wok, and there's barely any room to manoeuvre. I have to squeeze past my parents and Po Po to get to the cutlery drawer.

Before I head back outside with all the cutlery, Mum stops me in the living room.

"Elsie," she says, "I just wanted to say… It's nice to see you so happy with Joan."

"Mum…" I say, shifting from foot to foot, embarrassed.

She stands close to me and says in a low voice, "I remember, you know, after she moved back to Hong Kong, you talked about her a lot, how much you missed her, how she wasn't replying to your letters or emails. The adventures you used to have… And then you stopped talking about her. You stopped talking about anything much. You still seemed sad but you kept telling me everything was OK when I asked you. And it was my fault too. I wasn't speaking to my parents, and that was, of course, the biggest thing on my mind, but I didn't want you to know about that. But the situation's different now. I hope we can talk more, even though you're going to leave home and go to university."

I blink away tears. "Yeah. I'll try. We can read more manga together, Mum."

"Good," Mum says. "Little onion, you really seem happy."

"I am," I say, and she ruffles my hair.

Chopsticks and porcelain spoons weighing down paper napkins. Cans of Coke and a few cartons of Vitasoy at the centre of the table. As I arrange all of this neatly, Mum brings out the first few dishes and returns to the kitchen to collect more.

I switch on 'Do not disturb' on my phone. I'm determined to forget about *Eden Recoiling* for now and not hope too much for canon Zaria/Mayumi. I'm going to enjoy this afternoon for what it is, and there's going to be *so much* food.

Joan hugs me from behind. It's the best feeling to be held by her like that, to feel her so solid and strong against my back. I turn round and give her a kiss, quickly, while my family members are still out of sight.

"Look, your favourite," I say, pointing at the stir-fried egg with shrimp, the egg a perfect golden yellow with glimpses of juicy pink-red shrimp nestled inside.

Joan lets go of me as my parents and Po Po spill out of the house, carrying the rest of the dishes. I'm almost afraid the garden table will sag and break under their combined weight, but it holds.

"This looks amazing, Po Po," Joan says, pulling out a chair for my grandmother.

Po Po pats Joan's shoulder. "Honestly it's like I've gained

another gwaai syun. I'm so glad Yan Yan has a friend like you."

Joan smiles, eyes crinkling in the way that I love so much.

"Yan Yan, do you think you can take a photo of the food and send it to your uncle?" Po Po asks, her voice heavy for a moment.

"Yeah, of course."

As I'm doing that, Mum says, "It's a pity Uncle Kevin can't come, but... Shall we take a family photo? We should probably have something to remember this occasion by. You're going to Cambridge!"

"I'll take it," Joan offers.

"No, no," Dad says. "This is why we have a tripod!" He goes into the house to find it.

I gaze sadly at the food – I'm so hungry, and I'm not sure where Dad has stored this tripod. I can't remember the last time I saw it, which means it must be buried somewhere deep in the attic, and we might never get to eat at this rate.

I truly wish Uncle Kevin and David were here to share this food with us.

But I'm also overwhelmed by how much my family is welcoming Joan. She takes a seat beside me and holds my hand under the table, running a thumb over my knuckles. I still haven't made up my mind about whether I want to come out properly, but it doesn't seem to matter so much in this instant.

Any moment now, I hope, Dad will emerge with the tripod, and we'll take a family photo, and Joan will be in it, and we'll all smile sincerely for the camera. And then there's going to be beef with sha cha sauce, and deep-fried tofu, and soy-sauce chicken wings, glistening darkly and sure to make all of our fingers incredibly sticky. And then, after that, there's still an entire month left before uni starts, time enough for me and Joan to keep holding hands and kissing. Time enough for us to work out who we're going to be together, for the rest of this summer and beyond.

The future is wide and glittering, and I'm taking Joan with me into it.

ACKNOWLEDGEMENTS

This is a book inspired primarily by fandom – by the people I've met in fandom whom I've learned so much from, and who have given me the strength to achieve things I never thought possible. So my first thanks must go to them. To those who nurtured my writing since I was a preteen, especially Tilly and Jennifer. I Internet-married Tilly when I was thirteen (it was Facebook official and everything), and she was the first person to read the first draft of this novel, twelve years later. She is, in some ways, my Ada.

When I was little I dreamed of becoming a published writer but I put that dream away for several years and stopped writing entirely. I found a life-changing fandom in my early twenties that illuminated this path for me again, so thank you to everybody in that space who supported my writing and cheered me on, including Gemma, Lou,

Melanie, Sus, Mer, Laura, Sheila, Cristina, Hale, Jess, Cait, Cillian, and my Nemesis. Above all, thank you to Zoë, whom I met during one of the most surreal and exciting weekends of my life, and who has stayed a true friend (and the best Dungeon Master!) ever since, for some lovely notes on my first draft. Thank you dearly to Ashley for the same.

I have so much gratitude for my brilliant agent, Alice Sutherland-Hawes, who took a chance on me before I ever had anything close to a novel draft to show anyone. Thank you to my wonderful editor, Mattie Whitehead, and the other excellent editors I've had along the way – Ruth Bennett, Katie Jennings and Ella Whiddett – who believed in this book and helped it find its shape. Thank you to Jane Tait for copyedits, Leena Lane for proofreading, Dannie Price and Summer Lanchester for publicity, and to the rest of the stellar team at Little Tiger. Huge thanks as well to Charlie Morris, who's been an incredible champion of this book and who played an integral part in the early edits. Her support around the publication of *Proud* gave me the confidence to keep going and write a whole novel.

Thank you to Nadia So and Kimberley Chen for this absolute dream of a book cover.

Thank you to Dr. Peta Fowler, who nudged me over and over again to become a writer. I really needed that nudge.

Thank you to the friends I made at uni who made me feel like I could truly be myself, for the first time in my life. Gayatri, Rhys, Bridie, Rex, Dennis, Izzy – you are all gems. Extra thanks must go to Gayatri for reading a draft of this book and being very kind about it.

Karen Lawler and Sheena Cardoso were also extremely encouraging when reading drafts – thank you.

Shout-out to Amy, whose presence in my life is a constant source of joy. Thank you for calling yourself my #1 fan. Your friendship means the world and your enthusiasm is a glittering ray of sunshine. London feels so much more magical when I'm hanging out with you. I miss our chats over late-night cups of tea so very badly. Let's try and find somewhere else to get herring and egg sandwiches from, shall we?

Thank you to my family. To my grandparents: my 爺爺, whom I miss with all my heart and think about every day, and my 嫲嫲, who doesn't read any English, but whose warmth is hopefully in every word I write. To my delightful cousin Dorothy, whom I've only recently got to know properly – I'm so glad we're friends now. To my mum, who read *The Little Prince* to me when I was little and taught me the wonder and power of stories from an early age. To my dad, who is always steadily and quietly supportive in his own way.

And lastly, to Olivia. I told my friends I wouldn't start dating again until I'd written a novel because I didn't want any distractions. The first person I went on a date with after I finished the first draft of this book in 2019 was Olivia, and she's stuck around ever since. Thank you for loving me so patiently, my darling. You completely changed the way I think about love.

ABOUT THE AUTHOR

Cynthia So was born in Hong Kong and lives in London. Their work has been published in speculative fiction magazines such as *Uncanny*, *Strange Horizons* and *Anathema*. They are also one of the new voices in *Proud*, an anthology of LGBTQ+ YA stories, poems and art by LGBTQ+ creators, published by Stripes in March 2019. When they're not writing, they can often be found at the theatre, entranced by a play or a musical. They're also extremely enthusiastic about board games and tabletop role-playing. *If You Still Recognise Me* is their first novel.